I0603209

W.P Angus
Requiem Rising

For any enquiries: Walter@fictionbites.com

Published by: W.P Angus

ISBN-13: 978 0 64893 580 3

Requiem Rising

W.P Angus

Chapter One

In the grey twilight of early morning, a young man walks through the streets of Glasgow, his black coat billowing behind him as a stiff wind blows. Shrugging further into it, he pulls the scarf closer around his neck to fight the pre-dawn chill. Hurrying across an empty shopping plaza, he stops for a moment as he catches his reflection in the glass of a nearby shop window. His piercing green eyes have a tired look about them, and his coat and clothes are shabby after days spent out of the city. Brushing a strand of black hair out of his face, he rubs the stubble on his chin and sighs.

"I need a shave," he mumbles to himself. Turning from the shop window, he walks up the stairs to the entrance of the hotel which dwarves the nearby buildings. Stepping through its rotating door, he shivers a little as the warmth from inside washes over him. Ignoring the unapproving looks from the nearby wealthy patrons, he walks towards the lifts, unwinding the scarf around his head.

"Ah, Mr Aelfdane. Could I possibly borrow a moment of your time, Sir?" Stopping as he hears his name, the young man turns away from the lifts and walks over to the front desk.

"Yes?"

"A letter came for you while you were out, Sir. Here." Taking the envelope from the clerk, he turns it over and looks at it. Plain white, with no seals or a return address. Frowning, he walks past the front desk and steps into an open lift. Within moments, he arrives at the door of his room. Unlocking it, he steps inside, shrugging out of his coat and flicking a light as he walks forwards and sits down heavily on the sofa. With a sense of foreboding, he tears open the envelope. Inside, he finds a folded note and a first-class train ticket. Ignoring the ticket, he pulls out the note and reads it. As he reaches the bottom, anger fills him and he crumples the note. Feeling a presence in his mind, he stops as a man's voice talks to him.

"Calm down, Leon." Taking a deep breath, he unclenches his fist and smooths the note out. "She wouldn't have sent you a message if she didn't have a good reason and you know that."

"Yeah, but it doesn't make this crap any easier to swallow. We should be on our way. The quicker we get this over and done with, the better." Getting to his feet, Leon quickly gathers his meagre possessions and stuffs them into an old, worn rucksack. Pulling on his coat and scarf once more, he does a last sweep of the room before stepping out of the door and tucking the envelope into his pocket. Reaching the ground floor a few minutes later, he hurries over to the front desk and rings the bell, bringing the clerk running over.

"Yes, Sir?"

"I'm checking out. What's the rest on my tab?" Pulling out his wallet, Leon removes a card as the clerk taps away on the keyboard.

"It appears your account has already been settled, Sir. According to the notes, we've forwarded the bill to Schola Divini in London, Sir. They were very generous with their tip. Please pass on our thanks when you arrive." Putting his card away as the man bows to him, Leon grinds his teeth.

"I will be sure to thank them when I get there. Thanks for all your help."

"My pleasure, Sir. We hope you enjoyed your stay and look forward to the next time you choose to stay with us." Picking up his bag, Leon hoists it over his shoulder and leaves the hotel. Stepping out into the cold once more, he shields his eyes as the first rays of sunlight peek over the horizon. Setting off at a brisk pace, he crosses back over the plaza and into the empty street adjoining it. Keeping his brisk pace, he ignores his surroundings and gets lost quickly in thought. Touching his chest pocket, he sighs and comes to a stop as he bumps into a large man.

"Sorry. I wasn't watching where I was going." Turning to look Leon in the eye, the man takes an aggressive stance forward. Stepping back, Leon lifts his hands in apology.

"You picked the wrong part of town to come wandering into pal." Looking around, Leon realises the upscale buildings had given way to ramshackle huts and run-down buildings.

"I don't want any trouble, mate." Smiling menacingly, the big man cracks his knuckles and advances towards Leon. Jumping back a few paces, Leon takes a wide stance and flings his coat back, bringing his hand to rest on the metal cylinders clipped to his hip. Catching sight of the pieces of steel clipped to Leon's belt, the big man's eyes widen in fear and he backs away quickly from Leon, stuttering out an apology.

"My apologies, my Lord. I meant no offence; I was only playing." Reaching the corner of the street, the big man turns and flees before Leon can do anything. Relaxing slightly, Leon glances around the slums and quickly finds his bearings. With a sigh, he turns and picks up his brisk walking pace again, heading back in the direction he came.

* * *

Finding himself back on the main street a few minutes later, Leon hurries along as the streets fill with the morning foot traffic. Avoiding contact with those around him, Leon finally reaches the terminal for the station. Walking down the stairs, he heads to the nearest helpdesk, pulling the letter from his coat and removing the ticket. Placing it on the counter, he addresses the man behind the window.

"Good morning. I'd like to book a seat on the first train to London if I could please." Reaching over, the man takes the ticket, his eyes widening as he reads the text on it.

"Sir, this is a VIP First-Class ticket. We won't have a train with a carriage available of that calibre until later this afternoon."

"That's not a problem. Put me in a lower-class carriage on the first train. The sooner I can get to London the better." Frowning, the man turns to his computer and begins typing. After a moment, he gets out of his chair.

"I'll have to talk to my manager about this. I'll be back in just a moment." Stepping away from his computer, the man walks through a small door at the back of the office. Sighing to himself, Leon turns away from the helpdesk and surveys the train station. For the early hour of the morning, the amount of people hurrying around the station surprises him. Stretching out his shoulders, Leon removes his coat and folds it carefully on to the top of his bag. Rolling up the sleeves on his shirt, he yawns and rubs the tiredness from his eyes. Stepping clear of a man in a business suit, Leon catches sight of a small girl and her mother as they hand their luggage to a porter, who hurries away with their bags on a small trolley. Looking his way, the little girl smiles at him. Smiling back at her, he gives her a small wave. Waving back, she tugs on her mother's sleeve.

"Mummy, why does that man have pieces of metal on his belt?" Catching Leon's eye, the woman smiles at Leon before squatting down to the girl's height.

"They're anima. He has them because he's a keeper."

"Oh. You mean like Uncle...?" Laughing, the woman replies.

"Yes, like Uncle." For a moment a look of intense concentration covers the little girl's face.

"What's a anima?"

"They're what allow the keepers to keep us safe. The keepers are the ones who fight the nocturna."

The little girl's look of concentration deepens for a moment before her eyes light up with the discovery of her realisation. Letting go of her mother's hand, she runs over to Leon. Stopping in front of him, she drops into a small curtsy.

"Thank you for keeping us safe, Mr. keeper." Smiling, Leon drops to her level and looks her in the eye.

"You're very welcome, young miss. I think you should head back to your mother; you don't want to miss your train." With a last laughing smile, she turns on her heel and runs back to her mother. Taking the girl's hand, she bows her head slightly at Leon before heading through the turnstile and further into the station. Standing straight, Leon turns back to the ticket booth at the sound of the door opening. The man from earlier comes through accompanied by an older gentleman.

"I'm sorry, Sir, but we cannot transfer you to another train on this ticket. If you'd like, I can get you on the train that leaves in fifteen minutes, but you will have to purchase a replacement ticket."

"Fine." Gritting his teeth in frustration, Leon pays for his ticket. Taking it from the clerk, he jerks his bag up onto his shoulder and enters the station. Boarding the train moments later, he quickly finds his cabin and enters it quietly. Dumping his bag onto the seat, he removes his anima, stashing them into the top of the bag. Stretching out a kink in his back, he puts the bag in the overhead compartment before taking a seat by the window. Relaxing into his seat, he pulls down the shade as the last of the passengers board the train. Closing his eyes, his breathing slows as he drifts into a restless sleep.

* * *

Turning around, Leon looks over the table at Andrea, leaning against the kitchen bench.

"I take it my father isn't here?"

"They called him away on urgent business, Leon. It couldn't be helped."

"It never can be." Sighing, Leon gets up from the table and drops his dishes into the sink.

"Where did he get called to this time? America, or Russia perhaps?"

"He's in Brazil. In Rio I believe." With a humph Leon turns away from Andrea and walks towards his room, turning to the tv with a start as the emergency broadcast sound emits from it.

"Breaking news. We are just receiving reports that an as yet unknown disaster has devastated Sao Paulo. Reports coming in claim that a giant energy wave destroyed the city, as well as the surrounding areas." For a moment, the announcer stops talking and places her hand against her head.

"New reports coming in. Other waves have erupted in New York, Washington, Melbourne and various places in Europe." With a look of fear and terror, the lady looks over to her right.

"God help us all." With the sound of static, the broadcast shuts off and an emergency symbol fills the screen. Turning back to Andrea, shock covers Leon's face.

"Sao Paulo is right near Rio."

"Leon, we don't know anything yet. Don't panic. LEON!" Turning from Andrea, he bursts through the door and across the yard, ignoring Andrea's shout. As the memory fades to black, Andrea's shout lingers in his mind. Quickly replaced by a man's voice in his mind.

"LEON!"

"Fenrir?"

"Nocturna. Wake up!"

Waking with a start, Leon lands on his feet as he's thrown from the seat. The sound of grinding metal comes from outside as the train's brakes struggle to bring it to a halt. Reacting quickly, Leon grabs a single metal cylinder from the bag above. Reaching the door, he wrenches it open with a crash and runs down the corridor towards the front of the train. Narrowly dodging passengers, he ignores the shouts and curses that follow him as he charges through the train. Reaching the door between his carriage and the next, he kicks it open, stepping out into the air. Without a sound, he leaps up, landing lightly on the roof of the train. Looking forward, he starts to run as he notices gigantic figures moving around at the front of the train. With a flick of his wrist, the steel cylinder becomes a single edge sword, a wolf's head etched into the side of the blade.

"Let's go Fenrir." Increasing his speed as the first screams reach his ears, the world around him blurs. Sliding to the edge of the frontmost carriage, Leon leaps off the train, blade flashing in the weak sunlight. Landing heavily, he barely feels any resistance as the blade passes through the first of the nocturna by the train. Not waiting for the beast to fall, he launches himself around it, blade plunging into the chest of the next creature before it even knows he is there. Wrenching his blade free, he twists to avoid the claws of the third nocturna. Dancing away from the creature, Leon brings his blade upright in front of him. Gripping it firmly, he focuses on the next nocturna.

"Howling Wind Shard!" At his shout, wind bursts forth from the hilt, swirling around the blade. Stepping forward, Leon waits a moment for shards of ice to form and start spinning around the tip of the blade before swinging it towards the nocturna. With a scream that raises the hairs on his neck, the wind and ice rips into the creature, tearing it apart. Breathing heavily, Leon sags for a moment, driving the point of his sword into the ground and leaning heavily on it. Looking around, he takes in the carnage he caused in such a short amount of time. The sounds of breaking glass and screaming bring him back to reality, panic making him break out into a sweat. Hefting his sword, Leon runs to the other side of the train and comes across a sight that fills him with sadness and rage. Lying on the ground in a pool of blood next to a few other bodies, is the lady from the station, deep claw marks across her chest. Her daughter lying a few feet further away from her, as still as if she was peacefully sleeping. The little girl's lifeless eyes bore into Leon like an accusation. Looking up as more screams come from the train, rage fills Leon at the sight of nocturna, reaching in through the window. With a scream, the rage inside explodes out, and Leon launches himself towards the nocturna. Stepping under its arm, Leon kicks off the ground and drives his blade up into the creature's chest. Holding the blade as it rears backwards, he's lifted off the ground. Fixing its sight on Leon, the nocturna swings its clawed hand towards him. Letting go of the sword, he falls backwards, the force from the creature's swing rustling his hair as it goes past. Landing on his shoulder, Leon rolls clear of the creature's arms and comes to his feet. Bringing his hand up, his finger glows. As if he was writing on paper, he scrawls a symbol of light into the air. As he joins the two ends together, he flicks it towards the nocturna. From the symbol, missiles of light explode outward and arc from every direction towards the creature, engulfing it in an explosion as they connect. Breathing heavily, Leon keeps his hand raised, the symbol of light still against his finger. With a thump and burst of dust, the nocturna falls forwards and hits the ground. Lowering his arm, Leon walks forwards and kicks the creature over. Reaching forward, he wrenches his blade out of the chest of the creature in a spray of blood. Turning away from it and heading back towards the train, he suppresses Fenrir, returning him to his dormant form. As he reaches the door, a deafening cheer comes from inside of the train. Before he can take two steps, the Chief Conductor steps from his cabin and stops in front of him.

"You just saved us all, son. If it weren't for you, none of these folks would be going home to their families tonight." Looking around at the people's faces staring at him and the look of relief on them, he gestures outside, as he suppresses the grief rising from his chest.

"There's some who won't. Don't leave them behind." Without another word, he pushes past the conductor and with one glance at the look on his face, the people in the corridors step aside to let him pass. Arriving back at his carriage, he steps inside and closes the blind on the door before shutting it tight. Turning from the door, he takes two steps into the cabin before he falls to his knees, tears running down his face. In his mind, Fenrir's voice echoes strongly.

"There's nothing you could have done, Leon. We just saved a whole train full of people." closing his eyes, Leon replies.

"We didn't save a whole train. I did not save them."

"There's nothing you could have done, Leon. You know that."

"I know Fen. But it doesn't make it hurt any less." Kneeling on the ground, Leon hardly notices as the train moves once more, carrying him on his way to London as if nothing had ever happened.

Chapter Two

As the train rolls into the outskirts of London, Leon pulls his coat from the rack and shrugs into it, brushing the letter in his pocket as he does so. With a sigh, he reaches in and pulls out the slightly crumpled letter. Opening it, he reads the words written there once more.

'My dearest Leon,

I hope this letter finds you in good health. I know things haven't been great between us in the past, but that needs to be put behind us for the time being. Your presence is required at Schola Divini as soon as you can get here. I have a job that requires your expertise.

Look forward to seeing you soon,

Andrea.'

Putting the letter back inside his coat, he looks out the window. Sighing as the train enters London's shield, Leon reaches inside his mind.

"There's more to this Fenrir. There has to be."

"Perhaps Leon. But we won't know until we get there." Watching out the window as the train rolls slowly into Kings Cross, he looks at the ancient architecture. The sight of the station brings a small smile to his face, and a sense of awe still comes to him as the train rolls to a stop on the platform. Getting from his seat, he steps out into the carriage and quickly makes his way to the platform. Without another look, he follows the crowd towards the exit. Reaching the exit, he glances around at all the people gathered there. Family members waiting eagerly to see loved ones and taxi drivers holding up signs with names written on them. A startled shock runs through him as he recognises his own name scribbled on a sign held by a woman in a business dress. He walks toward her but stops as a commotion comes from the top of the stairwell leading back down to the platforms. A man is on his knees convulsing, black webbing already spreading up his neck.

"Nocturna!" Someone screams and in an instant, there's chaos everywhere as people fly into a panic. Swearing Leon tries to push back through the panicked crowd to reach the man.

"Move aside. Everyone, clear a path." Running from the man, people ignore Leon's cries and knock him around, as they crash into one another in their attempts to escape.

"At this rate, it'll be too late," says Fenrir inside his mind.

"Never again." Reaching around inside his coat, he removes an anima off his belt. Taking a wide stance, he holds the anima out in front of him.

"As the pack is led by the alpha, so too is the alpha led by the pack. For them, he must remain strong, to always protect those he leads. Come Fenrir!" The last words come out as a shout. With a flash, the cylinder becomes the wolf blade once more. A man's voice echoes into his mind.

"I can give you strength enough to get there, Leon, but that's all I'm capable of. I still haven't recovered fully."

"That will have to do. Lets go." As he finishes, a surge of energy fills his body. Pushing people aside, Leon leaps high above the crowd. With a grunt, he lands next to the man who is convulsing, the wolf blade returning to a cylinder. Panic fills Leon as he looks over the man. Grimacing as the man's arm becomes a monstrous claw, Leon draws a second anima from his belt, letting Fenrir's dormant cylinder fall to the ground.

"The light of the North, guider of those at sea and hope giver to all. The aura that washes away the darkness. Assist me now, AURORA!" With a flash, the steel disappears, becoming lazily flapping wings on his back, and a glove of pure white on his left hand. The infected man roars and black hair starts to cover his body. With inhuman speed, Leon grabs the man on the head with the gloved hand, stopping him from rising. White light emits from the point of contact covering both men, and Leon's voice rings out.

"Oh, Light of the North! Please, guide this lost soul back to the place he calls home. Wash away the darkness that has led him astray and show him the light once more." All the fleeing people stop and watch as the light wanes, finally disappearing, revealing both men. With a gasp, the infected man staggers and falls heavily on the floor.

"Thank you," he murmurs. Nodding, Leon turns from the man and returns Aurora to her dormant form. Reaching down, he picks up Fenrir and clips them both back on his belt as the young woman with his name on a sign hurries over.

"Mr. Aelfdane, I presume."

With a smile, he offers her his hand.

"Please call me Leon."

She takes his hand with force, and without another word, leads him from the station. Once they clear the crowd of people, the young woman talks to Leon over her shoulder.

"My name is Isabella Shandley. I am Headmistress Marques personal assistant. She sent me here to collect you." As they reach the car, she lets go of his hand and rounds on him. "Do you know the problems that incident will cause? As if we didn't already have enough issues. Who are you anyway, that the headmistress would send a personal escort to pick you up?”

“What’s it matter to you? And if it’s going to cause such an issue, then let’s get going and get this puppet show over with. I have no interest in staying around for whatever plan that old bat has....”

Slap!

“She’s a brilliant woman, and she deserves... Eeek!” Isabella lets out a little squeal as Leon lifts her to his height. Pinning her arms to her sides.

“Just so we’re clear. One. She’s a damn menace that has no problem using whomever or whatever she needs to get things done. And two hit me again and I will throw you in the Thames. Now let’s get going and see what all this is about, shall we?” Letting her go, Leon steps back and looks around at the city, a haunted look on his face. Stepping forward, Isabella opens her mouth to say something. As the wind blows, Leon’s coat billows open, revealing the three anima clipped to his belt. Shutting her mouth, she walks to the other side of the car, gesturing to Leon. Acknowledging her movement, Leon climbs into the car with an odd twisting feeling in his stomach. Without another word, Isabella gets in the driver’s seat and starts the engine, setting off towards the Schola.

Chapter Three

As the buildings on the outskirts of London give way to green fields, Leon shifts awkwardly in his seat as he catches sight of the edge of the barrier. Glancing over at the young woman driving, he studies her for a moment. Turning away to look out the window, as she speaks.

"There it is... Schola Divini." Looking out the front window, shock runs through Leon at the sight of the place. Even from a distance, he can easily see the Tudor style buildings above the walls despite them being further into the grounds. At his astonished stare, Isabella smirks and starts talking. "We built Schola Divini on the outskirts of London at the very edge of the barrier that keeps London City safe. The Mayor of London enforced the fact that it had to be built all the way out here, as he didn't want keepers near the city. The downside to that is, if something happens in the city, we're over half an hour away. That's too far to actually be of any use, should something happen." For a moment, Leon loses sight of the Schola as they drive down into a gully. From deep in his mind, Fenrir's voice echoes weakly.

"Leon, can you feel that?"

"Feel what?" Extending out his senses, a shock runs through him as he feels the power radiating from the school.

"Isabella, what the hell? Why does the school have such a powerful barrier over it?"

"I'm sure you know this already, but Schola Divini trains the largest number of keepers amongst all the Scholas. What you probably don't know is, that, the London Schola recently became the home base of the Chaos Guard. They moved here from London city about a month ago. They have their own barracks set up on the eastern side of the grounds with a dedicated training area and mess hall. When they moved here, it was easy enough to get permission to set the barrier up. We had to, so they could train and not have to worry about tiring out their animas in case they're needed urgently."

"That makes sense, I guess. So, anything else I need to..." Leon's words cut off as they round a corner and the white sandstone fencing comes into view in its entirety. Leaning forward in his seat, Leon struggles to see the top of the walls. Within moments, Isabella turns the car into a wide driveway and pulls up at a set of guarded gates. Stopping at the gates, she winds down her window and says a few words to the man in charge. As the gates open and they pass through, Leon notices some newly built buildings, well away from the main building at the end of the drive.

"Is that the Chaos Guard area?"

"It is. Most of the regular student and keepers here steer clear of them. They tend to think quite highly of themselves."

"How many Guards live here? It looks like you have enough room to support a small army."

"At the moment, we have about a dozen. Those barracks were built to house the full might of the Guard, which I think is around fifty right now. Gilroy's been sending patrols off pretty regularly for a few weeks now." At the mention of the name, a memory tugs at the back of Leon's mind.

"Gilroy?"

"Gilroy Roscoe. He's the leader of the Chaos Guard." As Isabella speaks the man's full name, a groan escapes from Leon's lips.

"Do you know him?"

"In a manner of speaking. It's probably best for everyone if we don't cross paths."

Isabella gives Leon a searching look and continues up the drive, pulling to a stop at the foot of the stairs leading up to the main building. Climbing out of the car, Leon looks at the hedges edging the square in front of the steps. Bending back down, he leans against the window and smiles at Isabella.

"Impressive. Where do I find Andrea?" Smiling back at him, she gestures towards the stairs.

"Go straight up those steps and through the double doors at the top. There will be keepers and other staff around. Someone will be able to point you to the Headmistress's office. Good luck." Leon stands clear of the car as Isabella gives the engine a rev and takes off down the driveway, the wheels spinning in the gravel. Leon can't help but smile to himself.

"In another life, in other circumstances, that may have been a fun time."

"Or a big regret." Fenrir says in his mind. Chuckling at Fenrir's words, Leon turns from the drive and heads towards the stairs with a sense of foreboding. Taking his time, Leon looks over the ground as he slowly ascends. Looking over towards the Chaos Guard area, he notices figures training out in an open field. Stopping, Leon looks closely, but can't tell from the distance if any of the men are Gilroy. Turning from the field, Leon walks up the stairs once more.

"What would I even say to him after all this time? 'Sorry for ditching you and what happened to your family.' It wasn't like I had a choice." After a moment, Aurora's voice echoes softly in his mind.

"I'm not sure, Leon. But depending on how long this takes, you may need to work it out." Closing his eyes for a moment, Leon stops and responds in his mind to Aurora.

"Hmm. Well, for now, I guess I'll just focus on what Andrea wants." Shaking his head, Leon takes a few steps before coming to a halt suddenly as he crashes into a person.

"Watch where you're going, mate." Looking up, Leon finds a face he barely recognises. Gone are the youthful, fun-filled eyes and long golden locks on a pretty boy face. Now it's all angles, hard eyes and golden crewcut. And where he was once lanky, he's now a solid wall of muscle. Dressed in a standard black Chaos Guard uniform, Leon recognises nothing in this man that was once his friend. Stepping back, Leon draws himself up to his full height and squares off against Gilroy, only barely coming up to his shoulder.

"Sorry about that. I wasn't watching where I was going. If you'll excuse me." At Leon's last words, a spark of recognition flares in Gilroy's eyes. Snarling, he grabs Leon and pushes him back down a few steps, pinning him to the railing on the stairs.

"You bastard. How dare you show your face here? I ought to kill you after everything you did." With a twist, Leon breaks Gilroy's hold on his shirt and forces the man back a few paces.

"Gilroy." He says coldly, anger threatening to get the better of him. Pushing himself clear of the railing, Leon makes a move to walk around the giant man and continue up the stairs.

"That's all you have to say after all these years. Fine!" With a surge of power, a battle axe appears in the big man's hands. The whistle of the axe as it swings towards him is the only warning Leon has. Twisting to the side, he avoids Gilroy's downward swing. As Gilroy twists the axe and swings it towards him again, Leon leaps backwards down the stairs, landing awkwardly on the square next to the hedges. The look of horror on a nearby person's face is the only warning he needs. Throwing himself left, he rolls clear as the battle-axe of Leviathan buries itself deep into the ground in the space he recently vacated. Regaining his composure, Leon shifts into a combative stance.

"Gilroy, you really don't want to do this."

"I really do. Now draw your anima or die where you stand, you bastard."

With a resigned sigh, Leon draws his first cylinder. With a flick of his hand, the wolf blade appears. Surprise and annoyance flicker across Gilroy's face.

"Surely you didn't think you would be the only one capable of a command summon? I'm not some novice keeper Gil. Even with everything that happened, do you really think I didn't train? Put your axe away. There's no need to do this. It won't end well." Sneering at Leon's words, Gilroy brandishes his axe towards him.

"Oh yes, there is. I don't care if you're an elite, Leon. I'll bury this axe into you regardless." Advancing the two men move slowly into a standard duelling pattern. Keeping exactly six paces between them, they start moving in a circle. Energy crackles through the air as the tension between the two peaks and wanes. Nearby keepers sense the growing energy and stop to watch, keeping a safe distance from the pair. Standing above, there's another who notices. Smiling to herself, she looks out the window and under her breath she mumbles,

"Well boy, let's see how far you've come in my five-year absence."

* * *

"Fenrir, can you overpower Leviathan?"

"Hmmm, it's not an impossible task, but not an easy one either. Leviathan is a double-S ranked anima. Aurora and I are merely S ranked. Valkyrie might have a chance as she's also a double-S, though you'll need more time to gather the energy to summon her. You're still not at one hundred percent from the fight earlier. On top of all that, her incantation takes a long time to say."

"Well, let's see if we can make that time."

* * *

The two men's eyes drill into each other. Both saying the same thing. Go on. Move. I dare you. Leon takes the initiative. Stepping forward, Leon channels his power into the blade.

"Howling wind!" A gale-force wind erupts from the tip of the blade and quickly surrounds it. With a swing, Leon unleashes it all at Gilroy. With a smile, Gilroy slams his axe, point first, into the ground and, like water against the prow of a ship, the wind passes harmlessly to each side of the big man.

"The wind across the valley cries into the moonlight like the howling of the pack. The alpha is needed, now that the pack has lost its way and finds itself in peril. Let neither ice nor snow hinder you. Come as swift as the northern wind rises over the mountain. Here you are needed, so come to me in all your glory and with the strength to save this lone wolf. Roar now, FENRIR!" At the last shout, the blade, which had been a glowing blur and spinning vertically at the end of his outstretched hand, disappears. Snow appears on the ground and howls ring through the air, sending chills down the watcher's spines. Out of the snow, three wolves appear. Two snow wolves and an old, scarred, dire wolf. The dire wolf dips his head and in an instant, a man stands there. Six feet tall, with long, shaggy, grey hair. An eyepatch covers his left eye. An ugly scar runs from forehead to chin. Scars crisscross his bare chest. The scarring on his back runs down below the top of his shaggy pants that are tucked into black knee-high combat boots. Held in his right hand the wolf blade seems longer and more alive now. Stepping forward with a voice like thunder and an edge of sharp ice, he speaks.

"So, you have called, I have come. No wolf shall standalone as long as I am alpha."

"So, you can summon your blade's phantasm form. It won't stop me." Gilroy can barely form the last words of his sentence; his lip trembling from barely checked rage. With a smile, Leon reaches into his coat and pulls out his second anima with his left hand.

"Come, Aurora." Wings explode out of his back with enough force to create a small shock wave. Instead of lazily flapping, they now flair straight out and up, like wings on a Valkyrie's helmet. The glove on his left hand is gone. Instead, an elegant rapier now rests on his left hip. With barely a sound, it comes clear of the sheath as he draws it.

"Guardian of the deep. Where the light of day fails and gives way to the currents that turn the world. From the blackest depths to the bluest highs let the king of the deep blue come forth and crush the enemies before him. Roar LEVIATHAN!" Gilroy's shout echoes strangely in the afternoon sun. The great battle-axe that was previously in front of him is now gone. In its place, a giant sea serpent towers behind him. Like a Chinese dragon of old with no wings, this serpent has four legs. Stretching its front legs, long razor-sharp claws slide out and gouge into the ground. Looking behind at its tail, Leon grimaces at the row of sharp spikes that can impale the unsuspecting. Its mouth is like a whale, but with multiple rows of razor-sharp teeth. With a hacking cough, it spits up a new battle-axe that Gilroy catches.

"Enough games you bastard. It's times for things to get real. And this time you die." The surge of energy is the only warning Leon gets. Raising his blade, he twists and narrowly manages to deflect the beam of energy from Gilroy's axe. As the beam curves away from Leon, he dashes towards the big man, ignoring the resounding explosion from the building behind him. Rapier flashing, he pushes towards Gilroy, the speed of his blade quickly cutting through the big man's defences and opening a series of small lacerations.

"If this is all you have, Gil, give up now, mate. Cause you're far from a level that can take me." As Leon's words reach Gilroy, the big man's eyes flare in anger and he shoves Leon back with the axe. Racing forward, Gilroy whirls the axe overhead like a madman and slashes at Leon with reckless abandon. Ignoring the wounds Leon's rapier inflicts, Gilroy swings the axe towards Leon again and again. Finally connecting with Leon's blade, he knocks the smaller man off balance for a moment. Not forgoing the chance, he brings the blade whistling back towards Leon.

Twisting to avoid the axe, Leon stumbles and grunts in pain as the axe slashes through the edge of his shoulder. Regaining his footing, he dances back a few steps from Gilroy and raises the rapier once more. With a maddening grin, Gilroy advances towards Leon.

* * *

As the two men clash in front of the school, on the other side of the Schola, a young woman sits down with a cup of tea in her hand. Looking around the open cafeteria, Estelle Hardwyn smiles and takes a small sip of her tea. Placing the cup of tea on the table in front of her, she breaks out into a cold sweat as a burst of energy comes from the front of the school building. Leaping from her seat, she sprints towards the front of campus, ignoring the shouts that follow her. As she nears the front of the building, a violent tremor shakes the ground as an explosion sounds, sending a burst of dust from one of the side hallways. With a curse, she dashes towards the explosion. Turning the corner, she stumbles into the wreckage of what was once the front of the building. Cursing, she sees older students dragging the younger ones clear of the wrecked classrooms that had been standing intact moments before. From a wrecked doorway, a young boy stumbles out and walks towards Estelle, trying to staunch the blood running out of a gash on his forehead.

"Mistress Hardwyn! Stop them, please. They're out of control. They hit the side of the main building and caved in three rooms." As the young boy finishes, he wobbles. Estelle moves fast enough to catch him before he falls.

"Who is out of control?"

"Th... Commander and... some new guy..." As he mutters out the last word, he falls unconscious. With care in her movements, she lifts the boy and places him softly on the ground, clear of all the rubble. Grabbing a passing young woman, she gives her the order to take the boy to the infirmary. With one last look at the ruined rooms with a growing level of anger, she heads towards the front of the building.

* * *

Holding onto his shoulder, Leon tries to stop the blood dripping out of the deep slash. Looking at the surrounding area, he bites back a curse. Fenrir's familiars are no longer moving. Fenrir himself has multiple cuts and is almost about to fade back to his dormant state. Closing his eyes, Leon feels deep into his mind and finds that he has the strength to summon Valkyrie at last. Focusing his power inwards, he smiles as she awakens in his mind.

"Val, get ready. You're up. Fenrir is spent and Aurora is almost done as well."

"What are we facing, that can do that kind of damage?"

"Leviathan, in his phantasm form."

"Damn, hurry and summon me. Bypass Union form and go straight to phantasm."

"You got it" Opening his eyes, Leon readies himself to cast an incantation. With a nod to Fenrir, he steps back, letting the anima take a vanguard position.

Fenrir raises his blade and steps forward, as Leon takes a wide stance, his hands stretched out in front of him.

"From the depths of the valley and the height of the mountaintop come to me winds of ice. Howling Wind Storm!" The wolf blade glows blue and is once again coated in wind. This time, however, small shards of razer ice swirl amongst the wind, as Fenrir runs towards Gilroy and Leviathan. Lowering his arms, Leon removes his third anima and stepping forward he chants.

"From the halls of Valhalla where the heroes of old rest. The defender of all that is good, just, and right. Heavenly queen upon a steed of light. Warrior Queen, fight with us one last time. Before we shed this mortal coil and join the warriors of old, bring forth your radiant light and smite all enemies that oppose us. Defend now and fight. VALKYRIE!" Lightning crashes down from the sky and where it hits, rays of light flicker for a moment. Then, with a blinding flash, she appears. A woman in plate mail armour carrying a round buckler and a double-edged long sword. Gilroy looks at Leon with a slight tinge of uncertainty. With a groan, Fenrir collapses into the dust and with a flash of light, goes dormant. Valkyrie steps forward and raises her sword as Leviathan roars, his tail lashing the ground, leaving two-foot-deep gouges behind. Leon readies the rapier and time slows down. Both men know the fight will be over in the next move. As they raise their weapons to strike, a woman's voice rings out.

"That is enough!" Before either can react, an explosion knocks both men off their feet. With ringing in their ears, the two men release the energy sustaining their anima and almost instantly they disappear and return to their dormant states. On the top of the stairs leading to the main building, stands a young woman wearing a blue guard's uniform with the Captain's shoulder patch. The wind catches her long brown hair and blows it around, giving her a wild appearance. The crimson bow in her hand crackles with energy as she leaps down the flight of stairs, landing lightly on her feet. Walking over to the two men, she knocks another arrow on the bow, drawing it halfway.

"What is the meaning of this? Commander Roscoe, you know better than to unleash your animas full power on campus. Several students are injured thanks to your actions. I will not tolerate it." Gilroy gets up and spits on the ground.

"I don't answer to you. You have no authority over me." It happens so fast that even Leon has trouble keeping up with it. The Security Captain covers the distance to the commander in an instant. Before he can react, she twists his arm to the side and sweeps his feet from under him, flipping him through the air. With a grunt, he lands on his back a few feet away. As he struggles to rise, she walks and places a foot on his chest. Pointing the arrow on her bow at Gilroy's heart, she leans down and peers into his face.

"That's right, you don't answer to me. But you will respect this school and its students by adhering to the rules. If you do not. I will burn down that pathetic building you call your guard room and throw the entire Chaos Guard out onto the street. Let's see how long you last dealing with London, given how they feel about your last performance."

Turning a pasty shade of white, Gilroy looks away from the Guard Captain. Satisfied, she removes her foot from him and steps back a few paces. With an effort, he raises himself to his feet and bobs a deep bow to the guards woman. Catching Leon's eye, Gilroy's eyes flare with anger and collecting his anima, he walks away with heavy steps. Visibly relaxing as the big man fades from sight, the guards woman turns to Leon and looks him over.

"That's no simple thing, having a stare down with Gilroy. You, newcomer, what's your story?" Leon slowly gets to his feet and collects his anima's dormant forms, clipping them back to his belt.

"I was invited here to see the headmistress. But upon arriving, I was forced to deal with Gilroy's old grudge against me. He used force, so I responded in kind."

"Well, if your story checks out, we'll know soon enough. Seeing as I think you're late enough; I'll take you to the headmistress myself. My name is Estelle, by the way. Estelle Hardwyn. I'm the Schola's Guard Captain."

"Pleased to meet you, Captain. Thank you for your intervention." Gesturing for her to lead on, Leon smiles.

"Now if you could please lead me to Andrea's office. I'd like to bring this unpleasantness to an end." She frowns at his last words but leads on towards the Schola's main building.

Chapter Four

Arriving shortly at an office with 'Headmistress' written on the door, Estelle steps forward and knocks three times.

"Enter" replies a women's deep voice from inside. As they walk in, they find the headmistress seated on the edge of her desk. Looking over her half-rimmed glasses, she catches Leon's eye and a sly grin crosses her face.

"Thank you, Estelle. Please wait out in the hall. I need some time alone with our guest." Bowing to the headmistress, Estelle quickly backs out of the room, closing the door behind her. As the door clicks shut, Andrea slides off the desk and paces over towards Leon.

"Well boy, you certainly know how to put on a show. Now..." Cutting her off, Leon takes a menacing step towards her.

"Cut the crap, Andrea. What do you want? I take it my father is aware you've called me. I can only assume that's why nocturna attacked the train not long after I left Glasgow to come here."

"I would imagine he does, and I assumed he would try as much. He has much to fear from you being here and as much as I hate to admit it, he has eyes and ears everywhere, so there's no telling what he knows."

"So, it's your fault that once again I'm forced to watch innocent people die. Always pulling the strings, huh, Andrea? You never could let things slide." At Leon's scathing words, a dark look comes over Andrea's face.

"Boy, you listen now, and you listen well. Things have changed in the last five years. The time when you could sit idly by and watch the world pass is gone. And your arrogance, which I will admit, I found amusing once upon a time, is less so now. You are your father's son in that regard. But enough of this, let's see how far you've come." She finishes with a brief smile. Raising a finger, a blue circle appears at the tip. Before Leon can react, Andrea steps forward and places it on his forehead. Power surges through him and bursts from his shoulders. Symbols and arcana swirl around Leon, their dazzling colours reflecting off the wall.

"Well boy, you've certainly gained strength and a good head for tactics it seems. I can see now what drives that arrogant swagger of yours. Mind, it doesn't prove to be your undoing in the months ahead." Taking her finger off his forehead, she turns from Leon and heads back towards her desk. Ignoring the thump as Leon falls to one knee, his strength momentarily drained from his aura being forcefully displayed.

"Months ahead? What have you done, Andrea? The hell have you gone and gotten me tangled up in now?"

Ignoring his question, Andrea removes a small wooden case covered in arcana writing from her desk. Opening it, she removes a thin cylinder wrapped in black velvet. Carefully unwrapping it, she flicks the steel out of the cloth towards Leon. Reflexes born from battle get the better of Leon and he catches the tube. Instantly, a deep wave of sorrow hits him, followed by mind-numbing pain. Before he can stop it, a screaming female voice rips through his mind.

"No more. I can't take it anymore. Sigmund save me!"

"Leon let go of the casing before she breaks your mind!" Aurora's voice yells over the screaming in his mind. With an extreme amount of effort, he drops the tube to the floor with a loud clatter. Sweating heavily, he looks at Andrea.

"What the hell was that?"

"That is the double S ranked anima Cleo. Cleo was previously wielded by Lord Sigmund Maur, one of the strongest and most well-trained keepers alive."

"I've heard of him. He was London's Council of Nine rep, right?"

"And the Leader of the Chaos Guard here as well."

"Hold on. If his anima's here and in such terrible shape, where's Sigmund?"

"He's dead. We found Cleo next to his body three days ago."

"How did he die?"

"We do not know. The only thing we know is that it was one assailant."

"There's no way one person kills a Council member ordinarily, let alone, someone as strong as Sigmund."

"Not just Sigmund. His six-member honour guard was slain as well. From what we can piece together, it seems like they never even had the chance to raise a finger. They died where they stood, leaving Sigmund alone against an as yet, unknown attacker. It seems he put up quite a fight before finally succumbing." Stepping past Leon, she bends down and carefully picks the anima back up, returning it to the wooden case. Placing the case on her desk, she moves back around to her chair and takes a seat. Watching as Leon slowly gets to his feet, she shuffles through some paperwork on her desk, before sliding a sheet out of the pile.

"The council has yet to make a formal announcement regarding his death. They were holding off until his successor was chosen. Now that it has been done, the formal announcement of both will be tomorrow."

"That explains why I heard nothing about his death. It changes nothing though and has absolutely nothing to do with me. So once again, why the hell am I here?" As Leon finishes, Andrea slides over the piece of paper towards him, a sad look crossing her face. She goes silent for a moment as he picks it up and reads over the page.

"What the hell is this, Andrea? What have you done?"

"It's simple, Leon. You're the next London Council of Nine representative and the new Lord Captain." Leon stares down at the paper in front of him, shock and anger coursing through him.

"This is your doing, isn't it? Haven't you meddled in my life enough?"

"I had a fair say in it. And in all honesty, Leon, I'm tired of your crap. You can blame me all you want for what happened five years ago. And I can't say that blame is misplaced. But everything since then, that's on you. It's about time you grew up. There's a war going on and if your father has his way, there won't be a world left." Striding around the table, her eyes flare with anger as she rounds on Leon.

"Now you have two choices boy, continue wallowing in the past or stand on your own two feet and move forward. The choice is yours. But know this; I will not be around to pick up the pieces this time."

"So, I get no say in this? What if I don't want to be The Lord Captain or the Council of Nine Representative?"

"No boy you don't. In two day's time, you'll be officially sworn into the council. Who have vowed, that once that is done, they will all go after this assailant. Leon, if you're not ready for this fight, you won't survive it. The reason you're here before you're sworn in, is so I have some time to train you. You never finished the training we started years ago, and I will be dammed if I let the past repeat itself." Turning away from Leon, she looks out the window at the setting sun, mumbling under her breath.

"I can't handle losing you too." Feeling the full weight of his guilt, Leon slowly walks around the desk to her side. Turning to face him, she wipes away the single tear running down her cheek. With a small sigh, Leon steps forward and pulls her into a hug.

"Dry your eyes. I was trained by the best keeper alive. My Godmother. Don't worry, I'm not about to die." Wrapping her arms around him, she pulls him tight and lets the tears flow.

* * *

Deep in her thoughts, Shizuri Kawamura barely notices the letter being placed next to her. Turning slightly, she finally notices the seal on top. Almost falling out of her seat, she tears the letter open with gusto. Reading quickly, she smiles, bursting into laughter as she reaches the end.

"So, he's appeared. Finally! Mr. Leon Aelfdane. Now, we shall see if you're truly the strongest keeper. Yes, we will. Kimiya?" At her call, a man comes out from the corner of the room.

"Yes, My Lady?"

"Prepare everything to leave at once. We're going to London."

Chapter Five

Leaving the headmistress's office, Leon breathes a heavy sigh and closes his eyes. Reaching inside his mind, he seeks Fenrir's presence.

"Well, now what do we do Fen?"

"I don't think we have much choice here, Leon. Whatever evil your father has cooked up, must be stopped. You know it as well as I."

"I know. I would rather be anywhere else but here." Stepping away from the door, Leon opens his eyes and pulls out the folded note from his pocket. Walking over to Estelle, he hands the piece of paper to her.

"Hello, captain. I was told to give this to you." Estelle takes the piece of paper and her eyes widen in surprise, which is quickly suppressed.

"Apparently, I'm to show you to the Lord Captain's Quarters. I wondered how long it would be before his replacement was selected. Guess that's the answer to that question." Scratching her head thoughtfully for a moment, Estelle looks Leon up and down.

"Given how things went with Gilroy earlier, I think I'll take you the long way around." Glancing at his arm, she frowns.

"I think we should go by the infirmary first, though. Get that arm of yours patched up." Looking down at his shoulder, Leon fingers the coat, wincing as he pokes the cut, causing it to bleed once more.

"Thank you, Captain. I would appreciate it." She beckons for Leon to head down the corridor.

"Please, call me Estelle. I'm not big on formality. It's too stiff for my liking." Smiling at the young woman's words, he walks, and she quickly falls into step beside him. Studying her from the corner of his eye, he chuckles a little at her inquisitive gaze.

"I feel you have about a million questions for me."

"At least two," she giggles.

"What do you guys do for food around here? After I'm patched up, how about we get something to eat and I'll answer what I can." Estelle frowns thoughtfully for a moment before smiling like she's won some kind of victory.

"Well, we have the cafeteria. The food there is decent, but it's nothing too special. If you want something fancy, though, you'll have to go to London. But seeing as its already getting dark, the Caf is the better option. Procuring a car with short notice at this hour would be nearly impossible. Sound good?"

"Sounds like a plan. So, tell me Estelle, how many people know about Sigmund?"

"Very few. Myself, the headmistress and maybe one or two more. And of those that know, only Andrea, Gilroy, myself and one other know the full story. We haven't revealed that part to the masses yet. It will be one of your first jobs as Lord Commander."

Emerging into the Main Hall, Leon glances over at the sealed-off corridor. Grimacing, as his eyes follow the red tape sealing off the area. Following Leon's gaze, she talks as if reading his mind.

"The students are fine. Most only had minor bumps and scrapes. They were lucky that shot only clipped the side of the building. They were mainly young students or newly admitted ones. So, they would've had no chance if it had hit full on the front."

"It should never have hit at all. If I hadn't been so arrogant and fought him properly, I would've been in the position to stop leviathans beam entirely rather than just deflecting it. And I wouldn't have got this stupid cut either." Shock covers the Security captain's face, and she stops walking for a moment.

"I've seen that beam before, and you're saying you could've stopped it? Are you crazy? How strong are you?"

"In terms of raw strength, when I'm in peak condition, Sigmund is the only person in all of Britain that would even come close to holding their own against me. Which I'm currently not."

"That's crazy. Why were you never selected as the Lord Captain prior to this?"

"Truth is, they wanted me for it. But my father got involved and dragged me away from the Schola and this life before they could enforce it. That's where Gilroy's anger stems from. He feels like I abandoned him and in a way I probably did. That was before Requiem rose to power and the rest of the world went to hell."

"I see. That makes sense. It can't have been easy for you, living alone for all this time?"

"It wasn't. Which way to the infirmary from here, this shoulder is still stinging a bit."

"It's down this corridor." Turning left, the pair head down another corridor leading away from the main entrance. Turning left once more at the end of the corridor, they enter a door marked with a caduceus. Inside is a spacious room occupied by about a dozen hospital beds. At the end of the room behind a desk sits a Middle-Aged red-haired woman in a white doctor's coat. Looking up, she addresses the newcomers.

"Well, don't jus stand there looking foolish. Get ova here and let me look at Ye." Leon smiles at her abrupt manner. Walking over to the end of the room, he tries hard to place her accent.

"Highlander?"

"Oh. Well, aren't you a knowledgeable sort? Is it just that wee little scratch on yore arm that needs tending to?"

"Yeah. Got winged during that earlier fight." Clicking her tongue, the nurse gathers bandages and sterilizing equipment.

"So that was you and that fool captain that did all that damage out front. Nawt a wise move picking a fight with him on yore first day here."

"I didn't exactly get given a choice. It was fight, or die."

"That lad do have some anger issues. That he does. But for sure, there be a way to talk out whatever problem he may have wit ye?"

"I hope so. Maybe tomorrow after he's cooled down a bit."

"That's the spirit boyo. Don't giv up till the big lass sings. Well, there ye are. All patched up. Now run along and keep yore self clear of mischief, ya hear? I don't want to be patching up a pretty lad such as yore self all the time." She finishes with a wink.

"Oh, and boyo, one more thing..." Leon turns to face her, and she grabs him by the front of his shirt, dragging him to her. Before he can object, she reaches up and pulls him into a kiss, much to Estelle's horror. After a moment, she releases him.

"Well, maybe ye should get injured just a little more. Don' think I'd mind if you come round here more often." And with a little laugh, she spins on her heels and goes out the back, leaving a very shell-shocked Leon standing near the desk. It takes a moment before he comes back to his senses. Turning to Estelle, he asks.

"Does she do that often?"

"Never."

"Huh." They both stare at the door for a moment before leaving the infirmary.

* * *

As Leon and Estelle head towards the cafeteria, on the other side of the compound in the Chaos Guard barracks, Gilroy sits patiently on a chair. His second-in-command Annalie Leifsson fussing around over his wounds. Grinding her teeth in anger, she curses Leon in her head.

"How dare he? How dare a newcomer do this to Gilroy." Noticing her scowl, Gilroy grabs both her hands, stopping the shaking from her pent-up anger.

"Anna, calm down, please."

"But that man! Look at what he did to you. How can you not be angry at him for doing this?" Gilroy sighs, knowing how she feels.

"Anna. I came to the realisation that it's not Leon I should be angry at. All these years I spent hating him for something he couldn't even change. Leon's father pulled all the strings, not Leon himself. And by the looks, it wasn't a peaceful life for him either. He should have been the Lord Captain of London, but he was taken from here before he could be." Looking at the young woman whose hand he has enclosed in his, he sighs before continuing to talk. "It's not Leon's fault this happened. It's mine. I picked a fight with him when I had no right to."

"But..." Gilroy holds up a hand before she can interrupt completely.

"Please let me finish. After our fight today, I realised something. I had everyone here at the Schola. He's been alone all along. And I can't even imagine what it must have been like for him for the past five years. I have only seen the images of San Francisco. He was there on the ground. I can only imagine what living with that must have been like. I was a fool." Sighing, Gilroy looks down at the young woman sitting next to him. "Come the morning, I will apologise to him. Now, how's about you finish patching these cuts and we can...." He never finishes the sentence as the young lady leaps into his lap and pushes her lips against his. For a moment, silence reigns. Once their lips part, he gets to his feet, lifting her with him. Wrapping her arms around his head, she kisses him again. And while still kissing, they retreat to his quarters. The rest of his wounds, and the med kit still sitting on the table, quite forgotten.

Chapter Six

Leon is surprised as he and Estelle enter the cafeteria. Set in a circular pattern, it has over a hundred tables spaciously placed. Opening his mouth slightly in awe as he looks around, Estelle smiles at his reaction. Taking a seat at a table beside the window, Leon relaxes. Sliding into the booth seat opposite him, Estelle reaches over and grabs two menus, handing one to Leon.

"How hungry are you?"

"I only had a small bite before I got on the train this morning. So, I'm famished." They both laugh as Leon's stomach grumbles its agreement.

"Well, in that case, I would recommend the super burger. Great for an empty stomach. Or a killer hangover."

"Talking from experience?"

"Maybe," she replies, poking out her tongue. Leon smiles and puts down his menu.

"So, how'd you end up being the captain of the guard, Estelle?"

"I'm the one that's supposed to be asking questions here." She frowns at Leon but gives in and answers anyway.

"Fine. It was my last year here when I got Athena. At that time, the current Guard captain was a real creep. Always making passes at the younger women. Anyway, one night while I was walking back to the dorms, I overheard raised voices. The Guard Captain was harassing a young girl but this time he went too far. Maybe he'd had too much to drink that day or something, but he snapped. He pushed her down and began to undress her. Before he got the chance to get much further, I ran in and kicked him off her. She escaped, and he rounded on me. To cut a long story short, we had a fight, and he lost. The next day he was stripped of his anima and thrown out. They found him in the river three days later. No one was surprised because he wasn't well-liked. And after that, they offered me the Captain's position which I gladly took up."

"Is that how you got that scar on your chin?"

"I'm surprised you noticed it. It's so faint now I hardly even remember it's there." She finishes with a sad smile. Leon sits there and shifts in his seat as the silence stretches between them for a moment. The arrival of the serving girl breaking it up. Food ordered, Leon smiles as Estelle turns towards him, a look of questioning on her face.

"Now it's my turn for some questions, new boy. Let's start with how you got here and where you came from."

"Well, I came on the train. Before that, I was spending some time in Glasgow. Not in the city itself, but up in the mountains. There was a rumour floating around about a powerful anima that had made its way into the area. I've also heard rumours that Requiem's hunting for powerful anima. Given I'd rather them be in my hands than theirs, I went searching. I spent about a week trekking through the mountains, but unfortunately found nothing except nocturna. I spent every day up in the mountains fighting. It was good training in a way and a good escape."

"I suppose it would be. All the time spent fighting doesn't really leave much room for doubt or reflection."

"Correct. I would have stayed out longer, but with my supplies dwindling and suffering from a few minor injuries, I decided it was best to return to Glasgow. I got back in early this morning and instead of spending my time in bed as I had hoped, I found the summons waiting. So, I left, and I boarded the next train outbound. I'd like to say the ride here was uneventful, but that would be a lie. A small host of nocturna attacked the train a few hours out of Glasgow. I dispatched them without too many issues, but not everyone made it." Turning away from Estelle, Leon blinks his eyes clear for a moment. Pretending not to notice, Estelle casually looks around the room.

"I heard about what happened at London station. How did you save that man?" Smiling at the sudden change of subject, Leon leans back as food is placed in front of the pair.

"I see news travels fast around here. My anima Aurora can stop the change, if it's not too late and heal minor injuries. But, it's not a passive ability, it's an active one, and it takes a lot out of me to use it like that. That stunt at the station will leave me drained for a few days. Not like, majorly exhausted but I'll feel it for a while."

"That explains why you're here now. It makes sense that the headmistress would send such an urgent summons to bring you here But I'm curious, why did you stay away from the Schola for so long? Surely someone with your skills could've easily climbed the ranks."

Shifting uncomfortably in his seat, Leon looks away before answering.

"I don't really have a good excuse as far as excuses go. My father is the leader of Requiem. So, I guess that's one reason. I've no interest in dealing with all the problems that kind of information brings. And I was at the destruction of San Francisco. Afterwards, Andrea wanted me to become the London Council of Nine Representative and replace Sigmund. See, they wanted me to take up that mantle before he was selected. But some stuff had happened, and I no longer had any interest or willingness to be a part of this institution. That's probably the primary reason

I stayed away. But I don't have a choice anymore. Requiem are getting too ballsy and it seems they're now targeting council members. The only reason I'm staying is to put a stop to my father. Once and for all."

"That's pretty intense. I never knew you were originally supposed to be the Representative before Sigmund. Well, for what it's worth, I'm glad someone as strong as you, is taking over for Sigmund. And you don't have to worry, I'll keep your identity to myself but there are plenty who would already know. Your last name is pretty unique."

"Thank you. I appreciate it. Taking over this role is going to be hard enough, without that hanging over my head as well." Smiling at Leon's words, Estelle eats her food. For a moment, silence hangs between the two. To be broken by a young woman's voice.

"Hey, Stelle. Hey newbie. Good job. First day here and you destroy half the school building." With a cheeky grin, Isabella comes striding up to the table and slides in next to Estelle. With a grimace, Leon looks at the young lady from earlier in the day.

"Hello, Isabella it's nice to see you too. I'm sure I can find a pond to throw you in as the Thames is a little far to go."

"Oh, come on now. I didn't even whack you once. Impressive fight by the way." Taking a chip from Estelle's plate, she turns to the brown-haired woman.

"I feel sorry for you. I assume the headmistress stuck you with the job of showing Mr. Entitled over there the grounds?"

"Why y...." Leon starts but is cut off by a kick to the shin from Estelle.

"Nah, Bella. I'm taking our new Lord Captain to his quarters. But we were hungry, so we stopped by here to grab a bite to eat first." Isabella's jaw drops and she turns in shock towards Leon. Her shock quickly giving way to anger.

"As if you're the new Lord Captain! Like you could ever live up to Lord Sigmund's shoes! I'm telling you right now, it'll be a chilly day in hell, before I ever acknowledge someone like YOU!" As her last word comes out as a shout, Isabella slides out from the table and storms off across the cafeteria. Her heavy steps echoing through the half-empty hall.

"Now what did I do to piss her off?"

"It's not you. She was quite fond of Lord Sigmund and took his death hard. If it wasn't for the headmistress taking her under her wing, she would've been in a lot of trouble a long time ago. I shouldn't have been so rough about it, though. She just gets up in everyone's face. It's what she's like. Don't take it personally, I'll find her and sort it out later." Folding his serviette up, Leon drops it onto the plate in front of him.

"I can deal with it. She's no trouble. As much fun as this has been, any chance I could get you to show me to my quarters. I'm still pretty exhausted from the trip here and I'm going to need to get some rest before I present myself to the Chaos Guard in the morning."

"Umm, you won't just be presenting yourself to the Chaos Guard. You'll be presenting yourself to the Schola's Guard as well. As Lord Captain, you have superiority over both."

"That's just great, even more people to hate me." Laughing, Estelle slides off her chair and gestures to Leon.

"Well then, my Lord Captain, if you'll follow me, I'll show you to your quarters." Standing up from his seat, Leon shakes his head and follows the Guard Captain across the Cafeteria and out into the night air.

Arriving at the Lord Captain's quarters a few moments later, Estelle unlocks the door and lets Leon in first. Flicking the light on, Leon blinks in surprise. Looking around the room, he whistles at the quality. A nice dark hardwood desk sits in the corner and a proper four-poster bed rounds out the room with deep maroon and blue colours. Walking over to the dark mahogany wardrobe against the wall, he opens the door to find clothes in his size already stored inside.

"Wow, I've stayed in supposed grand hotels that weren't half as nice as this."

Laughing, Estelle walks in and gestures to a suit of clothing in a plastic bag.

"Leon, here is your uniform. You'll need to wear it tomorrow." Looking towards the uniform, Leon lets out a small groan as she pulls out the black military coat. Adorned with all the rank badges of Lord Captain.

"Do I really have to wear that? What's wrong with my normal clothes?"

"Yes, you do. Unfortunately, for ceremonial and formal events like tomorrow, you need to wear this. The rest of the time you'll be fine but on big occasions, you need to wear the uniform."

With a sigh, Leon takes it from Estelle and hangs it over the back of the chair next to the desk.

"Well then, good night Lord Captain. See you nice, bright and early."

"Define bright and early?"

"Hmmm, the first call is it at seven-thirty A.M. You need to address the crowd at eight."

"Seriously?"

"Yup. Goodnight" Winking at Leon, she closes the door and leaves. Looking around the room once more, Leon talks out loud to himself.

"Eight A. M, huh? Best get some sleep then." Peeling off his shirt, he stops as his shoulder tweaks. Turning to look in the mirror, he can't help but grimace at the three jagged scars running down the length of his back. For a moment, he looks at the scars, sadness and sorrow crossing his face. With a sigh, he finishes undressing and turns out the light. Climbing into bed finally, his head barely hits the pillow before the day's exhaustion catches him and he's asleep.

* * *

Looking out over the wrecked and abandoned city, a man pulls a smoke from his coat and lights it. Taking a long drag, he removes a ringing phone from his pocket and answers it.

"This had better be good." Replying in a higher pitch, a woman's distorted voice comes through.

"You ordered me to keep you up to date on any expected changes. Leon arrived in the academy today, Sir. Had a small fight with the Chaos Guard Captain."

"The fight is irrelevant. What's interesting is the fact that he's there."

"What would you like me to do?"

"Do nothing. He's far more than you can handle. I'll deal with this personally." Closing the phone, the man flicks the butt of his cigarette out the window, watching as the red tip fades from view. Smiling, he pockets the phone and turns towards the wreckage of what was once a pleasant office.

"So that's your play, Andrea. You think to use him against me. Well, we shall see how well that works." Walking towards the doorway, he gestures towards a dark corner.

"Come girl. We have someone to go visit." From the corner, a young girl with black hair steps out and falls into step behind the older man. With a look of sadness and fear crossing her face, she follows him.

Chapter Seven

The moonlight filtering down on the tarmac lights up everything enough for Leon to see. Holding Fenrir in his hand, he watches as an anima rolls past his feet. Turning quickly at the growl behind him, Leon doesn't make it in time. Pain rips down his back and with a blinding flash, he wakes. Light streaming through the window blinds and confuses Leon for a moment. Looking around carefully, he stares up at the bed from which he fell. Pulling himself up against the side, his light blinded and sleep-filled eyes make out a female silhouette moving around the room with purpose. Looking down, Leon carefully gathers up the sheet from the floor and ties it around his waist. Sliding up onto the bed, he looks over at the woman.

"What's going on? Surely it's too early for this."

A familiar female voice answers over the clattering of dishes.

"It's quarter past seven Lord Captain. You have forty-five minutes until it's time to address the Chaos and Campus Guards."

"Isabella?" The young woman walks in front of the window, blocking out the light as Leon's eyes finally adjust.

"Lady Andrea asked me to assign you an assistant until you get the hang of things. I volunteered, and she agreed."

"Why would you agree? You weren't exactly jumping for joy last night. Is that coffee?"

Isabella smiles and hands a cup to Leon. Before her face becomes serious again.

"I'm sorry for my outburst last night. I knew that someone would be assigned to the vacant post sooner or later. Lord Sigmund and I grew up together. He was like an older brother to me. He helped me through the early days here at the Schola. I'm not really a fighter like most people here. I'm always the one supporting from the back. But I want to change that. I know I have no real right to ask this, but can you heal Cleo? I would like to test for compatibility with her if you can." Scratching his head for a moment, Leon takes a sip of coffee and looks over at the young woman looking at him with pleading eyes.

"Well, Aurora is back to full strength now, and I've had a good night's rest. I'm still a little tired, but maybe this afternoon we can see how we go. But Isabella, you need to be aware. I may do nothing for Cleo. It seriously damaged her. What happened with Sigmund." Stepping up from the bed, Leon stretches. Walking to the desk, he pulls out a sheet of paper and quickly scribbles down a note, handing it to Isabella.

"While I'm addressing the guards, take that to Andrea. She'll get every-thing sorted."

"Will do. But are you sure?"

"I am. Let me have a shower and get ready."

"Who's Farah?" Leon spills his coffee at the mention of the name.

"How... How do you know that name?"

"You talk in your sleep. Is she your girlfri..."

"She's dead." Leon says, cutting her off. He lets out a small sigh before continuing.

"By my hand. She was turned before I could save her. Not for a lack of trying, though. It's how I found out, that keepers aren't immune, to the nocturna virus." He turns away from her and for the first time, she sees the scarring down his back. Three long scratches, similar in size to a nocturna's claw, run from shoulder to hip. Walking behind his bed and into the bathroom, he fires up the shower. Climbing in, Leon lets the hot water soak into him. Using a trick he learned long ago, he focuses on nothing and soon, his depressive state washes away. Getting out, he quickly towels himself dry and pulls on his new clothes. They're a slight-ly tighter fit than he's used to but well cut and tailored. Looking in the full body mirror, he looks himself over. The black uniform with its rank patches and insignia pins makes his eyes shine even brighter. And the scar on his left cheek diminish. Walking out of the bathroom, he sits on the edge of his bed and tugs on his boots. Standing up, he turns and sees Isabella staring out the window.

"So, what do you think? Impressive enough?" She turns from the win-dow and her eyes widen.

"Wow. You clean up nice." Chuckling, Leon walks to the bedside table and collects his anima. Glancing at the clock on the wall, he gestures to the door.

"We should get going. There are only ten minutes. Where do I go to address these people?"

"You need to go around to the front of the barracks. Follow me." A few minutes later, they arrive at the front of the barracks. Leon takes a seat on the stairs leading up to the stage.

"Hey Isabella, don't suppose you smoke, do you?" Before she can reply, a man answers from the corner of the stage.

"I thought you quit."

"I did, but you know public speaking and all that. Not really my strong suit." Gilroy walks over and hands Leon a smoke and a lighter.

"I need to talk to you, Leon. About yesterd..." Leon holds up a hand and stops the big man. Lighting the smoke, he hands the lighter back to Gilroy before speaking.

"There's nothing to discuss. Oh, and I accept your offer by the way."

"My offer?"

"Yeah, the one you just made. Your shout at the pub tonight." The big man shakes his head and sighs.

"You never change. Meet you around eight. Front of the main building." Smiling, the big man walks off. Giving Leon a strange and confused look, Isabella shakes her head.

"Men," she mutters, shaking her head and walking off towards the front of the school building.

Walking up the stairs, Leon stops just outside of the view of all the people assembled. Swallowing his nerves, he crushes out his smoke and walks out at Estelle's gesture.

"And now I'd like to introduce our new Lord Captain, Leon Aelfdane." Taking the mic from Estelle, he waits until the scattered applause dies down.

"I take it from the look that some of you are giving me, that you would rather I wasn't who you got for Lord Captain. Perhaps you would rather have Sigmund. Unfortunately, he's dead. So, unless you all get over it, I guarantee that's where you'll find yourselves as well." Stepping up to the edge of the stage, Leon looks down over all the men and women assembled in front of him.

"I'm going to make one thing abundantly clear. I don't really want to be here, but whilst I am, I will do everything in my power to stop Requiem. But if any of you feel you can do better; I'll make you all a deal. If any of you can defeat me in combat, the job's yours. But until such a time as I am no longer in charge, when I say jump, you jump. You don't even ask how high. Requiem is out there, and you can be damn sure they won't show mercy when the time comes to face them."

"Requiem's right here on the stage too!" As a man's shout comes from the crowd, a small fist of rage knots up inside Leon's chest.

"If you've got something to say, come out and say it to my face. Don't hide in the crowd like a coward." With a shuffle, the crowd slowly disperses and a red-haired man steps forward, clear of everyone. Throwing down the microphone, Leon leaps from the stage and lands lightly in front of the man. Squaring up to him, Leon looks into his blue eyes before speaking.

"You got a problem, soldier?"

"I do, as a matter of fact. I don't want some damn traitor leading us all. Especially not the son of the man, who would bury the world and everyone in it." Clenching his face, Leon struggles to remain calm as he replies.

"You think you can do better? Come and take the job then." As the words leave his mouth, Leon realises his mistake. Leaping backwards, he winces as a whistling blade passes close to the front of his face. Holding a bastard sword, the man smiles menacingly.

"With pleasure." Quickly summoning Fenrir, Leon barely gets the blade up in time as the man advances. Knocking the man's sword aside, Leon quickly steps back to gain his footing. Establishing his stance, Leon attacks, smiling to himself as the crowd spreads out into a giant circle.

"I'm going to give you one chance right now to drop your blade and walk away from this." Laughing with a crazed gleam in his eye, the man turns to Leon and lifts his blade.

"Not a chance, traitor. Now shut up and DIE!" Reading the man's movements, Leon waits until the last moment before striking. Sidestepping the man's thrust, he follows up with a light slash to the back of his calf, sending the soldier sprawling into the dirt. With a look of rage, the red-haired man gets up and chants something under his breath. Feeling the surge of power, Leon focuses for a moment and moves. World blurring, Leon twists his head slightly, allowing the bolt of red energy to crackle past his cheek, the radiant heat from it leaving a slight sting. In an instant, he covers the distance and with a single strike, blood sprays into the air. Turning at the scream echoing from behind him, Leon sweeps the soldier's legs out from underneath the man. Landing heavily, the soldier whimpers and cradles the bleeding stump of his arm. Levelling Fenrir against his throat, Leon stares coldly down on the man.

"Any last words?"

"Go to hell." Smiling, Leon lets Fenrir vanish and drawing a sigil places his finger on the end of the man's arm. From the tip of his finger golden thread burst forth and connects the severed limb back to the arm, before settling into a bubble around the cut. Leaning down, Leon puts his arm behind the man and helps hoist him to his feet.

"What's your name, soldier?"

"Dell. Sergeant Dell Tonquin. Why didn't you finish it?"

"Because despite your flaws, you show spirit and defiance. And we're going to need that, in the days to come. And I would rather not kill a man unless I have to." Stepping back, Dell studies Leon for a moment. Before extending his good hand.

"I would be glad to serve under you, Sir. I was very much mistaken in my comments earlier." Taking the red-haired man's hand, Leon smiles.

"Good to be working with you as well, Sergeant. Someone, take Dell to the infirmary." Waiting a moment for another man to take away the wounded soldier, Leon vaults back onto the stage.

"Now that we've sorted out that, I can get back to what I was saying. I have one rule from here on out. Do your job or I'll cut you down myself. What happened here today is the only time I'll show any leniency against insubordination. Am I clear?"

"Sir, Yes Sir."

"Excellent, you're all dismissed to your respective duties." Standing straight, Leon watches as all the soldiers leave. Turning from the stage, he walks down the other side to find Gilroy and Estelle waiting.

"Right first things, unless we're in front of other people I'll have none of the Sir crap I made them go through. Now onto business Gil, I need a list of all your subordinates, with added notes on their anima and abilities. Also probably send someone to check up on Dell. With the arcana I cast on it, the infirmary should be able to fix him up."

"Estelle, you're coming with me. I've had Cleo brought into a secure area where I can look at her. Do you know where the quarantine rooms are?"

"They're in the lower levels of the main building. If you'll follow me, I'll take you there." He gestures for her to lead on. As he passes Gilroy, the big man reaches out a hand and puts it on his shoulder.

"You could have gone a little easier on him. You made enemies of at least a couple of them out there today.

"They don't have to like me. They just have to follow me. Is it better to be feared or respected?"

"Hard call on that one, mate. Well, let's hope nothing more comes of it."

"Let's hope." Leaving the big man standing by the stage, Leon follows Estelle and the two head towards the main building and quarantine area below it.

* * *

As the train doors open at King's Cross Station, a young Japanese woman steps out from a first-class carriage. Behind her walks a man carrying two small briefcases. Ascending from the platform, the young lady strides straight up to the information desk. Looking up from his screen, the clerk gives his attention to the woman. Looking her up and down, a strange look passes over his face and he talks to her in a mocking tone.

"How can I be of assistance My Lady?" She gives no outward signs of being offended by the young man's mocking tone.

"Can you tell me the name of a good hotel close by? I didn't have time to make all the proper arrangements. I left Tokyo in a bit of a hurry."

"No problems Miss. The royal hotel on the north side of London is good. It's only a three-star hotel, but it's small and discreet and has excellent service. Will that suit, or would you like something, a bit, flashier?"

"That will be fine. Thank you for your help."

"My pleasure, miss."

As she walks away from the desk grinding her teeth, she flexes her hand above an anima tucked in behind her back.

"Easy Shizuri, we don't need to bring attention to ourselves."

"I know. But I swear if another upstart little prick acts up, I'm going to clobber them. Exiting the station, Shizuri waits as the man behind her walks over to the street and hails a taxi. Getting in to the back seat, Shizuri looks out the window as her companion talks to the driver.

"The Royal Hotel please."

"No worries. Buckle up folks. We'll be there in a jiffy." With an engine rev, the taxi pulls into the street and speeds off up the road.

Chapter Eight

The bite of the shackles on her wrists has long since faded. The only thing that hasn't is the feeling of the cold stone wall against her back and the mind-numbing exhaustion. From nowhere specific, a tickle comes to the edge of her mind. With an anguished cry, she puts up the shield in her mind and opens her eyes. In the dull light, the black anima tube on the ground in front of her seems to glow with a menace and lust for destruction. The pressure increases and soon a voice echoes at the edge of her mind.

"Let me in dear. I promise once you do, all this needless suffering will end."

"Never. You killed Lord Sigmund and all those other people. I will never let you in again!" The voice becomes menacing.

"You will let me in. And through you, I will destroy this fragile world. There isn't anyone left that can stop me now." As he finishes, the pressure disappears. "Have it your way. But I will get in again. Your soul belongs to me now." As his menacing laughter fades, she lifts her head to look out the window of her cell, pleading desperately to the night sky.

"Someone, please, help me". The only answer is the deafening silence of her isolation.

* * *

Walking down a long line of stairs, Leon and Estelle find themselves in a tunnel leading to an already open door. Walking up to the door, Leon steps just inside and looks around at the specially made cell for keepers and anima. The black marble floors, walls and ceiling are all covered in the heavy angular script of arcana writing. Resting on a pedestal in the centre of the room, the anima Cleo gleams faintly in the low torchlight.

"That's some serious arcana. You ever had to use it for something like this before?"

"No, fortunately enough we haven't. You can't summon in there either, so you'll have to summon your anima outside before entering."

"So, it's basically a prison for rogue keepers. I guess this is where that Guard Captain was held until they passed sentence."

"Actually no. They built this after him because he broke out of his original cell."

"Ah, fair enough. Well, let's step out of here so I can summon."

Once outside the room, Leon removes Aurora from his belt.

"Let's do this Aurora." With a flash, the flapping wings and glove appear. As he steps towards the door, Aurora's voice fills his mind.

"Leon, you'll need to summon Valkyrie in her phantasm form as a precaution."

"A precaution for what?"

"I believe Cleo may go phantasm once I begin to heal her. If that happens, she could go nova."

"You have a valid point. We can't afford for that to happen here. Can you contain her Val?"

"Cleo has the opposite affinity to me. It won't be easy to contain her. Leon, if she goes nova, we will not have any other choice but to destroy her."

"I know."

"Well then, let's do it."

With a grim look, Leon chants. Moments later, Valkyrie is standing beside him.

"Are you sure you need more than one anima Leon? That seems a little excessive," Estelle asks. Before Leon can reply Valkyrie answers.

"What do you know of the anima condition known as nova, Miss Estelle?"

"Only rumours. I've never heard of an actual case."

"It's not a rumour. When an anima goes nova, they become highly unstable. If not destroyed quickly, the power they build up is extreme. All that power must go somewhere eventually and it usually all comes out at once. Before that, however, the output level of the energy brings nocturna from everywhere. And not just your average soldier class but it brings goliath types as well. If a Nova is not subdued or destroyed before they burst, it's the equivalent a nuclear bomb going off. Everything inside of a few miles is vaporised. And the aftershock will be felt fifty miles away in extreme cases."

"If she goes nova and we can't stop her, there will no longer be a Schola or London. But even before that happens, London will be overrun with nocturna. That is why Valkyrie is here." Nodding to Estelle, Leon enters the cell with Valkyrie at his heels. With a backward flick, he closes the door behind him. As Leon steps into the cell, Estelle draws Athena out and hugs the anima to her chest. Closing her eyes, she reaches inside her mind, feeling out Athena's presence.

"It's okay Estelle. That man will not allow that to happen."

"How can you be sure, Athena?"

"The look in his eyes. I know you saw it just now as well. That's a look of determination. He has dealt with a Nova incident before. Of that, I am sure."

Approaching the dais slowly, Leon can feel the pain emanating from the corrupted anima. Radiating outwards like heat from an open flame, it quickly becomes suffocating as Leon and Valkyrie get within a few feet from the pedestal in the middle.

"Ready Aurora?"

"Go Leon. Hurry!" Looking at the pedestal at Aurora's cry, he sees the reason for her panic, and a surge of icy fear strikes into Leon's heart, making his stomach turn. From the pedestal, Black miasma spills out from Cleo and begins to form around the base of the dais like a thick cloud. With a curse, Leon leaps forward and grabs the anima with his gloved hand. Radiant light billows out from the point of contact, and Leon staggers as pain and sorrow assault his mind. With a growing level of pain, Leon's vision fades and screams echo in his mind. Trying to push away the pain, a fog clouds his mind. His vision darkening, another wave of pain forces Leon down to his knees, his hand holding onto the anima by a sheer force of will.

"Hold on, Leon." Aurora's voice sounds as if she's far away. Blinking rapidly, Leon tries to clear his vision and regain his footing. Looking up, everything turns white and his composure fails as his mind is assaulted by a vision.

* * *

Approaching Leon is a girl dressed in black plate mail armour. A giant great sword with a blade as black as night crackles with energy as she strides towards Leon. Attempting to step aside, a shock runs through Leon as he looks into the black anima eyes staring out from under her helmet. Turning as she passes, he watches as she casually walks over to a big man in bright blue armour, taking no notice of the bodies lying around her. A chill runs down Leon's spine as Sigmund removes his helmet, letting it clatter to the ground, revealing his blood-smeared face. Stepping forward, Sigmund hefts a spear and a short sword. Covering the remaining ground to the knight in a moment, he lunges with the spear, moving almost too fast for Leon's eyes to follow. Stepping to the side, she delivers a kick to Sigmund's stomach with ease; the blow throwing him through the air like a rag-doll. Landing heavily a few feet away, Sigmund rolls to the side, quickly coming up to his feet. With a roar, he charges the woman once more, Energy crackling over the spear. With barely any movement, she deflects the spear and thrusts with her blade before Sigmund can recover. Shock covers his face as the blade plunges through his chest plate like a hot knife through butter. With a slight flash, the anima returns to its dormant form. Throwing it to the side, he swings his fist at the girl, landing a hit on the bottom of the helmet. Letting go of her sword, she staggers back a few steps. With dying strength, he pulls the black blade from his chest and throws it to the side, far out of reach of the female knight. With a roar, Sigmund leaps forward and swings the short sword with ferocious speed. With a laugh coming from multiple voices, the woman easily dodges the blade, ducking down below Sigmund's line of sight for a moment. Flexing her hand, the great sword appears in her gauntleted fist. Coming upright, she swings her blade and with a sickening crunch; it cuts the short sword and his chest plate in half. Staggering forward, Sigmund falls to his knees, the blade falling from his hand. As it hits the ground it reverts to its dormant form, but within seconds it shatters, small white lights filling the surrounding air. Holding his chest together, Sigmund coughs, and a spray of blood comes from his lips. With a flash of light, his armour disperses, and an anima appears on the ground in front of him. Reaching down, his fingers barely touch it before it shatters into an abundance of lights as well. Blinking back a tear, he raises his arm towards the knight. With a flash of black and a sharp stabbing pain, Sigmund's sword arm falls to the ground. With a smile, he looks up at the woman with a defiant stare. Snarling, she swings the blade towards him, his eyes closing as her arm comes down. In the early morning light, blood sprays across the ground and Sigmund falls still.

* * *

"Leon. Snap out of it!" Aurora's voice rings in his mind, bringing him back to the current time with a shock. Emanating from the anima at the end of his left hand, blue light sends ripples of energy bouncing from the walls. Spinning rapidly, it becomes a spear. With a powerful blue glow, the spear releases a burst of energy, throwing Leon against the far wall. As his back hits the marble, the link to Fenrir and Aurora disappears. Powerful waves of energy emanate from the spear and as Leon staggers to his feet with a curse, the glow intensifies. Shielding his eyes from the glowing spear, he blinks at the sudden disappearance of the light. Standing where the spear was, is now a tall woman. Dressed in leather battle armour with her bob cut black hair, Cleo casts a striking figure in the centre of the room. Standing up straight, Leon pushes himself clear of the wall and reaching to the side, picks up an arcana sword from the table next to him. Turning towards him with tears in her eye's, Cleo raises her spear. With no warning, she lunges towards Leon with the spear in her hand. Tightening his grip on the blade, Leon moves to intercept but stops as a figure dashes in front of him. The sound of the spear hitting the shield echoes around the room. Lunging with her sword Valkyrie tries to land a hit on the rogue anima but Cleo nimbly evades the slash, dancing away from the shield-bearing maiden.

"Are you okay, Leon?"

"I'm fine. But if we don't do something soon, we're going to be in trouble." Gesturing toward Cleo, Valkyrie lets out a Norse curse as light blossoms behind the woman's chest. With an ear-splitting shriek, waves of energy pour out of Cleo. Looking around, Leon watches in fear as a crack appears in the marble wall, the sound echoing throughout the chamber. Looking up, Leon watches as a crack spreads across the marble roof, finally reaching the far side of the chamber. With a dull thud, the door falls to the ground as the frame cracks, revealing Estelle and Isabella standing there, eyes wide with fear as they get their first glimpse of the carnage within. Fear courses through Leon at the sight of the two girls standing there and for a moment, he stands still in shock. The sound of steel meeting steel breaks the shock and he looks around, finally realizing that he has full control of his anima once more. Stepping forward, he yells out loud.

"Alright change of plans. Aurora, you take care of healing her. I'll back up Val." Spacing his hands out and throwing the arcana sword aside, Leon widens his stance and chants.

"Light of the North, keeper of the stars. Let now your radiance shine down and guide those that are lost. Reach far and wide to all who are lost in the dark places. Guide them to the places they call home and back to those who make it so. Let the light of the North save now those that are in peril. Come now Aurora!" Dazzling colours shine off the wall. Standing next to Leon is a beautiful lady dressed in a Roman-style white dress. A rapier resting on her hip and white satin gloves covering her delicate hands. Almost glowing golden hair spills down her back between softly flapping wings.

"Here now I have come, to guide this lost wanderer." Her voice sounds like liquid honey and fills Leon with a feeling of contentment. Warily eyeing the woman, Cleo backs up and creates some space. Staring at one another, the two women approach. Reaching to his side, Leon pulls out and summons Fenrir in blade form.

"Now!" He shouts. Everything happens faster than a normal person could follow. Dashing forward, Leon and Valkyrie rush Cleo, their blades flashing through the air. Spinning her spear, she catches both blades, turning them harmlessly away. Landing behind Cleo, Aurora rushes in and attacks with the rapier. Without stopping, spear still a blur, Cleo turns and dodges past the rapier. Grabbing the wrist of the unsuspecting anima, she drags her forward and throws her in Leon's direction. Holding up his hand, Leon suppresses the women back into her union form and snatches the rapier from the air. As it connects with his hand, wings once again appear on his back. Taking a step back, as another crack comes from the walls and a chunk of roof falls, smashing the pedestal on the dais.

"Dammit, at this rate, the room won't hold." A surge of energy brings his attention back to the fight still raging between Valkyrie and Cleo. With a twist, Cleo moves her spear between the legs of the armoured woman and upends her. Before Leon can move to assist, Cleo's spear lashes out and hits Valkyrie hard, sending her smashing into the wall with enough force to return her to dormancy. Cursing, rage overcomes Leon and using the wings on his back, he propels himself to extreme speed, covering the distance to Cleo in a moment. Blades whirling, he engages her spear in a deadly dance. With every blow, her attacks seem to hit harder than the one before. The shocks of the impacts jarring the bones in his arms.

"Leon, she's going nova. If we don't shut her down now this whole place will be destroyed." Gritting his teeth, Leon breaks from combat and leaps back, pouring energy into Fenrir's blade at the same time. Landing heavily, he swings the blade around in front of him, releasing all the energy at once.

"Howling tempest!" A whirling tornado of ice shards launches from the blade as Leon swings it. Spinning her spear, Cleo steps forward and chants.

"Sandstorm helix!" At her chant, a sandstorm wall spills forth from the centre of the spear and changes the direction of the ice. Leon looks on in horror as it slams into the remnants of the door frame, freezing it solid. Just on the other side of the doorway, Estelle and Isabella let out a squeal as they stand together, trembling with fear.

"Get the hell out of here!" Leon shouts. Cleo takes the moment's distraction to launch an attack. Barely reacting in time, Leon dodges the point of the spear but not the butt. Impacting heavily against his cross guard, it knocks him clean off his feet. Blades spinning out of his grip, Leon lands heavily on his back, the wind knocked from him. Climbing to his feet, Leon looks at the anima glowing with energy in front of him. Raising her spear, Cleo steps back before launching herself forward. Streaking towards his chest, the spear ripples with energy as time slows.

"So, this is it, huh? After everything, this is where I meet my end. So be it." The thought echoes softly in his mind, and he shuts his eyes. Hot wetness splashes his face and, opening his eyes, he looks up to find Isabella in front of him. The spear sticking out of her back, below her shoulder, dripping blood on his face. With a cry, he leaps to his feet. Stopping in his tracks as Cleo reaches out a hand to the impaled woman. With a smile, Isabella takes the proffered hand and, with a flash of light and a burst of energy, Cleo's phantasm disappears. In its stead, her dormant case is now clutched in Isabella's hand. Turning to look at Leon, she whispers.

"I did it. I bound her." As the last word leaves her mouth, so does a trickle of blood. Her eyes roll back, and she falls. With lightning speed, Leon catches her and lifting her easily, he runs for the door. Estelle jumps out of the way as he charges through. Holding Isabella tightly, he sprints up the stairs and barrels down the hallway. Shouting people out of his way, he sprints toward the infirmary. Reaching the hall, a surge of energy fills him, and he powers to the door. Barely stopping, he smashes the door to the infirmary open, bending its hinges and scattering a cart of medical instruments all over the infirmary. Leaping from her seat at the end of the room, the Scottish woman from the day before begins cursing.

"What in the blazes is the meaning of...?" But as she sees the limp girl clutched in Leon's arms, she leaps into action.

"Bring her here. Quickly boy." Moving to the gestured bed, Leon places her down softly. Standing back, he starts as he gets shoved toward the cupboards.

"Don't jus stand there ya great lout. Get over there and hand me everything I say. She's lost a lot of blood. By the looks of this woun, she's been impaled by a spear." Throwing her coat to the side, she rolls back her sleeves and examines Isabella's wound. Carefully rolling her over, the nurse curses.

"Damn it all to hell. It's torn through her right lung and muscle. You, lad, give me that case there. The red one with the serpent on it. And bring over the suture kit next to it as well." Leon grabs both cases and comes back over, passing the red one to her first. Taking it from his hand, she places it on the table next to her. Opening the lid, she reaches in and pulls out an anima tube.

"Hearts passed and bound. Flowing blood and flowing life. Like an open valve, pour forth your energy and come to my aid, Victor." For the briefest moment, the tube glows red and disappears. Shining surgical gloves appear on the woman's arms. Stretching out her arm, the right-hand fingertips glow. Reaching over, she puts pressure on each side of the wound in Isabella's chest. A commotion sounds at the door as Estelle comes barging in, clutching Leon's three anima to her chest. Turning briefly from Isabella, the doctor looks over at the Security Captain.

"Leave this place and let me work. One fool here to help is enough."

"Boy, grab me a towel and close the damn door. This isn't a tent and I need to concentrate." Stepping around the beds, Leon quickly grabs a towel and hands it over. Nodding at the woman's fierce gesture towards the door. Walking over to the door, he ushers Estelle from the room, gently taking his anima from her.

"How bad is it?"

"I honestly don't know. But as soon as I know more, I'll come and find you." As he closes the door, Estelle leans against the wall, tears streaming down her face. Sorrow welling up inside, Leon pushes it away and turns from the doorway, heading back over to where the Scottish woman is working on Isabella.

chapter Nine

Rolling Isabella over and using the towel Leon gave her, the Scottish woman wipes away the blood covering the young woman's back, suppressing a wince as she does so. Looking at the wreckage of the young woman's shoulder, she suppresses the gasp forming on her lips. Concentrating, she feels deep in her mind for the connection to the anima she summoned.

"Victor, how's it all looking?"

"I've stopped the bleeding, but there is significant damage here, Esmeralda. I can repair the damaged muscle and collateral damage from the spear's blast and set the bones back into their rightful place, but they'll need to heal naturally, and so will the wound. We don't have the strength for more right now. If you used me more regularly, we could have been able to fix it all."

"It'll have to do. There be a reason for that Victor and you kno it. I can never forget that night. Nawt for as long as I live." Ignoring the exasperating sigh from Victor, Esmeralda concentrates and all the power from Victor flows into the girl's chest. Knitting the muscle together and setting bones. Looking over her shoulder, she sees the young man closing the door.

"Boy! Get me some bandages from the far cupboard." With a nod, Leon runs over and quickly gathers what she wants. Focusing on the wound, the gloves on Esmeralda's hands let off a faint purple glow. From underneath come the sounds of bones clicking back into place as Isabella's shoulder bubbles and ripples. Gesturing to Leon with a nod, he places the bandages on the table next to her as he arrives. Focusing, she feels her consciousness expand to explore the young woman's shoulder. Following the lines of the muscles, she reconnects them, one by one, to where they had come from previously. Ignoring the fatigue weighing down on her, she quickly reconnects and repairs the severed veins and tendons as well. Finishing up with all the major injuries, at last, she sags with a clatter as Victor returns to his dormant state and tumbles to the floor. Stumbling backwards, she knocks a tray over as the world begins to tilt. Sturdy hands grab her and stabilize her before she can fall.

"Thanks, lad." She croaks, as Leon helps her stand straight. Pushing clear of Leon's support, Esmeralda pours herself a glass of water and takes a long drink. Setting the glass down, she turns and grabs a pair of surgical gloves and the suture kit. Looking down at the young woman, she preps the needle. Ignoring her growing level of tiredness, Esmeralda leans over Isabella and begins stitching the gaping wound. Finally, putting the last stitch in, she looks out the window to find the light of late afternoon streaming in. Turning from the girl, she finds Leon standing nearby, rigidly staring out the window.

"Come here, boy. I've naught the strength left to lift and bandage at the same time. Yore going to haf ta help me here, lad." Coming over at the summons, Leon follows the surgeon's instructions, carefully lifting Isabella and helping Esmeralda to wrap her chest with bandages. Stepping back as Leon carefully places the brown-haired girl onto a clean bed, she looks over her handiwork. Nodding to herself, she turns away from the bed and moves slowly over to an empty bed nearby. Sitting down heavily, she lets out a sigh. Smiling as Leon comes over with a glass of water.

"Thank ye muchly. Well, lad, I've done all it is I can do. It's up to the lass now." Leaning back, she slides sideways, her strength finally giving out. Moving quickly, Leon stops her from collapsing.

"Are you ok?"

"Aye. I just need a wee rest. It takes a lot out of me to use Victor that way. Give me a hand to get to my room over there." Supporting her with one arm, Leon helps her to the bed in the adjoining room. As she lays down, she looks at the boy standing in the doorway looking back into the room.

"She'll be fine, lad. Now go to your quarters and get cleaned up. It'll do no good for anyone to see ye in the state yore in. I'll send a message once she wakes."

"I'd like to stay until she does."

"More's likely she won't be up til the morrow. Now off with ye. I'll let ye know as soon as she is." Looking down at his clothing, Leon finally takes in the jagged tears and blood covering the once pristine uniform. With a frown he peels off the jacket, throwing it in the nearby bin. Turning, he looks at Esmeralda, who dismisses him with a sleepy wave of her hand. With a sigh, he takes one last look at the bed and the figure of Isabella lying there. Turning away at the guilt and shame burning his eyes, he leaves the infirmary and sets out into the campus.

* * *

Stretching the crick in his neck out, Gilroy finishes putting his last signature on the paperwork for the injured guard from earlier in the day. Looking up at the clock, he smiles to himself as it clicks towards five in the afternoon. Turning away from the counter, he frowns at several people running around. Stepping out the door onto the steps by the main building entrance, his concern deepens as he notices small groups of people talking in whispers. Intercepting a young boy, Gilroy grabs the young man by the shirt, halting him.

"What's everyone talking about? There seems to be an awful lot of commotion going on" Bowing deeply to the big man, the boy stammers out an answer.

"Lo... Lor... Lord Commander Roscoe. Apparently, Lady Isabella has been injured badly. Some of the first-year students said they saw the new Lord Captain covered in blood carrying her towards the infirmary. They also said he left there a few hours later looking as if someone had died. Some say that Lady Isabella was already dead before he got to the infirmary, but no one has got near enough to find out. Least that's what they're all saying, sir." Squashing the anxiety in his stomach, Gilroy keeps his composure as calm as possible, as he talks to the young man in front of him.

"Thank you for the information. But I'm sure they're just rumours. I'm confident that Isabella is fine. Now I don't suppose you know where the Lord Captain went after he walked out from the infirmary?"

"A girl from my class said she saw him sitting over by the front gate. Apparently, his formal jacket's gone, and he's sitting by a tree with his anima laying on the ground next to him."

"Thank you. Now best get back to your studies. I'll go and see the Lord Captain myself." At Gilroy's dismissal, the young boy runs off. Biting back a string of curses, Gilroy hurries as quickly down the steps as he can, without seeming to rush. Crossing the grounds, he finally sees Leon. Sitting against one of the first oak trees by the gate, his anima laying on the ground next to him.

Ignoring the anima on the ground, Gilroy squats down next to him. Looking down at his bloodstained hands, Leon begins to talk softly.

"I thought I had come far enough. I thought I had the strength to protect those who needed it and to overcome any adversary. But once again I found myself covered in the blood of someone, I couldn't..."

THUMP!

Leon is interrupted by a fist crashing into the top is his head. Anger quickly replaces his features and, grabbing Fenrir, he quickly rises to his feet, rounding on Gilroy.

"What the hell was that for?" Laughing loudly, the big man looms over Leon.

"I haven't seen a face that funny in years. That, mate, was well deserved. What's with the self-pity crap? Man up, take responsibility for your screw up and don't let it happen again. Wallowing in self-pity and despair won't help anyone. Aren't you the Lord Captain? If the keepers here see you walking around the grounds covered in blood and looking like a failure, what do you think that's going to do for morale." Gesturing for Leon to look around, Gilroy runs a hand over his blond hair.

"Argh, listen to me chewing you out like a recruit. Come on, Leon, let's get out of here. I need a drink and you sure as hell look like you need one, too. But, clean up first." Leon smiles and puts a hand on Gilroy's shoulder.

"Thanks Gil. I needed that. A drink sounds good. But there's something I need to take care of first. I'll meet you at my quarters once I'm done." And with that, he picks up the remaining anima and sets off at a run. Shaking his head at the back of his friend, Gilroy chuckles as he heads towards his own quarters.

* * *

Wandering aimlessly through the grounds of the Schola, Estelle barely recognises the faces that swim in and out of her vision or the areas her feet take her. Trying hard, she still can't stop the tears streaming down her face. Shrugging off questions with half gestures and barely under-standable comments, she dodges her way past people. Starting towards the main building, she comes to a stop as a pair of arms wrap around her. Turning, she comes face to face with Leon. Looking into his face, she can no longer hold back. With a cry, she falls to her knees, Leon dropping with her and holding her tight as the tears pour out. Curled against his chest, she cries until she has no more tears left to cry. Wiping away the last of the tears from her eyes, she pushes herself gently off his chest and sits back on her knees, looking him in the eye.

"I'm sorry. I wasn't able to stop her from running in."

"It's not your fault, Estelle. She made her choice, as foolish as it was. The Doc did a pretty good job of patching her up. She seems tough, so I'm sure she'll pull through. And once she's awake, we can work out what she owes us. Now..." Rising to his feet, he holds a hand out towards her.

"I'm going to head into town and grab a drink with Gilroy. Care to join us?" Taking his hand, Estelle gets to her feet.

"I will. After today I could use one. However, I think I might get changed first," she finishes, looking down at her clothing. Laughing, Leon looks down at his own bloody and torn clothes.

"I think I'll second that idea. That was next on my to-do list after finding you. Meet us out the front of my quarters when you're ready." With a nod, she hurries off in the direction of the guard barracks.

"Always the lady's man." Says a male voice from behind.

"So, will the good captain be joining us this evening?" Turning, Leon finds Gilroy in casual clothes accompanied by a small woman in a black dress.

"Leon, this is Anna. Anna, this is Leon."

"Hi. Nice to meet you. I'd shake your hand except mine are still dirty. Anyway, yeah, Gil, she's coming with us. Now I need to get cleaned up. How are we getting to London, by the way?" Stepping forward, the young woman squares up to Leon.

"I'm driving. Someone has to stop you from getting into trouble. And just so we're clear. I haven't forgiven you for hurting Gilroy yet," Anna states fiercely. Taking a step back, Leon shoots Gilroy a, 'what the hell?' look. The big man merely shrugs, steps forward and puts an arm around the woman.

"Anna, we've been over this. Play nice."

"Hmmph." Shooting Leon a last glare, she stalks off toward the garage to procure a car.

"She hates me."

"Yep." With a sigh, the two men head to Leon's quarters.

Chapter Ten

The door to the cell opens and a tall man in a dark robe sweeps in. Raising her head, it takes a moment for her to realise the man's identity. Snarling, she tries to launch herself at him but is held back by the chains.

"Easy my dear, I mean you no harm."

"I swear, Baur, when I get free from here, I'm going to kill you!" snarls the girl. He walks closer and places a black anima tube on the ground in front of her.

"Really and after I brought you a friend to keep you company in this dreary place." Straightening, he looks the girl in the eye and gives her a sickening grin.

"No, please. No more. Just kill me already"

"My dear girl. If I wanted you dead, I would have left you lying on the ground, after that man of yours ran you through."

"He had no choice. Wait, why are you here? You've not come yourself since Sigmund."

"Well, aren't you the perceptive one? That man of yours survived the injury you gave him, by the way. I just thought you'd like to know that." As he finishes, a dark smile crosses his face. It's then she realises why.

"No. You can't make me. I'll never submit. Nev..."

SLAP!

She falls instantly silent as the back of his hand connects with her face. Tasting blood, she turns to him but before she can recover his hand closes over her throat, and she's slammed into the stone wall. The stench of his foul breath washes over her, making her want to gag.

"Oh, you will kill him. But as a special treat, I'll make sure it's nice and slow. By the time I'm done with you, you'll relish the feeling of destroying his life." Releasing her, he turns on his heels and strides out of the cell. As the door closes with a loud bang, she slumps down the wall, the strength in her legs gone. Looking through the bars nearby. She weeps.

Sitting in the back seat of the car a few hours later, both men shrug uncomfortably at each other. Opening his mouth to speak, Gilroy closes it as icy stares come from two women in the front of the car. Reaching up, Leon touches his nose to see if the bleeding has finally stopped. Reflecting on his early choices, he decides commenting on how good Estelle's body looked, may not have been the wisest move.

"Still, punching me in the nose in response was a bit dramatic," he thinks to himself. Laughing at the situation had made Gilroy just as bad as Leon, as both women rounded on him shortly after. Sighing heavily, both men turn their attention to their respective windows for the rest of the ride to London.

* * *

Parking the car a few streets away, the four keepers walk in silence, finally reaching their destination. Entering the bar, both women make a beeline for the bathroom, leaving the men to get the first round of drinks. Taking the drinks from the bar and finding a seat at a nearby table, Leon looks at Gilroy over the rim of his glass, touching his nose gingerly one more time.

"I still think that was uncalled for."

"Bahaha it was a good call but you, my friend, have about as much tact as a sledgehammer." Laughing, the big man gestures at the various women around the bar.

"If I've learned one thing so far, it's that, while they like you thinking such thoughts, they don't like you saying them out loud."

"Pfft," Leon replies before taking another sip of his beer. Rubbing his jaw, he looks around the small room.

"If that's the worst that comes from tonight, mate, I'll be happy. I think I've just about had it with nasty surprises." As he finishes, a woman's heeled boot clicks heavily against the balcony above him and a chill runs down his spine as a female voice calls out from above.

"Found you, Aelfdane."

* * *

Walking into the Ladies' room, Estelle and Anna go straight to the vanity. Looking at herself in the mirror, Estelle adjusts her dress to reduce her cleavage. Frowning, she turns to the shorter woman adjusting her lipstick in the mirror.

"I can't get this to sit right. Can you help me with this, Anna?" Putting the lipstick away, Anna helps Estelle by hoisting the dress a little higher. Looking over her shoulder, she addresses the shorter woman.

"Maybe I shouldn't have punched him in the face."

"No, you should've beaten him black and blue. What kind of country hick says that to a lady? If you hadn't punched him, I would have. On sheer principle alone. Not counting the fact, that I'm still angry for what he did in the fight with Gil."

The two women look at each other and break down into giggles.

"Well, at any rate, let's make him sweat a bit more before I 'forgive him'," Estelle says with a malicious grin.

"Definitely." Smiling, both women giggle into their hands. Their laughter dies quickly as they hear a shout from Leon followed by the sounds of shattering glass and splintering wood coming from the bar. Without looking back, the two women race towards the sounds of battle.

* * *

Letting his reflexes take over, Leon leaps backwards from the table as a flaming katana cuts it in half. Rolling from the chair, he kicks it towards the woman, barely dodging as the blade passes through it with ease. Reaching to his side, he draws Fenrir and as the blade materialises; he dashes forward, catching the katana. Sweating, he pushes the woman back, as the heat from the flames singes his hair.

"What the hell? Who do you think you are, lady?"

"It's simple Mr Aelfdane. My name is Shizuri Kawamura. And I'm the Japanese representative of the Council of Nine. And as for why I'm attacking you. It's quite simple, really. I'm here to kill you." At her last words, Gilroy's eyes widen.

"Lady Kawamura, you can't just openly attack a keeper. Council members are only allowed to fight other council members."

"Correct Commander Roscoe. We will announce your friend here as the newest Council of Nine-member tomorrow afternoon. This is but a taste of what he should expect." Stepping in front of the small Japanese woman, Gilroy draws his anima.

"That may be the case, My Lady, but as he has yet to be sworn in, they still consider him to be a normal keeper and therefore it is against the council's rules to fight him." Smiling a wicked smile, she raises the blood-red katana and steps towards Gilroy.

"Are you going to be the one to stop me, Commander?" Swallowing his saliva, he tightens his grip on the anima in his fist. Placing a hand on the big man's shoulder, Leon pulls him away from the woman.

"It's alright Gil. If it's a fight she wants, then it's a fight she's going to get. But not here. Let's take this outside." Without waiting for a reply, Leon turns from the woman and calmly walks out the door, making his way to the centre of the street. Turning slowly, he waits as Shizuri steps outside, her katana still burning lightly. Following behind Gilroy, the two women look over at Leon with worry. Shaking his head, he turns just in time to dodge a slash from Shizuri.

"I'd focus your attention on me if you want to live past tonight, rookie."

"Rookie? Who are you calling a rookie?" Leaping forward, Leon channels power briefly into his sword and the blade coats with a thin layer of ice. Clashing against the katana, a burst of steam comes from between the two blades as Leon pushes into Shizuri, knocking the smaller woman off balance. Smiling, Leon quickly traces a sigil and twists away, raising his hand overhead. Above his hand ice quickly forms and in moments a long spear hangs just above his palm. Hurling it with accuracy, Leon doesn't wait for it to land and he chases after it. Recovering from the first clash, Shizuri reacts and with flames roaring over the katana, she steps forward and cuts the spear apart in a burst of steam and shards of ice. Before her swing can finish, Leon emerges from the steam. Grabbing her by the arm, he twists her elbow, sending the katana clattering away. Pushing her back and dropping his blade for a moment, Leon drives a kick to Shizuri's midriff, knocking the Japanese woman off her feet. Stepping away from her, he retrieves the steaming blade from where it lays. Turning back towards Shizuri, Leon opens his mouth to say something when a burst of energy comes from behind, staggering him with its force. Before anything more can happen, the lights in the street flicker and wane before giving out entirely, plunging the street into darkness. Screams and yells coming from nearby, sends a shiver of apprehension up Leon's spine. As people run away from the river, Leon grits his teeth and pulling out a second anima, he runs towards the commotion. Turning the corner and coming out onto the main street, Leon freezes for a moment at the sight in front of him. Rising from the river is a goliath class nocturna. Its truck sized claw reaches out and lands on the bridge directly in front of him, cracking the bitumen and putting a strain on the support beams. Swearing out loud, Leon doesn't wait for the others. Running towards the claw he chants, causing the blade in his right hand and anima tube in his left to glow. Sliding to a stop as Fenrir and Aurora appear in their phantasm forms, he removes Valkyrie from his belt and begins chanting once more.

"Warrior Queen, lend now your strength to one that needs it. For a warrior finds himself alone amongst enemies devoid of a way to fight. Rise now VALKYRIE!" The anima tube glows and vanishes with a flash. In his right hand is a double-edged long-sword and his left arm is now covered in armour from shoulder to fingertip. Flexing his left hand, he smiles as a light steel buckler appears strapped to his arm. Looking out over the bridge, he watches the water splashing over the edge of the wall as the nocturna lifts itself completely upright. Closing his eyes, he focuses his attention on the creature in front of him for a moment.

"Aurora, Fenrir, try to slow it down." The two anima don't wait for a second command as they surge forward and begin attacking the monstrous creature. Footsteps come from behind and turning he finds the three women and Gilroy running towards him, anima drawn.

"It's a stage three goliath. This is going to be far from an easy fight. Estelle and Anna, you two need to clear the area. Co-ordinate with local authorities and get the civilians as far away from here as possible. We're going to need some room to breathe." Giving Leon a nod, the two women run off in separate directions. Turning to find Gilroy looking at him, Leon brandishes his blade towards the big man.

"Gil mate, you up for a little exercise?"

Brandishing his axe, he grins at Leon. "Is water wet?" Pushing past the two men before Leon can say anything, Shizuri dashes towards the Goliath.

"Stupid newbie, I'll take care of this." Sneering, she leaps high into the air, her katana glowing red in the dim light.

"Amaterasu! Bring forth the heat of the sun and burn everything before you." Exploding upwards from the hilt, dark crimson flames engulf the blade. Leaning back, Shizuri swings her sword, unleashing a ball of fire so hot nearby windows shatter. Engulfing the monster, the fire crackles angrily. Shock runs through Leon as the flames are stopped by a blue layer of energy covering the goliath. Running onto the bridge, Leon yells up to Shizuri.

"That's arcana. Idiot. Get out of there!"

Looking down at Leon, a look of confusion covers her face for a moment before a spiked tentacle whips out towards her. Thinking quickly, Leon writes a sigil and unleashes it in Shizuri's direction. Bursting from her shoulder, a green shield wraps around her a hairsbreadth before the tentacle hits, rebounding it back to the water below. As the flames disappear, the goliath roars in anger and swats the shielded Shizuri out of the sky with its fist, sending her through the wall of a nearby building.

"Dammit. That fool. Gil let's do this. Give us a boost." Running towards Gilroy, Leon brandishes his sword and shield before jumping towards the big man. Turning his axe flat side up, Gilroy swings it. The flat of the blade connects with Leon's feet and he's propelled into the air above the goliath. Rising from the creature's back, the tentacles twist and drive straight at him. Turning so the shields to the front, he deflects the first tentacle to the side and cuts down. The blade passes cleanly through and the tentacle falls, spraying bright blue blood into the air. Ignoring the liquid that lands on him, Leon twists his body and continues the dive towards the goliath. Blade flashing in the night, the second and third tentacles fall soon after the first. Lashing out, Leon narrowly misses the fourth tentacle, cursing as it changes direction suddenly. Swinging away from Leon, the tentacle turns and whips back towards him. Twisting, Leon braces himself against the shield. With bone-shattering force, it connects, and he's hurled toward the goliath with incredible speed. Ignoring the searing pain lancing through his left arm, he swings the blade down at the goliath's head. Instead of passing through, the blade bounces off the crown with a flash of blue light. Landing heavily and cursing, Leon releases the shield, quickly scribbling a sigil onto the side of the blade. Putting all his weight into a single strike, Leon drives the sword through the magical shield into the creature's head. Roaring in pain, the goliath rears its head, flinging him into the air.

"Leon, above you!" At Gilroy's shout, Leon releases the sword and summons the shield. Bracing himself for the impact, surprise covers his face as the spike on the tentacle passes by the shield. For a moment confusion covers Leon's face, but its quickly replaced by pain as the spike pierces through his shoulder. Strength failing, Leon releases the shield and draws a sigil on the side of the tentacle. With a roar, the goliath flicks the tentacle viciously. Crying out in pain as the spike tears free from his shoulder, Leon fights the urge to black out. Concentrating, he extends his good arm and clicks his finger. Smiling, he watches as the sigil glows for a moment, before it explodes, tearing the tentacle apart. As he falls, the pain ceases for a moment as the wind whistles past his ear. Coming back with a vengeance as he hits the water with enough force to shatter his ribs. Sinking through the water, Leon coughs and watches as a trail of red blood comes from his mouth. Landing on the riverbed, his eyes close and he feels his remaining anima go dormant. Opening his eyes and looking through the haze of water, he can see flashes of red and blue light. Smiling to himself, his mind wanes as the water fills his lungs and his injuries take their toll. As his thoughts become sluggish and his consciousness begins to fade, he reaches his hand up towards the lights before letting it fall. Landing in the soft mud of the riverbed, his hand hits a metallic object. Closing on it, a shock goes through Leon as a voice rings clear in his mind.

"Keeper, you are dying. This you know. I have power enough to save you, however, I'm not willing to give you that power unless you agree to my deal."

"What kind of deal."

"The kind that will save your race and mine. I'm known as Revenant. I am a Scion. But you may know me as a black anima. We aren't like normal anima. Once summoned, we cloak the keeper's body with a version of ourselves for a limited time. I promise I will explain the rest to you later. But know this, I mean you no ill will. I won't lie to you. You are strong and potentially the one I seek. But I am not doing this for you, I do this for my own reasons, now what say you?"

"Well, I'm not all that keen on dying today and seeing as I can't think of another way of living from here, why not? Let's do this."

"Brace yourself Leon Aelfdane. This will be like nothing you have ever experienced." As the man's voice fades away from his mind, a burst of energy pours through Leon's body and light emits from under his hand, engulfing him in an instant.

Chapter Eleven

anding next to Gilroy, Shizuri looks around at the state of the bridge and the rampaging goliath.

"This is bad." Shizuri pants. "Where's Aelfdane?" Shaking his head, Gilroy glances towards the water.

"After he saved your ass, he charged in. Took out all the tentacles before he fell. Last I saw Leon, he was hitting the water with enough force to shatter bones. He's bleeding out from a wound on his shoulder. If we don't get to him soon, you'll be looking for another council member and all because you had to be a hero. Some council member you are."

Shock crosses her face, and a deep feeling of despair fills her.

"There's no way he can be dead." Looking around the spot Gilroy pointed out, she sees and feels no trace of his anima or presence. Readying Amaterasu, Shizuri prepares to strike. Stepping forward, she stops as an incredible amount of energy comes from underneath the Thames. Exploding, the water sprays in every direction and a beam of light stretches up into the sky. Shouting comes from all around as a figure rises from the river, like something from a fairytale.

* * *

Leaning against her desk, Andrea sighs and looks out the window at the dimly lit grounds. Pushing off the desk, she walks forward and places her hand against the cool glass, pensive thoughts running through her mind.

"Did I do the right thing, bringing him here?" Sighing, she doesn't even register a response as a voice answers inside her head.

"I believe so Andrea. If you're worried about the events of today, then talk to the boy. But he'll be fine. He's made of tougher stuff than that, as you well know."

"I know, but it still doesn't stop me worrying." Turning from the window she stops as a beam of light arcs into the sky, energy rippling out from it. Fear courses through her veins, and a shard of ice drops into the pit of her stomach.

"Please no. Don't let him be involved," she begs. Grabbing her coat, she hurries to the desk and reaches for the holo-phone, starting as it rings before she can push a button. With an ominous feeling, she answers the call. Flickering green for a moment, a man's face appears in front of her. Finally, the image settles, revealing him to be in his early fifties. Smiling, a handsome face makes his brilliant green eyes sparkle.

"Hello, Andrea. It's been a while."

"Alastair, is this your doing?" She demands, scowling.

"Is what my doing?" Grinding her teeth, her scowl deepens.

"Don't scowl, my dear. It'll put wrinkles on your forehead." Lighting a smoke, he looks away from her direction for a moment.

"I have no part in what's happening in London right now. Though I wish I did. That boy has become a force to be reckoned with. If he had taken my offer all those years ago, there wouldn't have been any need for him or that pretty girl of his to suffer. That light will be troublesome though. I'm sure you know well enough what's causing it, don't you?"

Frowning, she turns away and looks out the window towards London once more.

"I'll have to shorten my timeframe considerably, I'm afraid. That boy has been more than a thorn in my side, its high time I did something about it, don't you?"

"That boy, is your son. And he has been through hell because of you. I should've killed you with the chance that Maria gave me."

Taking a long drag from the cigarette, he breathes out the smoke before replying.

"You should have, but if wishes were fishes, my dear. Anyway, I'm done with playing these silly little games. A new age is coming and, like Maria, you've chosen the wrong side. You should have left him out of this Andrea. I promise you..."

Screaming, she turns, and the call is cut off as her desk is obliterated, scattering paperwork and objects all over her office. Looking down as the ribbons settle into place on her hand, shock courses through her and she wonders for a moment when she called her anima. Opening with a squeal, the door to her office swings wonkily on the hinges and a black-haired young woman walks in.

"Are you ok headmistress?"

"Yes, Iris I'm fine, though I fear my anger may have gotten the best of me." She says with a sigh, looking down at the wreckage of her desk.

"Yes, well, it gets the best of us all, My Lady. Do you know what's happening in London?"

"I have an idea and I will be needed if its anywhere close to what's actually going on. Is your pilot's licence current still, Iris, and is there a small airship available?”

“Of course it is, and I believe there's a small runner in the Aerodrome at the moment. Why, what do you need?”

“To get to London as soon as possible. We don't have time to go through the normal channels. I need you to fly me there.”

“As you wish, headmistress.”

Picking her coat up off the floor, Andrea hurries from her office with the younger woman. As they step out into the night air, Andrea looks at the flickering light in London.

“Hold on, Leon, I'm coming,” she whispers to the night.

* * *

Pulsating, the light finally fades, revealing a black-clad figure hanging in the air. Blinking the afterimage of the light from his eyes, Gilroy tries to focus on the figure in the dim light. Ignoring the hanging figure, Gilroy gestures at leviathan. Barely waiting for the giant sea serpent to continue its attack, he races across the bridge towards the goliath. Leaping from the bridge, he swings the battle axe down with as much force as he can muster. Barely making a mark, the blade whistles off to the side as the shield covering the creature pulses. Roaring at the annoyance, the goliath swings a giant fist towards Gilroy. Narrowly dodging the arm, he winces as it hits the side of the bridge, sending concrete spilling down into the Thames. Falling towards the dark water, Gilroy twists and scrawls a sigil quickly in the air, landing lightly on the water as it activates. Looking behind him, surprise crosses his face as the black-clad man's eyes open, glowing red and contrasting against his long white hair. Extending his arm, a black blade appears with the twist of his wrist. Grasping the hilt in a reverse grip, he looks down and lowers slowly. Ripples spiral out as his foot lightly touches the surface of the water. Shifting the grip slightly on the blade, he glances towards the goliath. Smiling, he vanishes, an explosion sending water spraying into the air as he disappears, reappearing behind the goliath. Swinging the blade with a ferocious look on his face, he barely registers the spray of black blood splashing onto him. Roaring in pain as its arm splashes into the water below, the goliath rounds on the man and spits a hailstorm of needles towards him. Pushing off from thin air, the man creates some distance between himself and the creature, blade spinning in front of him. Ignoring the needles bouncing off the blade in every direction, the man traces a strange sigil with his free hand. Clicking his fingers, the sigil disappears and burning balls of flame appear around the goliath's head. Twisting, he raises his hand and closes his fist, sending the fireballs hurtling into the goliath, exploding on impact. Reeling from the damage, the goliath's needles stop. Lowering his fist, the man moves with lighting fast speed. Appearing in front of the goliath, he swings the blade. Almost seeming alive, the black blade seems to draw in the darkness as it cuts into the goliaths' chest. Roaring, the goliath rears back and lashes out with its fist. Twisting the blade around, the man blocks the claws, getting knocked through a nearby wall with an almighty crash. Leaning its head back, the goliath roars and gets ready to unleash a volley of needles. Crackling in the air, a beam of energy comes from leviathan, knocking the goliath off balance for a moment. Pushing free of the remnants of the wall, the black-clad man staggers to his feet and disappears. Re-appearing next to Shizuri a moment later, he drives the sword into the bridge and leans heavily against it. Blood trickles from a wound on his head and he breathes heavily. Looking carefully at the man, she sees a slight resemblance to Leon in the man's face.

"Who are you?" She asks cautiously.

"Never mind that now, Shizuri Kawamura. You have a job to do. Take that blade of yours and drive it into the wound on the creature's chest. Once you've done that, use the power of Amaterasu to burn it to ash. I believe your anima can negate the enchantment." He says gesturing to the goliath.

Nodding, she readies her katana. Pushing off his own blade, he glances down at a gloved hand as Gilroy makes his way over to the pair.

"We're only going to get one shot at this. This body can't sustain my form much longer and by the looks of things, you two are at your limit. So, here's how it's going to work. Gilroy, get its attention and I'll create a clear path to the beast itself. That's when you strike. Is everyone ready?" Waiting a moment for the two to acknowledge his statement, he turns back towards the goliath.

"Let's go." Running forward, Gilroy twirls his axe next to leviathan, driving the tip into the bridge. Placing his hands out to either side of the blade, he chants.

"From the darkest depths of the blue, where light reaches not. Let the power of the deep reaches come forth now and destroy this enemy before us. Let the union of souls decimate all who stand against the power of the deep." Finishing the chant, he cuts his hand on the edge of the axe and smears blood across the centre. Twisting, he rips the axe from the ground and drives it into leviathan's chest in one motion. Stepping back, he waits for a moment as the blade glows an unearthly green. Pulsing, the light quickly engulfs leviathan and Gilroy. Moments later he steps clear of the light, his right hand covered with a scale gauntlet. Roaring, he runs toward the goliath. Leaping from the edge of the bridge, Gilroy lands heavily on the creature's shoulder. Twisting, he swings his fist hard against the creature's face, shielding his eyes as a blinding beam of energy erupts from the point of impact. Roaring in pain, the goliath stumbles away from the energy, its skin bubbling beneath the beam. Leaping away from the goliath, the energy crackling from his fist, Gilroy lands heavily on the bridge, his ribs creaking from the impact. Gasping, the beam dissipates. Rolling to his stomach, Gilroy tries to stand, only to collapse against the cobblestones. Rolling across the ground, leviathan's dormant anima form glitters in the twilight as his vision wanes. Swiping at the bubbling skin on its head, the goliath advances towards Gilroy. Stopping suddenly, as the black-clad man appears above its head, driving his blade into the top of its skull. Roaring, the goliath flails around trying to hit the man, punching itself in the face. Twisting away from the goliath as it swings at him a second time, the black-clad man leaps off the creature's head. Missing the claws by millimetres, he gasps as the remains of a tentacle clips his hip, sending him hurtling to the bridge. Bouncing off the stones with a dull thump, he lands just behind Gilroy.

"Flames of the sun, burn all those who would make night eternal. Ignite Amaterasu!" Finishing her incantation, Shizuri leaps towards the goliath. Crossing the distance quickly, she drives the flaming katana into the wound on its chest, twisting the blade in deep.

"Hakka Suru" Shouting, she smiles as purple flames erupt from the inside goliaths chest. Leaping clear, Shizuri watches in satisfaction as the goliath burns to a blackened shell in moments. Coming from above, the lights of an airship shine down onto the bridge, brightening everything. Turning from the creature as the flames dwindle away, she sees the man in black getting to his feet. Holding his side, he staggers forward a step before falling to his knees once more. Flaking away, his clothing starts to disappear, quickly engulfing him in a swirl of black. Disappearing as soon as it came, the black swirl bursts into the sky, revealing Leon kneeling on the ground, a black anima case clutched in his free hand. Smiling as a trickle of blood comes from his mouth, his eyes roll back into his head and he collapses on the bridge.

* * *

Standing at the door of the airship, Andrea watches with a grimace as the goliath burns to nothing. Looking down at the situation, she can't take her eyes off the man in black. Gasping out loud, she realises at last who it is as the black swirl surrounds him. Heart racing, she leaps from the airship and plummets straight down. Ribbons burst from her chest and quickly cover her arms as the wind whistles past her ear. Tracing a sigil as she falls, Andrea twists and activates it metres from the ground. Landing lightly on the stones, she barely makes a sound. Blinking forward, she appears next to Leon, ignoring the pain as her knees land on shards of broken glass and rubble. Panicking, she traces a sigil on his back. Tears come from her eyes as she analyses the damage to his body. Digging deep inside, she summons her full power. Standing, light emits from her fingers and forms tendrils that attach themselves to Leon's chest. Bursting from the point of contact, more tendrils of light shoot out to where his anima lay. Picking them up, the tendrils recoil back to his chest and bind themselves to him. Losing their light, they fade to ribbons. Frowning at the black tube on the top of the pile, she quickly traces a sigil in the air above him. Appearing from the palm of her hands, a clear bubble drifts down to envelop Leon and his anima. Clicking her fingers, the bubble solidifies and lifts a few feet off the ground. Sighing with relief, she turns to survey the damage. Stepping on shattered glass and rubble, Andrea inspects the wreckage of the buildings around the river. Cracking, a large piece of the railing breaks off from the destroyed bridge and plummets to the river below.

"Headmistress ..." Turning, she finds Estelle coming from a side street, blood running down a slight cut on her forehead.

"Captain Hardwyn. Report on the situation."

"Well, ma'am, most of the civilians were successfully evacuated to other areas. Still, there were plenty of injuries. The hospitals are barely coping with it right now. Also, from the few early reports that have come through, seems to be about a dozen casualties."

"Damn. How did a goliath even get into the city? Why didn't the wards pick up its breach of the shield?"

"I can answer that, My Lady." Supporting Gilroy with one arm, Shizuri calls out to Andrea. Frowning at the young woman, Andrea fixes her with an icy stare.

"Councilwoman Shizuri, why are you here? And your answer had better be a good one girl."

Passing Gilroy to a soldier, Shizuri stands in front of Andrea.

"Well, it's a long sto..." Rounding on the smaller woman before she can finish, Andrea grabs Shizuri by the front of her top, drawing her in close.

"I'm pretty sure I can shorten it. You came here, to pick a fight with Leon. And because of that distraction, neither one of you noticed the Goliath entering the city until it was too late. And now, London is once more on the verge of losing another council member. Does that about sum it up?"

"Well, it..." Letting go of her top, Andrea pushes the younger woman to the ground, flexing a hand above her, sigil already forming on the end of her fingertip. Cowering, the young woman raises a hand to shield herself. Looking up after the blow doesn't fall.

Reading a report given to her by a nearby soldier, Andrea lets the sigil die away.

"Shielded you say. Hmm, and it's too late now to know who. Gather everyone and lets all head back to the Schola, there's little more we can do here tonight." Getting to her feet, Shizuri tentatively approaches the headmistress.

"If it's all the same to you, My Lady, I think it's best for everyone if I just head back to Tokyo."

"You're coming to the Schola with me. I still have questions and you are going to answer them. I don't think you're in a position to refuse my request. Do you?" Finishing coldly, she glares once more at Shizuri as the young woman remains silent. Turning away with a click of her heels, she heads towards Leon and the descending airship.

67

Chapter Twelve

Slowly opening her eyes, Isabella blinks in confusion at the plain white ceiling above her. Laying still, she closes her eyes for a moment as the memories from the sealed room come flooding back. Moving her left hand, she slowly runs it down the right side of her body. Wincing in pain as her hand finds the bandages wrapped around her chest. Feeling Cleo's presence in her mind, a smile crosses her face. Slowly sitting up, she looks at the pressure next to her left leg, shock crossing her face as she finds Estelle asleep on the side of her hospital bed. Reaching over, she carefully brushes a strand of hair from her face, revealing a bandage wrapped around her temple.

"She has been here every night, lass, waiting for ye to wake," Esmeralda says quietly as she comes over.

"How long have I been here for?"

"About three days, lass. Though once you find out what's happened since, maybe you'll wish you'd stayed asleep."

"What do you mean?"

"I don't think I should be the one to tell ye but, seeing as I've already stuck me foot in my mouth, I might as well. Look at the far bed."

Looking at the far bed, she takes a moment to realise whose still frame is lying there. With a stifled cry, she goes to get up but finds herself held in place by Esmeralda.

"Easy lass. Running over there and busting all your stitches won't help anyone. There'll be time enough for you to see him. That boy be going nowhere soon."

"How did it happen?"

"It was a goliath class," Estelle answers sleepily. Sitting up, she wipes the sleep from her eyes and turns to look at Leon's prone form before continuing.

"Appeared in London the same day you were injured. We went out for a quiet drink and things got hectic fast. Were it not for the headmistress and the doc, he wouldn't have lived at all."

"Aye. Though he owes his life more to our headmistress than meself. That stasis field kept him breathing long enough to get here, so I could work on him." Turning, all three women look at Leon lying motionless on the bed.

"When will he wake up?" Isabella asks softly.

"It's hard to say, lass. The damage he sustained physically on its own was traumatic enough. But the problem is the strain that new anima be putting his system under."

"New anima?" The two girls say together.

"Aye. A case as black as night. To know more, you'd best ask the headmistress. I believe she knows something about it."

"I do, in fact, know something of those kinds of anima," Andrea proclaims from the door as she walks in.

"Good morning Headmistress," Estelle stammers out as she gets to her feet. Waving her back to her seat, the headmistress walks over to Isabella.

"Well, it's good to see your awake Isabella. You've had the good Captain here in quite a mess since you were hurt."

"Mistress Andrea, what's the deal with the black anima?" Sighing, the older woman walks over to Leon's bed and sits on the corner. Looking over at Leon, she turns to the girls with a sad look in her eyes.

"What I'm about to tell you can't leave this room. And what I know is limited and mostly speculation." Nodding their agreement, the three women look intently towards the headmistress as she continues.

"The black anima aren't like normal anima. They're immensely powerful but the strain it places on the user is extreme. Most keepers don't survive more than a few uses. This is only the second instance ever that I've personally seen. Each one is distinctive and never changes from keeper to keeper. I've heard they call themselves Scions. A kind of anima Lord or some such. The last one was insane and had such a thirst for destruction we had to kill the keeper it was bound to. And after that, we locked away it in the deepest vault of Fort Knox, but that was before the west fell. As far as we know it's still there, but with the concentration of nocturna around the area now, it would be nearly impossible to retrieve it. That thing called itself Scion Regal, and it chilled me to the bone when I saw its form. Black plate mail armour from head to foot. And a massive black broadsword."

"Sorry to interrupt Andrea, but when you say full form, what do ye mean by that?"

"Esme, surely you would have come across host-parasite type viruses in your time at Glasgow General. The way these anima operate is eerily similar. These scions form a kind of host bond with the keeper. So, when they're activated, they take their own form using the keeper's body as the vessel. Regal's keeper hinted that if a powerful enough keeper came along that they could achieve an unparalleled level of power. But I'm not sure I believe it. Regal was insane from what I could gather."

"True, that he is." Rasps a man's voice from behind. Turning Andrea looks towards Leon as he pushes himself up on the bed.

"Leon! When did you..." Andrea falls silent as he holds up a hand. Turning towards her, red eyes glint brightly in the morning light.

"Mistress... I am not Leon. His consciousness is still recovering from the battle. I am known as Scion Revenant. You said Regal was being held in a prison somewhere. I'm sorry to alarm you, but that is no longer the case. From Leon's memory, I learnt Regal was the one who killed your Lord Sigmund. He got this knowledge from the vision that overwhelmed him when he was cleansing Cleo. I don't think his host is willing though and there's something not quite right about it, but to what that is, I am unsure."

"You mean to tell me, you can force yourselves onto a keeper?"

"In certain circumstances, but those circumstances are very specific. Though there are limitations to how long we can maintain a hold over an unwilling host, however, and they cannot wield us like a normal anima. There is a cost when it comes to using one of us. The power we wield is great, and the cost is doubly so."

"What about Leon? Did you not just use him?"

"Leon seems to have been lucky and fallen into the exception this time around. There was no cost removed from him, but there will most likely be next time. There are five of us in total. I know Regal is now in play. We must locate the other three remaining scions. Without them, there will be no chance of stopping him. We tried years ago in our own world and look at what happened. He ripped our world apart and created the rift in to yours. We have nothing to go back to now. But on my honour, I will do everything in my power, to stop what happened to our world repeating itself on yours."

For a moment silence reigns over the infirmary before the headmistress speaks. Getting up from the bed, Andrea walks over to the window.

"Ok, so where do we start?"

Chapter Thirteen

Wandering aimlessly around the Schola grounds, Shizuri's depressive mood settles over her like a dark cloak. Kicking stones around as she walks, she ticks off the problems in her mind.

"First, that boy hasn't regained consciousness."

"He will in time, Shizuri." Ameratsu's deep voice echoes in her mind.

"How can you be so sure, Am? The council members were right. I was a fool."

"Perhaps, but placing the worst of London's destruction at your feet, is a little over the top if you ask me."

"Maybe, but If I hadn't been so hell-bent on starting a fight with Leon, I probably would've sensed the Goliath before it even had the chance to show itself."

Sighing deeply, as Ameratsu's presence fades away, she beckons to a young girl nearby. Coming over, the girl looks at her shyly.

"Yes, My Lady?" She asks quietly.

"Tell me, little one, where is this Schola's training room?"

"Just past the east pavilion, miss. It's in a standalone building. You can't miss it."

Thanking the young girl, she sets off and, after a few minutes of walking, locates the building. Walking through the entrance, an elderly man greets her.

"You here to train as well, are you, girl? Well, room three is free. Knock yourself out. Take care, mind you, while the summoned training creatures here won't kill you, they can still do some serious damage." Thanking the old man, she walks towards the gestured hallway ahead of her, smiling as he sits on a chair next to his desk and continues reading a paper. Following the old man's directions, she walks out into the hallway, stopping as she walks past room one. Looking in, she watches as a black-haired woman standing in the middle of the room pulls out an anima. Ignoring the generated nocturna around her, she flicks her hand and blue bracelets appear on her wrists. Dashing forward with ridiculous speed, she despatches the first wave of nocturna in front of her. Leaping high into the air as a second wave forms, her left hand quickly draws a sigil, at the same time a blue blade covered in ice, forms in her right hand. Glowing brightly in her fist, she swings the blade through the sigil and unleashes a torrent of ice spikes that impale all the nocturna below. Twisting, the girl lands softly on the ground, sliding to a halt as shards of ice rain down around her. Stepping back from the doorway, Shizuri leans against the wall, clutching her chest. Warmth quickly spreading through her chest to her face. Breathing heavily, she closes her eyes.

"Why am I having this feeling now?" She whispers to herself. Peering around the door frame, she watches as the girl runs through another formation, dispatching more summoned nocturna.

Coming back stronger than ever, the heat rises and her face flushes.

"So, after all this time, I'm still cursed."

Breathing heavily, bitter tears well up in her eyes as the words of her father come rushing back to her.

"You're no daughter of mine, girl. I could never have Sired someone who is incapable of producing an heir for me. No child of the Kawamura household would do such a thing as to go against God, by tainting them- selves with such nonsense" Turning from the room in a hurry she goes to leave and runs into a wall. Looking up into a man's face, she's shocked momentarily at coming face to face with the Chaos Guard commander himself. Trying hard to regain her composure, she takes a step back from him. Leaning against the wall and looking into the room, Gilroy lets out a quiet whistle.

"Damn, she sure is something. What do you think, My Lady?" Regaining her composure, she turns to Gilroy.

"She's skilled. I'll agree with that." Smiling, Gilroy looks around the doorframe once more.

"Well, Iris is one of the few elite keepers capable of activating the phantasm form of her anima. I wonder if she finished perfecting that move. Would you like to meet her? I'm sure she'd be delighted to meet a legendary member of the council such as yourself." Moving off the wall, he goes to take a step into the room, but he's stopped by a hand tightly gripping his arm. Looking at her, he raises an eyebrow as she diverts her gaze from his face and blushes heavily.

"I can't. My apologies, Commander Roscoe, but I shall have to decline your offer. I just recalled an urgent matter that I have overlooked and must attend to. Perhaps some other time." Letting go of his arm, she starts to walk down the corridor. Looking at her retreating back, Gilroy calls out to the small Japanese woman.

"It isn't a crime, you know. And there's nothing wrong with you because of it." Faltering, she stumbles at his words. Turning to face him, she finds herself faced with an empty corridor. The sound of Gilroy's voice calling to the young woman comes from inside the training room. Shattering at last, her resolve and poise collapse. Turning, she sprints from the training area, tears streaming unchecked from her eyes.

Chapter Fourteen

In darkness deeper than night, Leon's mind races. Echoing through the dark, voices flit around at the edge of his hearing. Reaching towards the voices, Leon wades through the darkness, cursing as the voices remain out of reach. Blooming around him, blinding light banishes the darkness and colours start to form images. Spinning quickly, the colours blur becoming clearer. And suddenly, he finds himself sitting at a desk in an office building. Gazing at a black anima in his hands, Leon's father stands with his back to him. Looking around, Leon glances at the room, finally remembering.

"I've been here before. Why am I relieving this now?" Swallowing heavily, his words echo into empty space and the memory plays.

Walking over to the desk where Leon is sitting, his father speaks.

"Well, Leon, have you considered my offer?"

"Which one is that? The one to join you and your pack of brainless muppets at Requiem or die? If that's the one you're referring to, then you can stick it. I can't believe, I ever aspired to be like you."

"I see. Well, that's a shame." Without warning, the anima in Alistair's hand becomes a blade, and he swings it with ferocious speed at Leon. Cursing, Leon kicks himself backwards, rolling clear of the desk as it's obliterated into splinters.

Spitting, Alistair kicks the remnants of the desk aside.

"I see. I guess that fool of a woman trained you well. No matter, you will still die here." Advancing towards Leon, a menacing aura radiates from him, as armour materialises on his arms. Stepping towards Leon, he takes a few air swings of the blade. Raising the blade to strike at Leon, Alistair stops as the door to the office bursts open and a young woman comes running in. Sliding to Leon's side, she throws a ball of yellow energy at Alistair. Swinging the blade to deflect it, surprise crosses his face as it explodes, throwing him through the wall into the next office. Grabbing Leon's hand, the young woman drags Leon to his feet and into the reception area.

"Farrah, what are you doing here?"

"Andrea sent me. Requiem has damaged the shield protecting San Fran. The shield is failing already and nocturna are beginning to run rampant through the city. The lifts are out of action, so we'll need to use the stairs to get out of here." Running into the next set of offices, they dash between the cubicles towards the stairs. An inhuman growl is the only warning the pair get as a man steps out and swings a clawed hand at them. Leon's training kicks in and he summons the wolf blade. Stepping past Farrah, he catches the claw on the flat of the blade. Before the man can react, Leon pushes against the claw and slashes the man's chest open, causing him to stagger. Flowing into a pattern, a second slash removes the creature's head, sending the body falling to the floor. Looking up, they realise the stairs are no longer an option as more growls echo from behind the doorway. Raising his blade, Leon gestures towards the door.

"Do you have a Plan B?" Pulling an anima from her belt, Farrah chants. Wings sprout from her back in a moment, and a rapier rests on her hip. Drawing the rapier, she runs to the window with a slash, she shatters it, sending glass cascading to the ground below.

"That is so, not a great Plan B."

"If you've got a better plan, I'd like to hear it." Dodging a partially turned nocturna's swing, Leon beckons Farrah to jump as he dispatches the creature.

"Go. I'll be right behind you." Turning away from Leon, she jumps out of the window, the wings holding her up with a few beats. Turning as Farrah begins to soar away, Leon takes a step towards the window, stopping as a surge of malicious energy comes from the room where his father was. Emerging from the rubble, Alistair wipes away the blood trickling down the side of his head. The gathering nocturna shy away from him as he walks into the room. Turning towards his father, Leon backs slowly towards the window.

"Last chance to accept my offer, boy. There won't be a second one. Actually, I'm fairly certain you will never come to my side, so I think I'll save myself the trouble and kill you now."

"That's such a cliché move, old man. Killing anything or anyone that gets in your way. How about we do things a different way?"

Raising his eyebrow Alistair replies,

"Oh, and what different way would that be, boy? Shall we talk it out? Or perhaps you can try sacrificing yourself for the world, just like Maria. Perhaps both your bloodstains on my blade might be the key to fixing my madness. Is that your plan? It might work if I was mad, but I'm as lucid as I've ever been." At the mention of his mother's name, a dark look comes across Leon's face. Tightening the grip on his sword, Leon replies through gritted teeth.

"You have no right to mention her name. You're not worthy of ever speaking her name again. As for my plan, well I'll have you stay here frozen for all eternity." Raising his blade, Leon chants.

"From the heights comes upon the world a tempest that has yet been stopped. Once passed, nothing remains but the silence of eternity. Howling Tempest of the White!" Leon's last words come out as a shout and from the wolf blade, a raging blizzard springs forth. Driving the blade deep into the concrete floor, Leon turns and jumps out the window. As he leaps into nothing, he traces a sigil and slows his descent. Falling slowly for a few moments, he lands softly upon the rooftop of a building on the opposite side of the street. Turning back towards his father's office, he smiles bitterly as a wall of ice quickly engulfs the floor of building, freezing it solid.

"That should stop your madness from poisoning this world, you sadistic bastard." A hand touches his shoulder from behind and before he can do anything, Farrah pushes herself into his back.

"I was so worried when you said your father wanted to see you. After everything that happened with your mother, I thought you might take up his offer. I'm sorry I interfered." Turning around, Leon pulls her into a hug. Before she can say another word, he kisses her. Pulling away slowly, he takes a deep breath before talking.

"I'm glad you came. If it wasn't for you, he would've killed me, just like my mother. But at least I managed to stop..." A sound like shattering glass stops Leon mid-sentence. Turning back towards the building, the pair watch in horror as a black blade flashes out, shattering the ice and sending large shards of it in every direction. Standing on the edge of the office floor holding Fenrir, Alistair yells loud enough for Leon to hear.

"Nice try, boy, but you'll need to do better than that if you want to kill me. Here, I believe this is yours, have it back." Leaning backwards, he hurls the sword at Leon and Farrah. Stepping forward, Leon extends his arm and concentrates hard. As the blade reaches him, it returns to its dormant state, allowing him to catch it with ease. Looking up at his father, Leon is lost for words. Sensing the confrontation is over, Alistair turns his back towards the pair and disappears into the depths of the building. A tug on his sleeve brings Leon back to his senses.

"Come on Leon. Let's get out of here before more nocturna arrive. Without the barrier holding them back, San Francisco will quickly become an infested wasteland. You remember what happened to Moscow when their barrier failed. We need to be well clear of here before the goliath types arrive."

"You're right. There's nothing more either one of us can do. Let's go." Taking her hand, he leads her to the door leading off the rooftop and together they descend into the aftermath of a city in panic.

* * *

Slowly opening his eyes, Leon blinks at the sunlight streaming through the window, making patterns on the roof.

"A dream then. But why now?" Whispering to himself, he closes his eyes for a moment. Pushing the dream aside, he looks at the roof and tries to place his location. With a start, his memory comes flooding back. London, the goliath and his impact into the river. Rushing to sit up, he groans loudly as pain lances through his chest and left arm. Movement by his right leg brings his attention to a woman lifting her head off the side of the bed and blinking sleepily at him.

"Andrea?" he croaks hoarsely. Smiling, she reaches over to the bedside table and pours him a glass of water. Handing it to the still stunned Leon, she gets to her feet and stretches. Straightening her hair and glasses, she sits on the edge of the bed before speaking.

"How are you feeling, Leon?"

"Like I've been hit by a lorry. How long has it been since London?"

"You've been asleep for four days. The Council of Nine is in an uproar and London is panicking. The new Lord Captain gets hospitalised in his first fight with something unexpected. It doesn't bode well for either of our reputations."

"How long has it been since you slept in your own bed?" Catching her off guard, the question brings a shocked look to her face. Before she can reply, laughter erupts from the other side of the room.

"HAHAHAHA. That boy do got ye there, Andrea. She's been here every night since ye were brought here, boyo. Now that ye be awake I might actually hav my infirmary back to normal. With just the normal injured patients in here. Oh, and don't move too much ye hear. I didn't spend hours stitching ye up so you can jus bust em all open again."

"Thank you, Miss....?"

"Esmeralda boyo. The names Esmeralda. But you call me Esme, same as everyone else round here. Got that?"

"I think I can manage that," Leon replies with a smile.

"Good. I swear Andrea that boy do hav too pretty a smile." Chuckling to herself, Esme leaves the two by themselves and retreats into her room at the other end of the infirmary. Turning to Andrea, Leon places his glass on the table before talking.

"That goliath was shielded. I swear next time I see him; I'll kill him."

"Alistair wasn't responsible for the goliath Leon. He called my office at the same time you were fighting. He said to me that he wished he was responsible for it and I believe he was actually telling the truth regarding the situation. Which means..."

"Which means, that someone else out there is also hell-bent on destroying the world, apart from Requiem." Silence lingers between the two for a while as the ramifications of the statement sink in. Both sigh heavily as a depressive atmosphere sets in. Breaking the atmosphere, Leon speaks first.

"What's the council's stance on things?"

"Well, they hold Shizuri primarily responsible for the incident, as she should have detected the creature, but as she was distracted by fighting you, she did not. They also want you to officially accept the London position as soon as you're able to stand. Once you're recovered, they will hold a physical meeting in Athens. You're required to attend."

"I see. Well, I'll need to set them straight on the Shizuri situation. I take it you didn't tell them it was shielded? Regarding the incident, what do they know about the being who calls himself Revenant?" frowning Andrea puts her hand on the side of her head as if she's thinking deeply before replying.

"I didn't mention about the shielding. I determined that would have been best coming from you. As for Revenant, they already knew about him. Apparently, they have a Scion in their possession already. Its name is Wraith. Though there's currently no one in the council capable of wielding it so they have it in safekeeping."

"What are their thoughts on me keeping possession of Revenant?"

"Well, seeing as he has already bound himself to you, they've unanimously agreed that you will be the one to keep possession of him. From here on out he will be treated as another one of your anima."

"Well, that's good then. It's one less thing I need to worry about. How are the others doing after everything that happened in London?"

"We're all fine, though you did your best to give us all a heart attack."

"Gil!" The big man smiles at Leon as he walks into the infirmary, closely followed by Anna. Leon smiles as he comes over and stands next to the bed. Standing up from her seat, Andrea turns to leave.

"I've got a few things to take care of. Leon, I'll come by later and we can talk more. Good afternoon Commander." Without waiting for a reply from either man, the headmistress leaves the infirmary.

"How's the shoulder?" Leon shifts in his bed and tries to rotate his arm before replying.

"Sore and stiff. But given the extent of my injuries, it's better than expected."

"That's fair. How long are they keeping you in here for?"

"I'm not sure I haven't spoken to the doc yet. Can I get you to do me a favour, Gil?"

"Sure. What do you need?"

"Find Shizuri. Get her to call an emergency council meeting for this afternoon. Once she's done that, tell her to come here and see me."

"I'm not sure that's a good plan man, given how injured you still are."

"I don't have the option of not doing it anymore. I'm starting to think there are things in motion beyond what's happening on the surface. Nocturna attacks are up. The murder of Lord Sigmund and now this attack on London. It was just Requiem but now that other forces are coming into play, things have changed. I am certain the cause is still most likely, that Requiem is up to something and whatever they are doing is causing problems all over. We just haven't found out the full extent of what that actually means yet. I need to get in touch with the council immediately." Looking at Leon on the bed, a dark look crosses Gilroy's face.

"I hope you 're wrong, old friend. For the sake of the world, I hope you are. But I'll do as you ask." With a sigh, the big man turns and leaves the infirmary. His heavy footsteps echoing in the empty corridor.

Chapter Fifteen

Walking down the hall towards the council chamber, Shizuri watches the man next to her out of the corner of her eye. As he walks, his steps irregularly while holding onto his chest. Stopping, she turns towards him.

"Do you need to stop and rest for a moment?" Slumping against the wall, Leon replies.

"No I'll be alright. It's just these damn ribs. They're not set properly yet. If we just keep a constant pace, I should be fine. Let's go." Clutching his chest and pushing himself clear of the wall, Leon continues down the corridor. Shaking her head, Shizuri hurriedly follows behind him.

* * *

Reaching the council chamber a few minutes later, Leon leans heavily on Shizuri. Leading him over to the table that takes up most of the room, Shizuri's step falters for a moment and Leon crashes heavily into his seat. Sucking air in through gritted teeth, Leon pushes himself up and drops into the chair properly. Regaining her footing, Shizuri begins to apologise but stops at a gesture from Leon, as the other seats are filling with holographic images of people. Shizuri nods before heading around the table to sit in her seat. In a few moments, all nine seats are occupied. Leaning forward, a young woman with strawberry blonde hair and blue eyes talks.

"Well, well, you're certainly a handsome one, Mr Aelfdane. I didn't expect you to be up and about so soon. It was a surprise, when Shizuri contacted me and informed me you wanted a meeting. But I guess I should introduce myself. I'm the leader of the Council of Nine, Cassandra Howard. But people just call me Cassy. I'm based out of Sydney, Australia. And I guess you already know Miss Shizuri. So I'll let the others introduce themselves, starting with little Mai." As Cassandra Howard finishes, the girl to Leon's left frowns and speaks up.

"Some here could do with a lesson on etiquette. Apologies for our foolish leader, Mr Aelfdane. I am Mai Nianzu, the representative for China. Based out of Hong Kong. Pleased to make your acquaintance." A man across the table from Leon is the next to speak. In a deep voice, he addresses everyone.

"Good afternoon everyone. Welcome to the Council of Nine Mr Aelfdane. My name is Kazeem Alawari. I'm the member of the Middle Eastern states. Based out of Abu Dhabi. It is truly a pleasure to finally meet you." All the other members of the council introduce themselves. Dion

Shadwell from Washington, America. Ennelyn Abendorth from Zurich, Switzerland. Bernado Grimani from Venice, Italy. And Luka Yakovich from New Moscow, Russia. Once the introductions are done Cassy shifts forward in her seat.

"Well Leon, now everyone has been introduced to you, we can get down to business. What was the purpose of you calling this meeting suddenly? Especially, as you're barely able to walk, if reports about the severity of your injuries are to be believed." Leon shifts to lessen the pain radiating from his chest before responding.

"I believe you're all well aware of the events that took place in London a little under a week ago. But there are a few details they did not make you aware of. First, the stage three goliath that attacked was sent there on purpose. Not only was it shielded against magic, but I'm certain its abilities were also boosted beyond that of a normal goliath. I was also under the impression that Requiem was responsible, but this doesn't appear to be the case. Headmistress Marques was in contact with their leader at the time of the event and he claimed to have no part in it, which she believes and so do I. This means, we now have a serious problem. If someone other than Requiem is attacking cities, we need to identify and stop the person or persons responsible as soon as possible. We can't fight a war on two fronts right now." Once he finishes, he slumps back into his seat and silence reigns for a moment. Surprising everyone, the first to respond to the new information is Ennelyn from Germany.

"If what you say is true, this is troubling news indeed. And if Lady Marques has confirmed it, then I'm willing to believe in this second party. We had a similar incident a few weeks ago. Luckily enough for us, it was only a small group of nocturna. But it was the same as what you say. Immunity to magic and they seemed to be intent on destroying the city."

"Why didn't you report this at the last meeting Lyn?" replies Cassy. Shrugging, the German woman replies,

"It slipped my mind. Given we were worried about the loss of the British representative, it didn't seem important. I also believed it was just a standalone incident. Most probably from someone living on the outskirts of the city. We still have not finished the upgrade in order to bring everyone behind the barrier, so dissent is on the rise. But I'm beginning to think we may indeed be looking for a second faction." Pursing her lips in thought, the Leader of the council has a concerned look on her face. A hand slapping the table causes everyone to look at the little man sitting to Leon's left.

"This is a foolish notion. Do you really think that such a faction actually exists? There have been two attacks and as far as I am concerned, these are standalone incidents. Typical Londoner thinking, it is. Not everyone is out to get you." Grinding his teeth, Leon barely keeps his cool as he replies.

"Typical Londoner thinking, you say? Listen here mate, I know a directed attack when it comes. I'm sure you've all been made aware of my heritage. I have been fighting off directed attacks for years. This isn't the time to sit on our arses and do nothing as it appears the Italian's apparently want to do. Or perhaps you have another reason for wanting the investigation stopped. Got something to hide, Bernardo?" Bernardo goes a deep shade of red and starts to twitch.

"Why you...."

"Enough! Bernardo stand down. Leon, stop provoking him. I won't tolerate fighting between any of you. Now I'm also of the opinion after having heard these reports, that there is a rogue party out there aiming to stir up trouble. The problem is how are we going to identify and stop these people?" All the council members sit silently for a moment before the American representative Dion speaks up.

"The first thing we need to establish is where they're next likely to attack. Now given the very little information we have for the moment; I think we should each do a small amount of reconnaissance first. I propose that we all go our separate ways for the time being and reconvene in person in Athens two months from now at the World Council's meeting. It's as good a place as any to discuss all of our findings and it's a very good candidate for the next target as well. We may well end up killing two birds with one stone." Cassy nods her head at Dion's words.

"I'm going to agree with you, Dion. Currently, that seems to be the best course of action. Now Leon, as you 're still injured, you need to focus on healing, more than investigating. For the time being, Shizuri will remain stationed at the London Schola with you. Shizuri, you will be responsible for looking into the incident of the goliath and gathering any information that may be useful in locating the person or people responsible. Everyone else is to conduct their own investigations into the matter regarding these attacks. Any information you uncover regarding Requiem and their movements will also prove to be useful. I look forward to hearing your reports in person when we convene in Athens. Everyone is dismissed." With nods, the council members disappear one by one. Giving Leon a death stare, Bernardo reaches forward and turns off his own holographic projector. Leon, Shizuri and Cassy are the last three remaining at the table. With a sigh, she turns to Leon.

"I couldn't say this before, Leon, but I suspect Bernardo knows more than he lets on. Your provocations may have just put a stop to my investigations into him. With his guard up, gathering any information about his movements is impossible now. That's not your fault though. There's no way for you to have known what I was doing. After all, you haven't even been officially sworn as a member yet. Anyway, once you've recovered fully, I want you to head to..." Everything else she says is lost as his consciousness dims.

"Leon?" Shizuri inquires, looking over at him, but his injuries finally take their toll. Running footsteps and both women's voices are the last things he hears as everything goes black.

Chapter Sixteen

Sitting in her cell, the girl doesn't even move at the sound of approaching footsteps. She doesn't know how long it's been since Bauer's earlier visit. How many times have they brought in Regal to break her? How many times has she just held out? She doesn't know and time has no meaning in the cell when she stares at the same four grey walls every waking moment. The door opens and closing her eyes, she braces herself for the inevitable mental assault.

"Hello, my dear. I hear you've been giving my subordinates no end of trouble." The man's voice causes her to start. Opening her eyes, she looks into an older man's smiling face. A smile that never reaches his eyes.

"Alistair!" Still smiling, he walks over to her, closely followed by a small girl with black hair and piercing green eyes.

"Victoria?" The young girl looks up for a moment before bowing her head back down as Alistair continues walking over. The look in the older man's eye causes her to lean back into the wall as far as she can. Squatting down in front of her, he reaches out a hand and places it on the left side of her neck.

"I do apologise for this, my dear, but you really aren't leaving me any other choice."

"What are you going to... AAiieee" Her pain-filled scream echoes in the cell as black energy comes out of Alistair's hand. Black webbing spreads along her neck from the point of contact. Her screaming stops and, gritting her teeth, she stares defiantly at the older man. With a dark smile, the black energy increases. Her eyes widen and a touch of fear enters them. Sweat begins to bead on Alistair's forehead as the girl continues to resist.

"It's futile to fight me, my dear. You can't win. Give in already."

"Never!" she states as defiantly as she can. Anger fills his eyes, and he lashes out with his free hand, striking her. Shock briefly registers on her face before her eyes go blank. Pulling his hand away, Alistair stands and steps back before wiping the sweat off his brow. Raising his right hand, he mutters a word and the shackles release.

"Come here and let me take a look at you." Slowly rising to her feet, she obediently walks over and stands in front of Alistair. Reaching up, he pulls her shirt to one side and examines the area where her neck meets her shoulder. A black mark, almost like a brand, now resides there.

Turning towards the door with a satisfied look, he shouts into the hall.

"BAUER!" At his shout, footsteps come running down the hall before the man known as Simon Bauer appears.

"You called?"

"I did. Take our lovely new employee and get her dressed. After that, make sure you're both ready to leave. I have a job for you."

"As you wish, Alistair. What are you planning to do about that son of yours?"

"You need not concern yourself with him, Simon. He will be dealt with shortly." Glancing down at the girl standing next to him, he smiles a cold smile.

"I have a present I'm sure he will enjoy." Chuckling, Baur collects the blank-eyed girl and leaves the cell. Walking over to the window, Alistair pulls out and lights a cigarette. Taking a drag, he looks up into the night sky.

"Be seeing you soon Leon."

Turning, he exits the cell, the young girl following closely behind.

* * *

Driving through London the morning after the council meeting, a feeling of surprise washes over Shizuri as she watches the people go about their lives normally. Men and women hurry through the streets to get to work and children dressed in uniforms are walking around, laughing, as if nothing had ever happened. Finally, nearing the bridge where the attack took place, she looks around with sadness at the many damaged buildings from the fight. Arriving at the blockade in front of the bridge, she thanks the driver and gets out of the car. Walking past the police barrier, she sees Gilroy standing at a makeshift table, talking to men in safety vests and hard hats. Walking past them, she steps out onto the bridge, looking at the damage to the bridge in the daylight. Whistling softly at the destroyed guardrail and the heavily damaged buildings on the far side of the river, she doesn't notice as Gilroy comes and stands next to her.

"Yup, it sure made a mess of things, but we'll rebuild." Looking up at the big man, she turns and leans a foot on a broken piece of a guardrail.

"Was anyone able to examine the Goliath?"

"No. It had turned to dust before we got back. Any evidence that may have been on it, is long gone."

"I suspected as much. Anyone who would go to such lengths to control a Goliath, wouldn't be foolish enough to leave traces behind." Turning towards the spot where the corpse had been a few days before, she looks over the damaged rail into the river. Breaking through the clouds at that moment, the sun lights up the area and a glint of metal catches her eye, causing her heart to leap inside of her chest.

"Surely we wouldn't be that lucky?" she whispers to herself. Without a word to Gilroy, she strips off her clothes as she steps away from the destroyed section of railing. Gilroy turns bright red and quickly turns away before talking over his shoulder.

"What are you doing, Lady Kawamura?"

"Going for a swim. Back in a moment." Dropping her dress and boots in a neat pile, she runs barefoot to the edge. Shouts come from the workmen as she dances past the broken masonry to the edge of the bridge. Without a shred of fear, she leaps from the edge, the wind whistling past her ears as she plunges to the river below. Her breath is knocked out of her from the frigidness of the water as she enters with barely a splash. Composing herself quickly, she swims towards the area she had locked in her mind. Going deeper towards the riverbed, she sees the glint of metal ahead of her. Closing the last of the distance, she reaches the object. Looking down at the piece of metal, she discovers it's a twisted spearhead. Reaching down, her hand grips the spearhead and visions dance in front of her eyes.

* * *

A girl looks out from behind a cupboard at a slightly older man who is on a phone call. While she hears no words, she can feel the girl's shock at the words spoken by the man. The vision shifts and the young girl is running on the top of a building, her brown hair flying in the breeze. She leaps from the building and lands lightly on the head of a nearby goliath. Pulling an anima from her belt, she summons up a cutlass and, driving it into the goliath, slides down its back. When she's about halfway down she stops, removing the spearhead piece of metal from her belt and with a twist, drives it into the heart of the behemoth chanting as she does so. With a roar, the behemoth flails around crashing into buildings. Reaching over its shoulder, it tries to grab the girl on its back. Dodging its hands, she continues chanting. Then, with a slight twist, it catches her. With a scream, she's lifted high into the air above the behemoth. Before it can do anything to her, she draws a second anima, and another cutlass appears. Slashing with her second cutlass, the blade bites deep into the monster's hand, causing the behemoth to let go of her with a grunt of pain. Landing heavily on its shoulder, she quickly scrambles back to her feet and leaps down to where she was, picking up her chant once more. After a few moments, the goliath staggers to a stop. With an almighty crash, the creature falls to its knees. Dropping to the ground, the girl walks around to the front of the goliath and says something. With blank eyes, the goliath reaches its hand down for her to climb on before regaining its feet and shambling off. The girl stands steady on its shoulder, as if she now owns the monster. Shock runs through Shizuri as the girl looks up.

Forgetting she's underwater, Shizuri inhales and her lungs fill with water. Panicking, she tries to take another breath and more water fills her lungs. As the blackness closes in, a wave of strength courses through her. Pushing hard off the riverbed, she swims for the surface. Every muscle shrieking with pain as her lungs cry out for oxygen. Growing lighter, the water gets easier to swim through and the surface shimmers just above her. Hope wells up in her chest as she nears the surface. As quickly as it came, the strength dissipates and a wave of exhaustion washes over her. Dazzling just above her, the sunlight seems to mock her with every reflected ray. Just as she begins to give up, a woman's figure plunges into the water and quickly swims down to her level. Grabbing Shizuri around the waist, she summons a pillar of ice just below them. With a muffled rushing sound, the ice erupts and spits them both from the water like a cork from a bottle. They stay airborne briefly, before landing heavily on a platform of ice. Laying on her side Shizuri coughs up water, as she lays panting on the ice. Her eyesight blurs from the water and she can't make out the face of the woman coming towards her.

"Lady Kawamura, are you alright?" Still blinking water out of her eyes, she's lifted slowly into a sitting position. As the water finally clears from her eyes, she sees for the first time the woman who rescued her from the river. The same one she saw at the training centre. Blushing slightly, she gets to her feet, still coughing. Standing on a shelf of ice floating in the middle of the river, Shizuri shivers from the cold. Turning back to her rescuer, Shizuri steps around a blue sword embedded in the ice and bows deeply.

"Thank you for coming to my aid. If you had not, I would have surely drowned."

"It's my pleasure, My Lady. I have your clothes over here. Perhaps you should put them on before the men get too side-tracked from their work." Looking at the bridge, Shizuri turns bright red as she realises all the bridge workers are watching her with big grins on their faces. With a squeak, she covers herself and drops to her knees. Stepping forward, the young woman grasps the hilt of her sword in the platform. Within moments, the chuckles from the men on the bridge are cut off as a wall of ice surrounds the small platform. Turning back towards Shizuri, she smiles a warm smile.

"There you go, My Lady, now you get dressed in private." Walking over to the pile of clothing, Shizuri quickly pulls on her clothes. Before long, her wet body soaks through her clothes and she shivers. Walking over to the girl, she summons her anima.

"Here, let me repay the favour of helping me. I'll dry us. This won't take but a moment." Reaching out, she extends her pointer finger and places it on the woman's forehead. Closing her eyes, she exhales deeply. As her eyes open, warm air circles around the two women. Stepping back, Shizuri drops her arm to her side. The warm air persists for a moment before dissipating softly. Feeling her clothes, the young woman smiles.

"Thank you, My Lady."

"It's no problem. After all, you did just save my life. It pales by comparison. What's your name?"

"Iris Aegelmare, my Lady."

"If you don't mind my asking My Lady, but what reason could you have for risking your life like that?" Taking off her jacket, Shizuri picks up the broken spearhead and shows it to Iris.

"This is why. I'm not sure if you're familiar with its like, but this clue into who attacked London was worth the risk."

"May I take a look, My Lady?" At Shizuri's nod, Iris walks over and takes the device carefully from her. Rotating it in the light, she examines it closely.

"I'm very familiar with these devices, My Lady. My family were heavily involved in the manufacturing of such devices a few years ago. I do not know who made this one, but I can tell you with certainty that it was not manufactured by any of the local dark dealers. All the local dealers make plain items, so they are nearly impossible to trace back. However, this piece is intricate, almost a work of art. Whoever made this wanted everyone to know they made it. I imagine you will find an answer elsewhere. Once we are back, I can give you the names of the local dealers if you'd like to question them."

"I would very much appreciate that." Iris's smiling response causes butterflies to erupt in Shizuri's stomach. Blushing heavily, she takes the device back from Iris before wrapping it carefully in her jacket. Turning back to Iris, Shizuri beckons to the younger lady. With a wave of her hand, the ice wall surrounding them dissolves and forms a set of stairs running back up to the bridge. As she marches up the stairs, all the workmen that were watching her from above disappear as if by magic. The only one who remains is Gilroy. As she walks up to the big man, his smiling face becomes worried, and he seems to shrink at Shizuri's anger.

"Mr Roscoe. If you're quite done watching the view, do be so kind as to summon my driver. I need to return to the Schola immediately."

"Ye...yes. Certainly My Lady." Trying hard not to run, he turns and walks toward the parked car. Moments later, he arrives with a toot of the horn.

"Your driver has gone for a break; I can drive us back though."

"Step aside, I'll drive, and you're coming with us. You need to see what I found as well." Climbing out of the driver's seat at a gesture from the Japanese woman, he quickly climbs into the back seat. Without another word, Shizuri and Iris climb into the front seats, and with squealing wheels, head towards the Schola.

89

Chapter Seventeen

Letting the wind blow through his greying hair, the man relaxes slightly. Looking down over London, he can see the cranes and work crews trying to repair the damage the goliath wrought on the city. But it's not the bridge or the city that really holds his attention. It's the Schola behind the city. Only just visible from where he stands, It's still an impressive vision. Sensing its shield from where he stands, he smiles and gestures towards the school as a small woman dressed in black comes over.

"He's in there. Make it quick Victoria. Are you going to be able to kill him? He is your brother after all."

"If it's what you wish, father, I won't hesitate." The girl replies in a cold and lifeless tone.

"Well, I wish he'd never strayed from the path I set him on. But like your mother, he always believed in the greater good. Go now." Turning away, she walks towards the edge of the cliff.

"Oh, and Victoria? Don't fail me." With a nod, she vanishes over the side of the cliff. Still looking down, he smiles a twisted smile.

"You'll see our son soon enough, Maria. And you're the only one to blame filling his head with all that righteous crap." Never looking back, he turns and walks away.

* * *

Opening his eyes, Leon blinks slowly in the late afternoon light. Looking around, he realises he is in the infirmary once again. Slowly propping himself up to a sitting position, he touches his ribs gingerly.

"Easy boyo. We didn't go to all the trouble of fixing them wounds so ye could tear them open again."

Looking towards the sound of the voice, he sees Esmeralda coming across the room with a tray of food.

"How long has it been since the meeting?"

"Just a day. Now I'd like to keep ye here for a few more days, but life seldom works out how we wish ye know? Ye ribs are more or less healed now but they'll be tender a few more days yet. That left arm will take a wee while longer to be fully healed. After all the damage done to it, yore lucky it even works at all. Don't take dem bandages off for at least another week. They've been specially designed to help fix that muscle in your shoulder. Now get dressed and I'll let the headmistress know yore awake." Wheeling over a cart next to Leon, she places the tray of food down and then throws a bundle of clothes on the bed. Nodding, she turns and heads back into her office. Leon quickly eats everything on the plate and gets up. Standing in front of the full-sized mirror on the wall, he looks at the bandages crisscrossing his torso and left shoulder. Flexing his shoulder, he looks at his left arm and the tightly wound bandages down it. Unwrapping the clothes bundle, he blinks in surprise as his anima tumble out of the top. As he touches them, voices explode into his mind. Staggering from the onslaught, he breathes a sigh of relief as a stern male voice breaks over them all.

"Enough. Let the man get his bearings before you all scream at him."

"Thank you, Revenant. It is Revenant isn't it?"

"Aye. That it is. I'm sorry for not being able to reduce the damage to your body." Shaking his head Leon replies.

"It's fine. Don't worry about it. If it wasn't for you, I'd be dead. So, I'm glad." Slowly but painfully, he gets dressed. Pants, socks and boots go on first. Just as he finishes attaching his anima to his belt, he senses a familiar presence approaching fast. With a start, he realises who it is. Moving from the bed, he walks a few paces before turning suddenly.

"You're in no condition to fight properly, Leon. You can't rely on your anima for this fight. The strain will be too much for your system." Warns Revenant.

"I'm well aware of that. Guess I'll have to rely on arcana. Damn. It isn't exactly my strong suit."

Extending his right hand, he scribbles a sigil of light. The window explodes inwards, and a small woman dressed in black leaps through. In her hand are two twisted, cruel-looking daggers. Finishing the sigil, Leon flicks it forward. Missiles of light explode from it and arc in every direction towards the bed. The girl's eyes widen for a moment before she's engulfed by an explosion that blows the side of the wall out and knocks Leon off his feet. Out of the flames the girl springs. Her clothing torn and blood trickles from a wound on the side of her head as she leaps forward. The muffler that was covering her face falls to the ground as she lands in front of Leon. Pushing himself slowly to his feet, he faces off against the young woman.

"Hello, Victoria. Still leaping before looking, I see." Wiping away the blood running down the side of her head, she replies through gritted teeth.

"Why brother? Why didn't you accept Father's offer? You clearly know why I am here. He wants you dead."

"I know. In time I hope you'll come to realise that father is as twisted as the nocturna that threaten the world."

"I'm well aware of how twisted he is. But what choice do I have? After your defiance, he made sure all his subordinates would obey. Even being his daughter doesn't grant an exception." Pulling down the left side of her shirt, she exposes the black crest on her neck. Sobbing, she steps forward into Leon's chest.

"Please brother. Come back with me? Don't make me do this." Patting her on the head, he quickly traces a small sigil with his left hand and attaches it to his right.

"Sorry V. I can't do that."

She steps back, and her blades flash in the light as she swings them at him. Leon swings his right fist forwards, meeting the blades. With bright sparks, the blade reflects off the red shield of light attached to his hand. Using the moment that she's stunned, Leon retreats a few more steps toward the back of the room.

"Sorry brother but you leave me no choice now." Bringing her blades around in front of her, she casts an incantation.

Reacting quickly, Leon pulls out Fenrir and command summons him.

"Leon, don't do it!" Shouts Revenant in his mind.

"I don't have a choice."

"Howling wind Scythe!" Slamming Fenrir's blade tip into the floor, Leon unleashes a blade of wind towards Victoria. Without stopping her chanting, she leaps to the side. But not fast enough. The edge of the wind blade catches her left shoulder, slicing it open as her twin blade's glow red. Ignoring the blood streaming from her shoulder, she rushes Leon. Summoning up his shield from earlier, Leon braces his sword against it and takes her attack head-on. Red lighting crackles as the blades connect. Followed by an explosive force that throws Leon through the infirmary door, turning it to splinters. Landing heavily, he continues sliding down the hallway before rolling to his feet and coming to a stop. Dropping to one knee, he grabs his chest as pain tears through it. The pain increases as he coughs, his mouth filling with the taste of blood. From the back of his mind comes Revenant's voice frantically.

"Leon, you've broken two ribs, and one of them has punctured your left lung. Your body is not currently in a condition where it can sustain my force. Likewise, you cannot summon Valkyrie either. However, if you release Fenrir and use Aurora, you should be able to stem the blood flow and lessen the effect of your injuries." Gritting his teeth in pain, Leon reaches behind his belt and removes Aurora's casing. With a quick chant, he summons her. Wings flap lazily at his back and a white glove appears on his hand. A white nimbus surrounds him and the pain in his chest lessens.

"Leon, I've managed to stop the bleeding and stabilise your ribs. But please take it easy. Your body can't withstand much more of this." Releasing Fenrir, he turns back towards the infirmary as Victoria kicks away the remnants of the door.

"I'll try but there are no guarantees here." Stepping out with her blades glowing red, she swings them and unleashes two scything lines of energy towards Leon. Stepping backwards into the main hall, he turns and jumps over the railing, landing on the floor below. The blades wink out halfway across, but not before leaving viscous tears in the walls and floor. Looking quickly around the hall, Leon makes a quick decision and starts running for the main door. Sensing energy from behind him, he turns and quickly summons a shield. Leaping off the rail, Victoria hurls a ball of energy towards Leon. Hitting the ground in front of him, it dissipates into the floor. Frowning, Leon takes a step forward. Light blooms from under the floor, and with a deafening blast, the floor explodes.

* * *

Sitting in the cafeteria, Estelle glances across at Isabella. Looking up from her meal, she meets the Security Captain's eyes.

"What's up Stelle?"

"How are you feeling? Have your wounds healed?" Stretching her arms up, she feels her ribs and grimaces a little.

"Hmm, mostly. They're still a bit tender though. And I haven't recovered enough to use even a training blade, let alone summon Cleo."

"You need to give it time. Don't push yourself. It won't do any good if you bust open all your wounds again."

"Yeah, I know." Sighing, the younger girl plays around with her food for a few moments before looking out the window in the infirmary's direction.

"How do you think Leon's doing?" Looking in the same direction, Estelle takes a long drink from her coffee before replying.

"I don't know but, he's tough. I'm sure he'll be fine."

"Yeah, you're probably right." Turning back from the window, Isabella pushes her plate to the middle of the table and leans back.

"I'm done eating. Feel like a trip to town? I need to get away from here for a night,"

"I'd love...," her words are cut off as an explosion comes from the front of the Schola's main building. Jumping out of their chairs, the two women look at each other. Isabella is the first to speak.

"You don't think he's involved, do you?"

"Of course, he is. He's always involved. You go and get the rest of the guard. I'll head there now."

Isabella opens her mouth to complain, but Estelle cuts her off.

"You're in no condition to fight, I'm sorry, Izzy, but this is all you can do this time. Now hurry." Turning away from Isabella, Estelle runs as fast as she can towards the front of the main building. Praying silently for Leon to be alright, she sprints towards the front of the school.

* * *

Regaining consciousness at the base of the stairs, Leon slowly pushes himself up. Blood drips onto the ground from the gash across his forehead. Looking around, he spots Fenrir's dormant form on the ground near his hand. He reaches over to pick it up, but a blow to his stomach knocks the wind out of him and turns him over onto his back. Standing above him, Victoria points one of her blades down towards his chest.

"You should have just agreed to come with me, Leon. Now, this ends." Raising her blade, she drives it towards Leon's chest. Energy surges through him and with a burst of speed, he rolls, narrowly avoiding the blade. With the sound of cracking concrete, the blade sinks into the ground where his chest had been. Continuing his roll, he uses his momentum and in one movement gets to his feet. Looking around quickly, he locates Aurora's dormant form lying near his foot. Without taking his eyes off his sister, he reaches down and picks it up. Muttering an incantation in a moment, wings flap lazily from behind his back once again. Breathing heavily, Leon backs up a little to put some distance between himself and Victoria. Finally pulling her blade free from the ground, she takes a combat stance before slowly advancing.

"Leon, you have no chance of fighting her now. You need to get away." Revenant says in his mind.

"I'm well aware, but that's easier said than done. She's not my sister for nothing." Clutching his ribs as another wave of pain runs through him, Leon staggers. Victoria doesn't waste the opportunity and with lighting speed, she charges towards him. Leon takes another step back and quickly changes Aurora into her rapier form. Waiting until the last second, Leon parries his sister's first strike and narrowly doges the second before retreating past her to the foot of the stairs. As he regains his footing, a slight whistle comes from above and an arrow streaks past his head. Blades whirring, Victoria knocks the arrow aside and takes a defensive stance, blades raised in a reverse grip. Looking behind him, a wave of relief washes over him as he sees Estelle coming down the stairs with her anima drawn.

"Jeez. Is it impossible for you to go one day without getting into trouble?"

"Well if I did, we'd all die from boredom."

"Think I'd prefer the boredom to be honest. Now step aside Leon, Ill deal with this." Raising her bow above her head as she comes off the steps, stopping next to Leon as red light covers the weapon. Lowering her arms as the light dissipates, the bow disappears, and a buckler and sword take its place.

"Now I'll show you what happens to people who mess with my Schola."

"Step aside, bitch, this is between my brother and me. You have no right to interfere!"

"I have every right as the Schola's Security Captain. If you think I'm going to let you walk in here and attack people, you've got another thing coming girl."

"Guess I'll just kill you first then."

"You're more than welcome to try." Before Leon can stop them, the two women cross the distance between them, and with the clash of steel, they fight.

Chapter Eighteen

As they approach the Schola grounds, Gilroy picks up the cloth wrapped piece of steel sitting in the middle of the back seat. Unwrapping the spear-shaped object, he pulls it out and holds it up high enough so that Shizuri can see it through the car's mirror. Turning it over, he inspects it before musing to himself aloud.

"So, this is all it takes to control a goliath, huh? Doesn't look like much." Meeting his eyes through the mirror, she sighs before replying.

"It may not look like much, Commander Roscoe, but that is indeed what can control a goliath, not to mention its numerous other uses. As you well know, it is forbidden to make such weapons from the remnants of a destroyed anima. The people who trade in this dark art are far and few between so it shouldn't be too hard to track them down one by one and get a name for the creator of this particular piece."

Gilroy nods before wrapping the spearhead in its cover once more and placing it back on the seat next to him.

"I hope you're right and it doesn't take long to track them down." With a shrug, he settles back into his seat and looks out the window at the scenery passing by. Open fields dotted with grazing animals and the occasional windmill lead to the sandstone wall of the Schola. Looking towards the main building, he notices the smoke rising above the wall. Sitting forward, instantly alert, he impacts the back of the seat with his arm, causing Shizuri to swerve.

"What the hell do you think you're doing, Commander?" She yells, regaining control of the vehicle. It takes only a moment for her to see the smoke rising from the school as well. Peering through the front window, Iris gestures towards the Schola.

"That doesn't look good, My Lady."

"I know Iris. Try contacting the guard station. See what's going on." Picking up a small phone from the centre console, Iris quickly punches in a number. Putting the phone to her ear, she waits for a moment before putting the phone back down again.

"No answer My Lady. I fear something may be very wrong." Nodding his head in agreement, Gilroy settles back into his seat. Without a word, Shizuri steps harder on the accelerator pedal. With a roar of the engine, the car springs to life and picks up speed. The fields begin passing by at a blur and before long; the sandstone wall of the Schola replaces them. As the gate gets closer, cold sweat beads on Gilroy's face.

"You might want to start slowing down Lady Kawamura." He says in a shaky voice. Turning to face him, the crazy look in her eyes causes fear to well up inside him.

"You might want to hold on to something Commander." Gripping the back of the front seats, Gilroy can only watch as the gate approaches rapidly. Pushing the pedal harder, Shizuri grips the steering wheel as the car gains more speed. With the sound of squealing metal, the car careens through the gates, smashing the windscreen and throwing the occupants forwards in their seats. As the gates clatter off the car's hood, the motor gives a rattle before smoke billows out from underneath the front of the car. Stalling, it goes into a spin as the brakes lock. Wrestling with the steering wheel, Shizuri manages to gain a sort of control and guide the vehicle away from the trees lining the drive. Moments later the car comes to a halt, halfway down the drive. Unbuckling himself, Gilroy tumbles out of the car onto his knees, breathing heavily.

"You're never driving again. Are you crazy? You could've killed us!" Climbing out from the driver's seat, Shizuri smiles innocently before replying.

"But I didn't. You need to live a little, Mr. Roscoe." The sounds of steel clashing nearby, focuses their attention on the situation at hand. Getting to his feet, Gilroy takes everything in from a quick look around. Smoke billows from the top of the stairs and at the feet, Leon is propped up against the banister. On the open field in front of the main building two women are locking blades in deadly combat. Shizuri steps away from the car, drawing her anima as she stops next to the smoking and crumpled hood.

"Commander! See to Leon. I'll assist the Guard Captain." Without waiting for an answer, she runs towards the ongoing fight. Sighing in exasperation, Gilroy gets to his feet and runs towards Leon. Arriving at the base of the stairs, he's shocked at the damage to the school. But, more so at the damage to his friend. Propped against the outside stone bannister on the stairs leading to the main entrance, Leon is bleeding from multiple wounds and clutching his chest. As Gilroy bends down level with his friend, Leon opens his eyes and smiles a pained smile.

"Bout time you got back. You missed the party."

"Looks like it was some party. How about we find you someplace better to rest though? Those stairs don't exactly look comfortable." Nodding in agreement, Leon shifts so Gilroy can get a good grip on his good shoulder and hoist him to his feet. As the two of them walk slowly up the stairs, Leon talks between breathless steps.

"Gil... You... need... to... stop... them. It's not... Victoria's... fault." The last word comes out as a croak. Stopping at the top of the stairs, next to a smoking hole in the concrete, Gilroy looks back out at the battle scene. However, all he can see is a wall of ice. Sighing, he adjusts his stance and lifts Leon up a little as he slumps against the big man's shoulder. Turning away, he carries the unconscious man inside.

Chapter Nineteen

Covered in wounds, Estelle leans heavily on her sword. The remnants of her shield lay a few feet away on the ground. The wounds inflicted by the young woman finally take their toll, and she wanes slightly. Standing across from her, Victoria tests the edge of one of her daggers. Closing the distance, she lashes out once again with her twin blades. Raising her sword quickly, ignoring her pain and the complaints from her muscles, Estelle manages to just parry both strikes. Leaping backwards, she creates some distance between herself and the young woman. Catching her breath, she tries again to read the woman in front of her, but cannot sense anything from the young girl.

"Mistress, you cannot continue this fight any longer. You must retreat. It's taking everything I have to stop your wounds from bleeding out. But I am almost at my limit."

"I know that Athena but, I swore an oath to protect this school and everyone in it. I will not allow her to get away with this. I cannot." The defiant words to her anima are let down by her injured body as her legs tremble and collapse beneath her. Landing heavily on her knees she pours energy into her blade, reforming the bow once more. Drawing and knocking the single arrow, she draws the fletching back to her cheek before releasing. Whistling softly as it leaves the bow, the arrow flies true. However, with a twist of her blade, the young girl deflects it harmlessly over her head and away from their fight.

"Seems you've finally run out of steam, bitch. Now I'm going to end you and finish what I started with my brother." Victoria mocks. Closing her eyes and getting ready for the final strike, Estelle braces herself as a shadow falls across her vision. When the strike doesn't fall, she opens her eyes to see her vision blocked by a wall of ice. Coming round the outside is a woman wearing a school dress. On her wrist, ice blue bracelets seem to shine compared to her white skin. Looking into her face, Estelle almost cries with relief and all the tension drains from the Security Captain as she slumps down.

"Iris! I'm glad you're back, but forget about me. Go save Leon." His name comes out as a strangled sob. Running over to the Security Captain, Iris bends down and hugs the woman.

"Don't worry Estelle. Commander Gilroy is seeing to Leon. Now give me your hand. It's not safe here anymore."

"What about the girl? She is dangerous and can't be left to roam the school."

"Leave her to Lady Kawamura. Now let's get you to the infirmary." Helping Estelle up, Iris quickly guides her away from the grounds and towards the infirmary. As they reach the top of the steps, an explosion causes Iris to spin towards the grounds. Letting go of Iris, Estelle moves over to the bannister. Watching the fight take place on the grounds below them, Iris cries out as Shizuri takes a slash to the ribs. Moving toward the fight, she comes to her senses a moment later and remembers her duty. Turning from the grounds, she goes to help Estelle once more. Waving her away, Estelle points at the raging fight.

"Leave me. I can make it to the infirmary from here. Go to her. She needs help and I can see you want to go. So, go."

"Thanks, Estelle." Turning away from the injured woman, Iris takes the steps three at a time.

* * *

Walking over, Victoria slashes at the ice wall. The blade bouncing off the thick ice harmlessly. Lashing out in anger, she drives one of her daggers deep into the ice.

"Now, now, anger is unbecoming of a lady. Don't worry, I'll be more than a match for the likes of you." Turning around after pulling her dagger free of the ice, Victoria finds herself face to face with Shizuri, who is examining the edge of her katana. Without replying, she charges the older woman. Sparks fly into the air as she catches both daggers with her Katana. Pushing Victoria away, Shizuri goes on the offensive. Sparks continue to fly as Victoria parries every strike. With a final push, Shizuri breaks the engagement, knocking Victoria off balance. Taking advantage of the moment, Shizuri leaps backwards, bringing her sword around in front. Running her hand down the length of the blade, fire seems to swirl around her fingertips. As she slides her hand off the tip of the blade, fire swirls through the air around her fingers. Finally, gathering to become a fireball the size of a grapefruit. Without warning, she hurls the fireball at Victoria. Regaining her footing just in time, Victoria kicks off the ground with force, diving under the fireball. Rolling out from under it, she comes up and slashes it with her blade, using the resulting explosion to propel her towards Shizuri with force. Slamming into the Japanese woman, she knocks Shizuri off her feet before landing lightly on the ground behind her. Stunned by the impact, Shizuri lies on the ground for a moment before springing back to her feet. Just in time to block Victoria's first attack, but not the second. Victoria's second blade catches Shizuri in the side, cutting her dress and leaving a long cut across her ribs. Putting pressure on the wound with her free hand, Shizuri jumps back, putting some distance between herself and the younger girl. Gathering fire in her hand once more, she presses the flames to her side, sealing the wound and causing her to cry out in pain. Not wanting to lose the advantage, Victoria attacks. Dodging her first strike by millimetres, it takes all Shizuri's concentration to dodge the follow-up attacks. Watching the girl closely, she backs away, keeping Victoria in her line of sight. Patiently waiting for her to make a mistake and give her an opening. It only takes a moment. Dashing forward, Victoria puts her full strength behind her attack. Lunging at Shizuri's wounded side. Ignoring the stabbing pain shooting through her ribs, Shizuri steps to the side and dodges it. Like lightning, she turns and strikes with her own sword. Cutting the girl across the shoulder, blood gushing out from the force of the wound. Stepping away from the younger girl in shock as she falls to her knees. Dropping her weapons and screaming, Victoria clutches her shoulder as black energy spills from her injury. Finally, collapsing as the energy dissipates; Victoria reaches out for her fallen weapons. Before she can reach them, Shizuri steps within striking distance, levelling her Katana against the girl's neck. Looking down at her, Shizuri composes herself to keep the pain from her voice before talking.

"Give it up. The fights over." Looking up at her with hatred, the look that crosses the girl's face is the only warning that she has. Slamming her fist into the ground before Shizuri can slice down, a cloud of smoke billows out from the impact. Stepping away from the smoke and raising her katana, Shizuri covers her mouth to avoid the smoke. However, she still breathes in some of it. As it reaches her lungs, a wave of dizziness comes over her. Staggering, she moves over the ice wall, coughing, and struggling to stay standing. Emerging from the smoke, Victoria is holding the wound on her shoulder. Looking over at the struggling Shizuri, she reaches down and picks up one of her daggers.

"This is where you meet your end, bitch. The gas doesn't last long, but I don't need it to." Finishing Victoria throws the dagger towards Shizuri. Raising her hand to defend herself, she's surprised as it's gripped by another. Stepping in front of Shizuri and raising her other hand, Iris forms a shield of ice between the dagger and them. With a jarring impact, the dagger pierces through ice, shuddering to a halt, millimetres from her outstretched hand. Breathing a deep sigh of relief, Iris releases the ice causing the dagger to fall, landing point down in the ground. Readying herself to fight, Iris looks around for the young girl but can't see her anywhere. With a puff, the dagger bursts into smoke, which dissipates quickly. Going to move away, Iris finds her hand tightly held by Shizuri. Colour slowly creeping up her neck into her face.

"That's twice you've saved my life now. Thank you." Turning to reply Iris, finds herself very close to Shizuri. So close that she can see the woman's brown eyes shifting colour in the light. Shuffling a little closer, she looks into Shizuri's eyes and replies.

"Anytime My Lady. I…" Losing her nerve, she looks away. The feel of a body pushing against hers causes her to turn once more, and she finds their faces almost touching. Blushing furiously, she looks into the older woman's eyes. Leaning in slowly, she can feel Shizuri's breath and the two women inch closer together.

"Are you guys ok?" Running from behind the ice wall, Gilroy slides to a halt. Battle-axe in hand, he looks around before his eyes stop on the two women. Stepping aside awkwardly, they look at the big man.

"So, I guess it's over then." Taking a step forward, he's stopped in his tracks by icy glares from both women.

"What?" With an angry look, Iris creates a giant snowball and throws it at him. Connecting with his head, it knocks the big man over. With a humph, both women stomp off in separate directions, leaving a stunned Gilroy lying on the ground.

Chapter Twenty

Sitting on a stool next to the bed, Andrea brushes a stray strand of hair out of Leon's face.

"He'll nawt be likely to wake tonight Andrea. Why don't you get some rest? Tomorrow will be soon enough to tell the lad anything ye need." Looking up at Esmeralda with a sad-eyed smile, she sighs.

"I know Esme. But seeing him like this reminds me of his younger days when he was just a boy. I was forever bandaging cuts. I guess I just miss those days where I could fix everything that was hurt with a bandage and a kiss to the forehead." Walking over, Esmeralda places a hand on Andrea's shoulder.

"He do be a strong lad, that one. I'm nawt sure he'd agree with Ye placing a kiss on he's forehead anymore."

Laughing, Andrea grabs Esme's hand and slowly stands up.

"I think you're right there. I'd better get some rest. I imagine he'll be raring to go come the morning. I imagine I will be quite busy afterwards, organising everything." Looking out at the darkening sky, she sighs a heavy sigh.

"I feel the days growing shorter. As if we're all running out of time. But that could just be night fancies taking me."

"Aye, but I feel the same as Ye. Almost as if there's a big storm brewing just beyond the horizon. And that lad is the only thing standing between us and it." Both women turn to look at Leon.

"That, is what worries me." After a moment, Andrea bids goodnight to Esmeralda and takes her leave.

* * *

Standing on the roof of the main building, Shizuri looks out over the Schola's grounds. In the light of the half-moon, I shroud the area from her fight earlier that day in darkness. Looking up at the moon's pale shape, she sits on the edge of the building. Holding her side, she grimaces at the pain coming from the wound. Thinking about the days' activities brings a blush to her face, as her thoughts turn to Iris and subsequently her reason for being on the roof. Parting ways after the fight, she ran into her coming from the infirmary, and had asked the young woman to meet her here. Checking the time, butterflies appear in her stomach and her palms begin to sweat. Leaning against the cold concrete, she looks up at the night sky and its beautiful stars, her breath making small clouds in front of her face. Walking out onto the roof, Iris's black hair fans out behind her. Catching the moonlight, it looks like liquid silver. Heart racing, heat flushes through Shizuri, making her chest ache. Determined not to let her see how much the younger woman's presence affects her, she turns away and faces the grounds once more. Trying to calm her racing heart, she takes slow, deep breaths. The hollow clicks of Iris's heels echo softly in the dark.

"I'm glad you came, Iris. There is something I wish to discuss."

The smell of her perfume makes Shizuri's heart race more as the wind shifts and blows in her direction.

"Good evening, My Lady. My apologies for being a little late. What is it you wished to discuss?" Mustering her strength, Shizuri turns to face Iris once more.

"I want to discuss..." At that moment, Shizuri's nerves fail and she stops talking. Looking down at the ground, she swallows the rising sick feeling.

"I can't do this. It was a mistake. I'm sorry." Without another word, she walks towards the exit from the roof. Reaching out to grab the door, she's stopped by a hand on her arm.

"Please don't go, my Lady." Turning to look at the younger woman, she finds her looking away, face glowing red. Feeling a renewed burst of strength, Shizuri grabs Iris' hand and leads her over to the edge of the roof.

"Perhaps we should take a seat." Taking a seat apart from each other, the silence stretches on as they take turns dodging the other's glance. Shizuri looks down at her hands and thinks.

'What am I doing here? I can't have this. My family will never allow it.' Sighing as her thoughts turn to what she has to say, she looks up and turns to face Iris. Finding the girl staring at the moon. Without looking down, she speaks.

"I apologise in advance for my frankness, my Lady, but I was always taught it's better to speak your mind. Since you arrived, I've been struggling to contain what I've been feeling. I saw you looking in on me in the training room and was almost clobbered by one of the training nocturna when I lost concentration. My Lady, I like you. And not in the let's be friend's kind of way. And I hope you feel the same and I'm not making a fool of myself here because I feel like surely, I would die if that were the case." Listening to the girl speak, Shizuri's chest gets tighter, almost to the point of being unable to breathe. Getting to her feet, she staggers a few steps away, breathing heavily.

"Are you ok My Lady?"

"I am not. I'm cursed. I thought I buried these feelings long ago. But you... You woke them up again." Clutching her chest and turning to face the now standing Iris, Shizuri steps forward and grabs the girl's hand, placing it on her chest.

"Just standing near you makes my heart race. No matter what I do, I cannot make it stop. And I don't want to. Even though I know it will destroy my family. It's a heavy burden, and it's killing me. And I can't..." Finally breaking, Shizuri falls to her knees and sobs. Kneeling and putting her arms around the sobbing woman, Iris pulls her into a hug before talking softly over her head.

"A wise man once said, 'The right thing to do and the hard thing to do are usually the same.' He's right to an extent. Though relying on others and sharing the burden makes that less difficult. I don't know what I can do, but if you ask, I will give you my strength and help you overcome any hardship." Stopping her sobbing, Shizuri stays where she is.

"I can't promise a future for us."

"With the world the way it is, you can't even promise me tomorrow. So, let's not worry about the future. It's the now, I'm interested in and what I want. I know what that is, the question is, what is it you want?"

"What I want?" Pushing herself away from the younger woman as she gets to her feet. Grabbing one of Iris' hands, she places it on her chest and places her own on Iris's.

"I want this. No more hiding who I am."

"Are you sure, my lady?" Instead of replying, Shizuri moves her hand to the side of Iris' neck and pulls her closer. Looking into her eyes, she whispers one word.

"Yes." Moving forward at the same time their lips lock. As the two women kiss on the rooftop, a star shoots across the sky above them.

* * *

Waiting until the presence of the headmistress disappears further into the building, the girl hides in the darkness next to the main building. Leaning against the wall, she takes a deep breath before pulling a flip phone from her pocket. Opening the phone, the girl pushes a few buttons and after a brief ring, a man's voice answers, echoing slightly over the line.

"Yes?"

"Agent eleven reporting in, Sir. Victoria failed. Leon still lives, though he is badly injured. Orders?" Putting the receiver down, the man on the other end can be heard addressing another. For a little while, all she can hear are the two men talking in the background quietly enough not to be overheard.

"Agent eleven. Good work. Regarding Mr. Aelfdane, you are to take no action. Continue monitoring the Schola and the woman who runs it. Report anything major immediately."

"Understood Sir. Agent eleven out." Removing the phone from her ear, she closes her hand tightly around the cell phone. Glancing up at the infirmary as she steps from the wall, light from a nearby window reveals the hatred in her eyes before it winks out and she's returned to the darkness.

Chapter Twenty-one

Slowly waking up, the first thing Leon hears is hushed voices arguing. Opening his eyes with a struggle, he blinks the blurriness away. Looking around in the dim light he can just make out Shizuri and Gilroy huddled together arguing over a map. Rolling over towards them, he tries to speak, but nothing comes out. Leaning over, he knocks a spoon off a nearby tray, sending it clattering to the floor. Stopping their arguing, they turn at the sound. Seeing him awake, Gilroy gets up and moves over to the bed. Grabbing a cup from the nearby tray, he helps Leon into a sitting position before placing the straw to his lips.

"Small sips. Try to take it easy."

"How…?" His words come out as a croak, and he takes another sip of water before trying to speak again.

"How long have I been here?"

"It's been six days. The sun's just about to rise. You should get some more rest."

 "What were the two of you arguing about?" Gilroy and Shizuri share a look as Leon takes another sip of the water. Meeting his friend's eye, Gil tries to push Leon back into bed as he talks.

"There will be plenty of time to fill you in later. You need to get more rest. Your wounds have mostly healed but you're still in no condition to be running around the place." Shaking off his friend's hand, Leon grabs Gilroy on the shoulder, looking into his eyes pleadingly.

"Please, tell me what's going on." With a sigh, the big man takes a seat on the bed. Walking over, Shizuri grips Leon on the shoulder before shooting Gilroy a look and leaving the infirmary.

"Shizuri got a tracking mark on Victoria during their fight. The mark went dormant near the ruins of San Francisco. Shizuri was against telling you this. She fears you'll run after your sister and leave the council and London exposed to an attack."

"I'd like to. It's my fault she's the way she is Gil. How many more are going to pay the price for my shortcomings? First, it was Farrah, then Victoria and Isabella. Not to mention the damage to London and of course the cream of the crop, San Francisco itself." Suddenly filled with anger, Gilroy grabs Leon on the front of his hospital gown, dragging him close and looking him straight in the eye.

"You think you're the only one here that's lost people? Well news flash mate, you're not. People die every day. Whether it's to Requiem or the nocturna. I read the report on San Francisco, their shield collapsed and there's nothing you could have done." Letting go of Leon, Gilroy settles back down on the bed. Looking at the palm of his right hand, Leon makes a fist before responding.

"I could've stopped my father. The shield collapsed because he tore a hole through it, allowing the nocturna to overrun the city. I had a shot, and I missed. And the price was San Francisco and Victoria. In the confusion, I wasn't able to get to her in time." Sitting on the bed quietly for a time, the two just stare out the window. Finally getting tired of the silence, Gil speaks.

"To be honest, that you could actually fight your father is amazing. Remember our fight when you first arrived here?" At Leon's nod, Gilroy continues.

"If you recall, the good Captain referred to an incident that put me out of favour with London. That incident was a fight with Requiem. We were running a standard training mission in a remote area of coastal Ireland. Three days in, some boats landed near our camp. When we went to investigate, we ran into a full platoon of Requiem soldiers led by Alistair. Rather than waste his forces, he entered the field of battle himself. It was a massacre. He destroyed the dozen men I had with me. When it was my turn to face him, he stopped and granted me free passage away. As long as I told Andrea his message. There was no doubt in my mind. I'm only alive because I was allowed to live. The sense of power coming from your father was overwhelming. I'll never forget it. That you squared off against him and lived to tell the tale is no small feat." Looking out the window as the sun crests the horizon, Leon smiles. Turning to Gil as the sunlight streams through the window, Leon talks.

"Thank you, old friend. Truly, I am grateful to have you here. Now, as I'm still healing, I'll have to plan everything from here. I need information on a few things, and we need to prepare everything for Athens."

"What do you need me to do?" Turning and looking out the window once more, Leon's despair washes away with the dawning of the new day.

* * *

Falling down the stairs leading into Requiems base, Victoria lies on the ground for a moment before slowly getting to her feet. Holding the wound on her shoulder, she tries to ignore the burning pain radiating through her shoulder. Leaning heavily against the wall, she pushes through the double doors and stumbles into the main room. Looking up from his desk, Alistair fixes her with an icy stare.

"You failed. Bested, by a few of Andrea's pet keepers."

"Father I can explain. I..." Anything more she has to say is silenced by a backhand that knocks her to the floor.

"Silence! That you are my daughter is the only reason you still live. But, as a reminder of your failure, I think I shall leave the curse as it is. You're still compelled to do as I say, but it seems you're no longer immune from the nocturna. Now let's have a look at that wound." At her father's last word, Victoria goes pale. Grabbing the wound with one hand, she backs away. Leaning down, he grabs her hand, pulling it out of the way. Before she can object, he grabs her wounded shoulder with his other hand. Black energy crackles around him and Victoria screams. Letting go after a moment, he stands up and looks down at his daughter. The wound on her shoulder is gone. In its place is a red, painful-looking scar that runs through the centre of his curse brand.

"Good. Now get out of my sight." Sobbing, Victoria picks herself up off the ground and runs from the room. Clapping from the other side of the room is followed by a man's sadistic laugh.

"Still the family man I see."

"What do you want, Baur?"

"I just came to show you our newest recruit." Stepping aside, Baur ushers in a woman dressed in black armour. With a two-handed broadsword strapped to her back, she emits a menacing aura.

"Very good. Now, I have another job for you. Take the girl and go to Athens. You'll be met by an associate of mine once you get there. He has the key to the next part of the plan." Turning to leave, Baur stops in the doorway.

"How do you want me to handle your associate?"

"Same way we always do. Now go." As Simon Baur leaves with the female knight, Alistair picks up a flip-style cell phone. Dialling a number, he draws and lights a cigarette. Taking a drag as the phone rings against his ear. Blowing out his first breath of smoke as a young man answers the phone, he waits for a moment. After a brief click, the young man's voice changes, becoming untraceable.

"You need to pick your times better. I had to fake an asthma attack to get rid of the people around me. What do you need?"

"I have a job for you. I need you to obtain the anima we discussed last week. Kill whoever is in possession of it. My sources tell me it will be where I suspected it would. An associate will meet you after it's done a few days from now."

"Understood. Anything else?"

"No that's all. Oh, and don't screw this up. Requiem does not tolerate people who fail in their responsibilities."

"I'm aware." With another click, the line goes dead. Closing the phone and taking another drag of his cigarette, Alistair goes back to looking over his map of the world.

Part Two

Chapter Twenty-two

Wiping the sweat from his forehead, Leon takes his stance once more. Standing in the middle of the field used for training manoeuvres, he practices his swordsmanship. Flowing from one form to another, he slowly makes his way across the field. Stopping before the dummies at the edge of the field, he shifts backwards. Ice and wind swirl around the wolf blade in his hand. Covering the distance to the dummies in an instant, he impales the first one. Ice explodes from the centre, tearing it in half and quickly expanding outwards, shards of ice tear the remaining dummies apart. Stepping clear of the wreckage, he surveys his handiwork. Returning the blade to its dormant state, Leon shivers as a stiff wind blows across the field. Instantly freezing the droplets of sweat running down his naked back. As he approaches the area where his clothes lay, Gilroy comes jogging over.

"Not bad. Considering you were in the hospital until two weeks ago." Clenching his right hand into a fist, Leon looks up and smiles before replying.

"I still have a way to go, though. I've regained most of my earlier strength and my skill with Fenrir has definitely improved, but still. I worry it won't be enough to stop Requiem and my father." Coming over and clapping Leon on the shoulder, Gilroy looks over at the wreckage of the dummies at the far end of the field.

"Well, old mate, let's worry about that bridge when we come to it. Stressing about it won't do you any good. Anyway, the reason I came all the way out here, The Headmistress, is back. She's requesting your presence immediately." Failing to cover the look of shock on his face, Leon reaches down and hastily pulls on his shirt.

"How long ago?"

"I don't know, maybe fifteen minutes. It took me a while to find you."

"Dammit! How about next time, you open with the fact she's looking for me."

"My bad." Turning from his friend, Leon sprints away from the open field toward the Schola's main building.

* * *

Sitting down at her desk, Andrea taps impatiently on the pile of documents in front of her.

"Where on earth can that damnable boy be?" Finally losing the last of her patience, she gets up from her desk and heads towards the door when it bursts open. Standing in the doorway sweating heavily and messily dressed, Leon smiles a wolfish grin before entering and closing the door behind him.

"Sorry, it took me so long to get here. Gil only just informed me you got back. I had to run all the way from the drill field. You couldn't have like called, this morning and informed me you were going to be back?" Walking up to her desk, he drops his anima belt on the chair in front of it and begins tucking his clothes in. looking over the top of her glasses with a unimpressed look, Andrea grinds her teeth at his tone.

"Good to see you too, Leon. I didn't call because I sent you a message that I would return this morning. I expected you to be here in my office waiting for me, seeing as it was you who requested this information, that I went to great lengths to get." Voice rising, she throws herself back into her seat before leaning forward on her elbows.

"Instead, I find that you're nowhere to be found. On top of which, I need to send someone to locate you. And you have the audacity to accuse me of not letting you know what's going on. I think after this is all done, you and I are going to have a serious talk about your mannerisms. But on to the reason I wanted you here. I have obtained some information regarding the Scions. And through calling in some favours and a little persuasive influence, I found out what the World Council's plan is. Which do you want to hear first?" Finally finishing getting dressed and buckling on his belt, Leon shrugs into his coat and takes a seat across from her before replying.

"Let's hear about the Scions first. What the World Council has planned, while most certainly is going to be interesting, is not as important as the Scions. How reliable is the source of information?"

"Okay. The information's reliable. I got it directly from the council's archives. Just, don't be too depressed about the lack of it. There is little in the way of actual intel regarding who or what the Scions are. According to what I could dig up, there are five scions in total. Their names are Regal, Revenant, Wraith, Faye and Kain. Those are also their ranks in strength. Regal, Revenant and Wraith are by far the three strongest of the five. At present, we know where both Regal and Wraith are and, of course, we also know where Revenant is. Faye and Kain are currently in the wind. There's no telling where they ended up when the breach was opened. Regal, as you know, is currently in Alistair's possession. Now I would like to say that Regal's influence is the reason your father is doing what he is, but that isn't the case. Alistair showed his true colours long before the breach occurred. Wraith is currently in the safekeeping of the Council of Nine. Cassandra knows its whereabouts. Currently, Wraith is not bound to a keeper. The reason behind this is simple. To use the power of a Scion, there's a cost that must be paid. I believe there are a few extenuating circumstances when this cost is negated but, there will always be a price for the power you obtain when using one of the

Scions."

"What kind of price are we talking? Years of your life? Your first-born child?" Andrea shifts uncomfortably in her seat before replying.

"As far as we can tell, it differs with every wielder and use. The last keeper who wielded Wraith was only able to use him twice before the cost took her life. The first use cost the keeper her left arm. A problem came up where she needed to use Wraith a second time and the cost was her life. I think it best if you leave Revenant here for the time being. At least until we've located the remaining two."

"Alright. I'm happy to do that. I don't foresee any time in the future when I will need that kind of power. Now, what's the World Council planning?"

"You're not going to like it. They're planning to launch an assault on Requiem, come winter. Now its common knowledge that Requiem has established themselves in the ruins of San Francisco. I've already tried to use my leverage to stop the attack, but my warnings are falling on deaf ears. The only hope we have now is for the Council of Nine to intervene and stop the attack. The problem is, they don't have enough Intel to call a stop on the assault. Cassy is out of ideas on what to do, and so am I. If the attack goes forward, I fear we will be handing what's left of the world to Requiem on a silver platter." Getting up from her seat, Andrea paces back and forth for a moment in agitation before turning to look out her window. Leaning back in his seat, Leon scratches his newly formed beard for a moment before his eyes light up. Getting up from his chair, he walks over to Andrea. Stopping next to her, he places a hand on her shoulder.

"I think I have a plan. How quickly can you get a two-man air skiff? And we're also going to need to keep it quiet. Only you and I can know about it."

"Pretty easily and like you need to ask. I invented subterfuge. What do you have in mind?" Smiling, Leon retakes his seat. As Andrea sits down once more, Leon begins.

"I need it loaded beneath the cargo hold of the airship that's taking us to Athens. Attached to the crawlspace beneath the decks. On top of that, I need Isabella and Estelle as well. I'm aware of how far my father's reach extends. Doing it this way, means, we'll get the jump on him. Which will be a first, for a change." Smiling, Andrea nods as Leon outlines his plan to gain the advantage over Requiem. On the opposite side of the Schola, a chill runs down Estelle's back as she sits down to eat.

Chapter Twenty-three

Peering around the corner of the building, a young woman makes sure the street is clear before dashing across it to a dark doorway. With barely a sound, she opens the door and slips inside. Walking through the darkened shop, she makes her way quickly and quietly to the back before descending a staircase. Stepping into the dimly lit basement, she looks around quickly. Spotting a man sitting at a workbench, a tool in hand, she walks over to him, being careful to avoid various other workstations on her way over. Without looking up from his work, he points at a cloth-covered object as she approaches. Moving to the bench, she twitches aside the cloth, revealing a gleaming spear. Down the sides of the blade, arcana writing glimmers brightly in the faint light.

"Impressive, but I no longer have a use for it." Sighing, the man puts down his tools and swivels to look at the young woman.

"And why would that be?"

"I have a new plan. I'm going to attack the council directly."

"You'll end up dead if you do that. There's no way in hell, he's going to let you expose him. That man will use any means necessary to keep his affiliations with Requiem hidden. You know this and yet you're still willing to take him on?"

"Do you have a better plan? Cause last I checked, the whole attacking cities with nocturna thing, isn't working."

"I don't. But are you sure you want to do this? If this plan backfires, everything we've worked so hard to achieve will be for nothing."

"I'm sure. Now how do I get in?" With a resigned sigh, the man gets up from his desk and walks over to a cabinet on the wall. Opening the door reveals hundreds of blueprints stacked away neatly in their own alcoves. Thinking hard for a moment, he selects a couple and brings them back to the desk. Rolling out the first, he weighs down the corners and steps back so the young woman can read it.

"You get in using this." Under the light, the Council Chamber blueprint is easily readable. Smiling, the young girl leans over the blueprint and begins studying it.

* * *

Walking down the stairs of the main building, Leon looks up at the setting sun. Rubbing the tiredness from his eyes, he sets off towards his quarters. Arriving a few minutes later, he finds Gilroy sitting on the seat outside his room. Taking a seat and the proffered cigarette, both men spark up before Gilroy speaks.

"Everything all sorted?"

"Yeah. We leave two days from now. Airship arrives tomorrow, so you will have just over a day for any final preparations. Remember, it's an eighteen-hour flight to Athens in which anything can happen, so make sure you have contingencies in place for any issue. Have you picked out your squad yet?"

"Four of my best, as well as Iris. She insisted on being a part of the squad. Either way, they should serve well enough as an honour guard for you. Once you've been escorted to the Council Chambers, they'll return to the aerodrome and wait on the ship until everything in Athens is sorted. You said it would only take a day, right?"

"I said, it should only take a day. But given recent events, who knows?" Going quiet for a while both men stare at the setting sun, enjoying the peace of each other's company. Getting up from his seat, Gilroy looks down at Leon.

"Well, I'm going to get some rest. I'll see you first thing tomorrow."

"No worries Gil. I won't be too far off myself. I just have a few things to wrap up before I call it a night."

"No worries. Take it easy. I'll see you tomorrow. Night mate."

"Goodnight." Turning from Leon's quarters, Gilroy heads off. Watching the big man walk away, Leon smiles to himself before getting up and going inside his quarters. Stepping inside, he finds Estelle and Isabella sitting on the other side of his desk. Taking off his coat, he hangs it on the coat stand by the door before walking over and taking a seat across from the two women.

"I take it you got my message then?" Pulling a small piece of paper from her jacket pocket, Estelle slides it across the desk to Leon before replying.

"We did. What's so important you needed to see us both? And why the secrecy in coming here?"

"I have a mission for the both of you. And as for the secrecy, I believe there's a traitor at the Schola and its imperative they don't know what I have planned. But before we go any further into that, Isabella, how are things progressing with Cleo?" Shifting in her seat, Isabella removes the anima from her belt and places it on the table between them.

"Good. My wounds are all healed now, so the strain on my body is no longer more than I can handle. As for Cleo, I'm still not able to command, summon her or shift into Phantasm form. However, I have access to most of the abilities of her spear form and the rest I will gain with a little time, I think."

"Okay. Then I think you should be fine with what I have planned."

Looking at Isabella, Estelle frowns slightly before turning back to Leon.

"Which is what exactly? You've still told us nothing about what you're planning. Clearly, it's something that may require us to fight."

"The two of you will be going to San Francisco to gain information regarding Requiem's movements. Before you get all up in arms over it, let me explain why I need this done." Stifling their objections, the two women focus their attention on Leon. Gesturing for him to continue, Isabella removes her anima off the desk.

"Thank-you. Now, we have a problem with the World Council. Well, more so with what they have planned, rather than the council itself. Come winter, they plan on launching an all-out attack against Requiem. Normally, this wouldn't be cause for concern. But given Requiem's lack of movement lately, the Council of Nine believes they are planning something from the shadows. We believe that, Requiem knows of the World Councils plan to attack. If that is the case, we'll be walking straight into their trap. If that happens, The World Council will lose too much of its main fighting strength. There will be no one left to stop Requiem when they initiate their true plan, whatever that may be. So, it falls to us to gather what information we can to put a stop to the actions of the World Council. Now, I'll answer any questions or objections you have." Rubbing the scar on her chin, Estelle looks over at Isabella briefly before turning back to Leon.

"I have no objections. Just one question. How are we getting there?" At Leon's smile, a chill runs down Isabella's back.

"There will be a small skiff airship attached to the airship that will take us to Athens in a few days' time. I read your personal files and saw that you've had training in flying that kind of craft, Isabella. Now here's the fun part. You both need to get aboard the airship without being seen. This entire mission revolves around being able to sneak aboard that ship quietly. If anyone sees you, the mission is over before it even began." Looking at Leon in disbelief, Isabella gets up from her chair and paces around. After a few moments, she walks back over and slaps her hands down on the table.

"How the hell do you propose we get on board? The World Council has its best guards stationed on ships that carry VIPs. While it's grounded, the whole thing will be lit up like a damn Christmas tree. So even at night, there are no shadows to even hide behind. It is impossible, to get on that airship."

"Not impossible, just difficult. Also, I'm sure I don't need to remind you both of what the World Council guards will do if they catch you trying to sneak aboard. I will, of course, deny any knowledge of your actions should the worse happen. You will be completely on your own. Any more questions?" At the two women's silence, Leon continues.

"Very well then. Here are the instructions on where the skiff's located and where you can wait until we're underway before launching it. I'll see you both onboard the airship in a few days' time. Good luck." Getting up from the desk, Estelle takes the folded sheet of paper from Leon and, taking her hand, leads Isabella out of Leon's quarters. Walking over to the window, he watches until the two women are completely out of sight. With a sigh, he turns back to his desk and re-takes his seat.

"They're gone. You might as well come out now." Opening the door to his bathroom, Shizuri steps out into the room. Glancing at the door, she takes a seat in one of the chairs before turning back to Leon.

"Are you sure about this, Leon? It's a big gamble and if it all goes south, everything we're working for will be for nothing. The Council will fail, and the world will fall."

"I don't see how I have any other choice. Do you? Because I'm all ears. I wouldn't have selected them if I didn't think they were capable. If it means stopping Requiem, there's no price too high." Looking at the door once more, Shizuri lets out a small sigh and whispers to herself.

"There is no victory without sacrifice, huh?" Turning back from the window, she watches as Leon pulls papers from the draw in his desk.

Chapter Twenty-four

Stepping out of the shower, Isabella towels herself dry. Stopping as she reaches her shoulder, she turns to look at herself in the mirror. The ugly red of the scar sticks out against the whiteness of her skin. Rubbing it softly, she sighs before taking a seat heavily on the edge of the bath. Looking over at the pile of clothes next to the shower, she stares blankly at the anima sticking out of the top of the pile. A soft knock at her door brings her back to reality. Getting up, she quickly wraps the towel around herself before walking over to the door. Opening it, she finds Estelle standing outside. Taking one look at her friend, she steps inside and closes the door behind her.

"Jeez, aren't you ready yet? We've got to go. The guards rotate shifts in ten minutes." Swearing under her breath as she glances at the clock and dropping the towel, Isabella runs over to her room. Hastily pulling on clothes, she talks over her shoulder.

"Sorry I didn't realise the time. Have you got everything we need?"

"Yeah, it's all been arranged. But it won't matter if we don't get to the ship before the guards change shifts." Doing up the last button on her shirt, Isabella scoops up her coat and anima.

"Well, let's go then." Without looking back, the two women leave the room. Reaching the ground's, they take cover in the building's shadows. Waiting until the night patrol passes, they dash from the side of the building to a small copse of trees nearby. Slipping quietly away, they make their way over to the training field. Arriving at the training field, they slide behind a small pile of training dummies as a spotlight beam slowly makes its way across the area. Peering around the edge of the dummies, Estelle looks at the distance from their location to the airship.

"Well, at least we made it this far without any issues." Picking at the grass beneath her, Isabella sighs before looking around the dummies with Estelle.

"Yes, well, the hard part is yet to come. And it looks like this is going to be far harder than I originally anticipated. With the extra guard rotations because of that attempted attack on the ship yesterday, it may be nigh impossible to sneak aboard now. At any rate, we'll need some kind of distraction if we're going to have any chance of making it." Pulling her anima out, Isabella grins.

"I have the distraction covered. I've been training hard for the last few weeks. Even though I can't reach phantasm yet, I can do plenty of other things. All I need from you is... hey, who's that?" From the edge of the field, a black hooded figure emerges into the light. Yelling out an inaudible command, the closer soldier draws his anima, which lengthens into a lance. Reaching their right hand behind their back, the figure draws an anima as well, clutching the tube in front of their chest, before lowering their arm to the side. With a flick of their wrist, it becomes a single-edged long-sword as black as night. Covering the distance to the soldier in a matter of moments, the figure sidesteps his lance. Catching the hood with the tip of his lance, it tears it off. He has only a moment to see the black-clothed woman before him, before her blade pierces his chest. Pulling the blade out in a spray of blood, she turns her attention to the remaining guards. Bringing their weapons into existence, the remaining soldiers converge on the woman. Pulling a veil of black material over her face, she hefts her blade and charges into battle with the men. Jumping to her feet, Isabella summons Cleo.

"Time to go." Turning the spear point downwards, she grabs Estelle before driving the point into the ground. With a rushing sound, the earth rises and swallows both women. Moments later they reappear in the middle of the field near the battle. Not wasting a second, Estelle summons her anima into its sword and shield. Dashing forward, she pushes a soldier clear of the assassin's blade and catches it with her shield. Shoving the woman back. Estelle quickly steps in to engage her. Keeping her shield up, she drives the assassin back with a series of quick stabs in the woman's direction. Leaping out of the reach of Estelle's blade, the assassin brings her blade up vertically in front of her face. Placing two fingers on the blade above the hilt, she whispers an incantation while running her hand up the length of the sword. Black flames burst out along the length of the blade as she steps forward. Raising the flaming sword above her shoulder, she charges Estelle with a cry. Stepping to the side, Estelle only just dodges the woman's first strike, barely bringing her shield up in time to block the second. With the sound of metal scraping, the sword comes to a stop against the edge of the shield. Looking over the edge of her shield into the other woman's eyes, Estelle shrinks back at the bloodlust emanating from them. Grinding her teeth, Estelle puts her weight into the shield and pushes the woman back.

"You're a strong bitch, aren't you, Captain? But I think it's time for you to die!" Her last word comes out as a shout and the flames on the sword grow and spread, quickly cladding the assassin in an armour of black flame. Sweat breaks out on Estelle's face as the heat from the flames wash over her.

"Estelle!" As Isabella's cry comes from behind her, the force pushing against the shield increases exponentially. With the terrible sound of screeching metal, the shield breaks in half. Passing through the shield, the assassin's blade carves a bloody line up Estelle's arm. Staggering backwards from the force of the impact, Estelle watches as the shield fragments burst into lights. Bringing her blade in front of her face, she can only watch in horror as cracks of light run up the length of the blade. With a sound like shattering glass, the blade breaks before becoming particles of light. As the lights begin to disperse the anima's dormant form returns to her hand. As cracks run up it, a voice echoes sadly through Estelle's mind.

"I'm sorry My Lady. This is the end for me. Don't be sad. We were never meant to exist in this world in the first place. Goodbye..." As the voice fades away, the casing in her hand bursts, sending more particles of light into the air. Looking up at the particles of light floating around, a tear falls from her eye.

"Watch out!" Looking up at the shout, a shock runs through Estelle as the assassin's blade pierces her chest, just below the shoulder. Spinning her spear above her head as the blade punches through Estelle's back, Isabella drives the point straight into the ground. A second later, the ground between the two women rumbles. Wrenching her blade free of the Guard Captain, the assassin jumps clear as the tip of the spear fills the space she just vacated. Pushing the attack, Isabella follows the assassin. Spear whirling, Isabella steps inside the reach of the assassin's blade. Sidestepping the black blade as its swung down at her, Isabella hits the women between the eyes with the butt of the spear. Reeling from the impact, the assassin swings her blade wildly. Leaning away from the wild slash, Isabella lunges in as the sword whistles past her harmlessly, driving the spear into the women's leg. With a scream, the assassin grasps the shaft of the spear. With a grunt of effort, she pulls the spear from her leg and drags Isabella towards her. Releasing her grip on the spear, Isabella puts her hand up. Lines of light quickly form and trace themselves into a sigil. Flicking her finger, the sigil bursts, sending lightning streaking towards the assassin. Stabbing her blade into the ground, the assassin throws herself backwards onto the ground. Hitting the dirt with her shoulder, the assassin rolls away from the blade. As she rolls to her feet, the lightning streaking towards her veers off and onto the blade stuck into the ground. With blinding light, the ground explodes, throwing dirt and debris into the air. As the dust begins to settle, small lights fill the air as the assassin's black sword slowly disintegrates. After a moment, it goes dormant before bursting and sending lights into the air. Running through the light Isabella goes to where she last saw the assassin before the explosion, only finding a small splattering of blood on the ground. With a frown, she turns, picking up her spear. In an instant, it becomes the dormant anima case once more. Clipping it to her belt, she runs over to Estelle as the guard captain cries out in agony.

Chapter Twenty-five

Clutching the wound in her chest, Estelle tries to control her breathing. Ignoring the sadness welling up inside her, she holds out her hand and particles of light quickly appear and form a sigil above her palm. Grimacing, she pushes the sigil against the wound in her chest. With a cry of agony, the sigil activates and begins to heal the worst of the injury. Sweat blossoms on her forehead as the muscles in her chest knit back together. Finally, the pain becomes too much and collapsing into the dirt; she releases her hold on the energy powering the sigil. Black flecks swim before her vision and the pain in her chest pulsates in time to the pounding of her heart. Moments later, she senses a presence next to her. Turning her head, she looks up into Isabella's eyes. Worry etched all over her friend's face.

"I'm fine Izzy. Help me up." Reaching down, Isabella helps hoist Estelle to her feet. Leaning heavily on the smaller woman, the Guard Captain staggers a little as they walk over to where the bodies of the soldiers lay. Running footsteps come from ahead of them and, looking up, they see a squad of security keepers running onto the field in their direction. Stopping, the two women wait until the keepers reach them. Running up to them the squad leader draws his anima and, summoning a pair of short swords, stops in front of the two women. Blades glinting in the light, he looks them over with a worried look.

"Lady Estelle. Miss Isabella. What happened here?" Letting go of Estelle, Isabella steps forwards.

"There was an assassin, Arren. The men guarding the ship never stood a chance. Luckily enough, we just happened to be nearby and saw everything unfold. And even then, we almost didn't succeed in stopping her. She's wounded. Gather your men and hurry after her. I'll get Estelle to the infirmary." Pointing to the blood splatter nearby, Isabella waits until Arren looks before talking.

"I last saw her in that direction. With a wound that bad, she can't have gone far. I also destroyed her anima. Now go."

"Are you sure you wouldn't like me to leave a few of the boys to help you?" Stepping forward shakily and coming to lean on Isabella once more, Estelle gives the young keeper a hard stare.

"You've been given an order, Arren. Now go. Gather the squad and stop that assassin. Inform the headmistress of what has happened. She will need to assign more troops to guard the ship." With a final salute, the young man gestures to the others behind him. With one last look at Estelle, he runs off in the direction of the blood splatter. Turning from the security squad, Isabella grasps Estelle once more and begins walking away from the airship.

"Come on. Time to get to the infirmary." Stopping, Estelle grabs Isabella on the arm tightly.

"No! We board the airship. Hurry, before more guards come. This may be our only chance." With a shocked look, Isabella looks her friend in the eye.

"You can't be serious. You're in no condition to carry out this mission. You're badly injured and your anima was..." Trailing off as a sad look enters Estelle's eyes, Isabella lets out an exasperated sigh.

"Fine! But once we're aboard, I'm going to contact Leon. He needs to know everything and I need to get some supplies to finish patching you up."

"That's fine. Let's go." Taking Estelle's weight on her shoulder once more, Isabella leads the injured woman over to the airship and into the hold.

* * *

Sitting at his desk, Leon looks down over the paperwork stacked upon it with a sigh. Signing off on the last page, he throws the pen down onto the table and leans back in his chair. Getting up, he rubs the tiredness from his eyes and walking over to the small table near his window; he pours himself a glass of water from the pitcher on top of it. Rubbing the stiffness from his neck, he surveys his room. Frowning at the scattered papers and assorted piles of junk lying around it, he places the glass of water back on the table. For a moment, fear runs through him as a small pile of sand grows out of the floor in front of him. Dashing past it, he grabs Fenrir and with a flick of his wrist, the wolf blade appears. From the pile of sand, a small scarab beetle emerges. Walking over to Leon, it grows as it approaches. Stopping just in front of him, it opens its mouth and a dull white light emits from it.

"Leon, are you there, can you hear me?" Recognising the voice, Leon puts away his blade, before squatting down in front of the scarab and talking at it.

"Isabella? What in the hell is going on?"

"There was an assassin. She tried to attack the ship when we got there to board it. I managed to get us on board without anyone seeing, but Estelle's injured badly. She stopped the bleeding, but the wounds still open."

"What do you need me to do?"

"I need bandages and a suture kit. As well as some cleaning alcohol. You should be able to get all that in the infirmary. Hurry."

"How do I get it all to you?"

"Take the scarab with you. Place everything inside its mouth. It will make its way back to me." As she finishes speaking, the light fades from the scarabs' mouth and it shrinks in size. Picking it up, he places the creature in his pocket. Grabbing his jacket off the rack, he steps out into the night air. Setting off at a run towards the infirmary, he dodges soldiers and guards as he makes his way over to the main building. Reaching the school building in minutes, he stops at the steps as a group of security personal run down them and out onto the grounds. Taking the steps three at a time, he races into the main building and up the staircase to the infirmary. Reaching the door soon after, he stops outside and waits for a moment. Listening closely, he cracks the door open and peeks his head inside. Stepping into the dark room, he carefully makes his way over to the supply shelf, feeling his way by memory. Reaching the shelf, he traces a sigil and a small werelight bursts into being, coating the area in pale white light. Pulling the scarab from his pocket, he places it on the ground and shudders as it grows once more. Raiding the shelves, he quickly gathers the items and places them inside the insect's mouth. With a flash of light, the items disappear, and Isabella's voice comes out once more.

"Thank you. Good luck in Athens."

"Good luck to you two, as well. Be careful. If anything happens, you're to abandon the mission."

"Will do." Shuddering, the scarab bursts into a cloud of sand that floats out of the hole in the wall. Watching the last grains of sand float out into the night, a sense of foreboding comes over Leon. Turning, he leaves the infirmary as quietly as he entered and heads back to his room.

* * *

Sitting against the wall of the airship, Estelle's breath comes out raggedly, her head lolling to the side. Looking at her friend with worry, Isabella concentrates on the energy flowing from her. Without a sound, grains of sand begin to enter the small room they're hiding in. Gathering in the centre of the room, the scarab quickly forms. Skittering over to Isabella, it dispels the medical supplies onto the floor. Smiling, she holds out the dormant anima casing. Jumping into the air, the scarab bursts into particles that quickly attach themselves to the anima case. Clipping it back onto her belt, she quickly gathers up the medical supplies and moves over to Estelle. Shaking her friend lightly, Isabella rouses Estelle softly.

"Hey, Stelle. The medical supplies are here. I need you to wake up. Remove your top." Coercing her friend into movement, Isabella helps shift the Guard Captain off the wall and remove her top. Getting her first look at the wound, she sucks in a gasp of air. Even after Estelle's rudimentary first aid, the wound is still open and red, weeping plasma. Folding up Estelle's shirt, Isabella pushes the woman down onto the deck of the ship, placing the clothing behind her head.

"Sorry, Estelle. But you shouldn't be awake for this." Tracing a sigil, she moves to place it against Estelle's forehead. Grabbing the younger woman's wrist, Estelle stops her.

"Wait, Izzy, please."

"Sorry Stelle." Ignoring her friend's pleas, she pushes the sigil onto Estelle's forehead. Within moments her breath evens out. Waiting a moment to confirm she's unconscious, Isabella gets to work. Quickly cleaning the wound with the alcohol before gathering up the suture kit. Drawing a sigil on the skin next to the wound, she activates it. As the skin pulls close together, she quickly and deftly stitches the wound closed. Keeping the sigil active, she focuses the energy into the wound below, reconnecting the nerves and veins together. As the night wears on and tiredness takes its toll, she continues to work on her friend. Rolling her over carefully, she begins the same slow process on Estelle's back. Checking the wounds, Isabella carefully wraps Estelle's chest and shoulder with the bandages. Checking her handywork, she finally releases the energy, and the sigil winks out of existence. Wiping the sweat from her brow, she looks at the window above her. No longer black outside, a pale colour fills the sky. Slumping down against the wall, exhausted, Isabella closes her eyes and falls asleep as the sun rises. Lying on the ground, Estelle rests peacefully, her wound finally stitched and bound.

Chapter Twenty-six

Blinking as the morning light hits his face, Leon rolls over in bed. Looking at the window, he sees Gilroy standing there. Sitting up, he looks down at his clothing in confusion. Then he remembers everything that happened the previous night. Getting up, he comes over to the window and stands next to the big man. Clapping him on the shoulder, Leon looks out at the bustling people.

"Nice morning for it. You ready to go Gil?"

Starting at Leon's touch, he looks at his friend with sad eyes.

"She wouldn't see me this morning, man." Turning away from his friend, Gilroy swallows heavily.

"Who Anna? Why wouldn't she see you?" Turning from the window, the big man moves across the room and sits down heavily on Leon's bed.

"I don't know. I knocked on her door this morning and she screamed at me to go away. So, thinking something might be wrong, I went and opened the door. She used a sigil to slam it so hard on me, it's a wonder I didn't go through the wall."

"What did you do? Man, talk about hell hath no fury..."

"I know right. I didn't do anything. Everything was fine last night when I said goodnight to her, right before I came to see you." Moving across the room and sitting on the bed next to his friend, Leon places a hand on the big man's shoulder.

"Well, I can't help you there, mate. My luck with women, hasn't exactly been great. Anyway, if she doesn't want to see you, there's little you can do. We had best get ourselves ready. Our stuff won't board that airship by itself." Moving his hand off Gil's shoulder, Leon gets up and begins gathering his bags. Hoisting them onto his shoulder, he gives Gil a push with his foot.

"Ready?" roused from his sorrow, Gilroy gets up and leads Leon out of his quarters. Stopping outside long enough for the big man to gather his own bags, the two men set off across the grounds toward the airship. Coming around the edge of the training room building, a magnificent sight greets their eyes. Stationed on the training field, early morning mist rolls off the ground around the legs of the airship and its boarding ramp. The early morning sun's rays of light cut through the mist, caus-ing the damp to glisten on the hull and reflect rays of light everywhere, like a mirror ball. Already, people run around gathering last-minute supplies, giving the whole area a feeling of organised chaos. Stopping at the edge of the field, the two men drop their bags and Gilroy offers Leon a smoke. Taking one with a smile, Leon lights it up with a sigil traced in the air. Taking a drag, he leans against the fence and watches the madness before him.

"You know Gil? Even starting this early it'll still take a few hours before she's ready to take off." Catching the tone of his friend's voice, Gilroy gives Leon a grimace.

"The answers no. I don't even care what it is your thinking Leon. Every time you say those words, with that tone, we always end up never being where we're supposed to be. And we always end up in trouble. Remember your old man's fortieth? Cause I don't. Well, not past nine P. M anyway." Choking on his smoke, Leon breaks out in laughter.

"Hey, that was a good night. What was that chick's name again? I don't remember, but she sure had a thing for you. And for the record, I didn't make you take those shots."

"No, you just accused me of being a pussy. And it was your idea to go to that bar in the first place."

"Pfft. Lies. I'm an angel I am. This bad influence version of me you seem to recall is false. I'm sorry to say but I think you're going senile mate. And so young too." At the grin on Leon's face. Gilroy breaks into a big, booming laugh. His voice echoing across the misty field. Turning from looking down at a list as she hears the laughter, Shizuri turns towards the men and raises a hand in greeting. Waving back, the two men put out their smokes before gathering their bags once more and vaulting over the fence. Walking over to the Japanese woman, they smile as she barks orders.

"How's it going?"

"How do you think it's going? So little has been prepared to go, and the stuff that has been, is organised so poorly, it's a damn nightmare."

Dropping his bags onto a cart nearby, he catches Shizuri's eye.

"Well, you seem to have it all under control, so, I'm going to head inside and have a look around. I'll catch you later, Gil."

"Yeah, no worries, mate. I've got to go make sure the guards are ready to go." At the mention of the guards, Shizuri blushes slightly and then renews barking orders out. Leaving them behind, Leon makes his way onto the ship. Dodging people wheeling in baggage, he ducks behind some crates, removing an arcane blade from a stack nearby. Crouching, he moves to the back wall behind a large crate. Waiting until the coast is clear, he pushes against a vent in the wall and slips quietly into the crawl space next to the hold. Bending slightly, he quickly moves away from the cargo hold and below the decks. Reaching a small panel, he pries it open softly and slips inside. Straightening up, he finds the two women asleep.

One on the floor, the other propped up against the wall. Moving quietly so as not to wake them, he inspects the wound on Estelle's chest. Still moving quietly, he grabs two blankets and places them carefully over the two women. Smiling as Isabella stirs slightly, he stands and heads towards the exit. Stopping just next to the panel, he places the blade on the ground and traces a sigil in the air. Flowing from it, shimmering words attach themselves to the wall. Smiling, he slips out of the small room and back into the crawl space. Emerging back into the cargo hold moments later, he blends back into the chaos and heads upstairs to his room. All thoughts of the two women banished from his mind.

* * *

Waking with a start as the floor begins to rumble, Isabella sits up, the blanket sliding off her. Blinking the sleep from her eyes, she looks at the wall above the doorway and the words shining there.

Good Luck. Stay safe.

Smiling as she gets to her feet and stretches, she walks over to the wall and tracing a sigil waves it over the words. Leaving them to fade, she turns and kneels next to Estelle. Tracing another sigil, she places it softly on Estelle's forehead. Going to their bags, Isabella gets out a flask of water and comes back over as her friend stirs. As Estelle's eyes open, Isabella carefully props her up. Holding the flask to her friend's lips, she waits patiently as Estelle takes a long draught from the flask.

"Are we moving?"

"Yeah, I think so. I just woke up myself." Looking at the window, shock runs through her as the colours of sunset show through the glass. Shifting slightly to look at her chest, Estelle touches the bandage there.

"How are my wounds?"

"They're okay for now. I've repaired the damage to your veins and nerves, so there shouldn't be any residual issues there. But I didn't repair the skin surrounding the wound. Doing that would've taken away energy that was better spent on your internals. For now, I've stitched them up. So, you'll have to take it easy for a little while. Try not, to tear out your stitches."

"Thanks, Izzy." Leaning into her friend, Estelle pulls the younger woman into a hug. Smiling, Isabella hugs back. Breaking off the hug, she gets up and goes to their packs once more. Rummaging around, she produces a new shirt for Estelle. Getting slowly to her feet, Estelle stretches and tests the stiffness in her shoulder. Looking around the room, she notices the blade leaning against the wall. Walking over, she picks it up and draws it. Hearing a blade being drawn, Isabella spins around, reaching for her anima. Holding the blade in her good arm, Estelle gives it a few swings. Smiling as she sheathes it, she looks at Isabella.

"This will do. It won't replace what I've lost, but it allows me to fight still. I take it this was Leon's doing." Throwing the shirt to her, Isabella stands.

"I assume so. There were words left on the wall when I woke. Good luck. Stay safe. He must've checked in earlier. He's done as much as he can for us for the time being. Get changed and let's go find this skiff." Gathering their things as Estelle changes, Isabella brings them over to the doorway leading into the crawl space. Waiting patiently for her friend to change tops and buckle on the sword, Isabella closes her eyes and focuses her attention inwards.

"Can we really do this, Cleo? I feel like it may be too much. But I don't want to let everyone down."

"It's okay Isabella. These feelings are only natural. I know how fond of Sigmund you were. And even he, for all his strength, still doubted. To doubt is to be human. Now come. Let us go before such thoughts overtake us." Pushing gently, Cleo sends Isabella back to reality. Opening her eyes as Estelle does up the last buckle on the sword belt, she carefully opens the door into the crawl space. Leading, Isabella steps into the crawl space and hunches down, waiting for Estelle to close the door behind them. Moving carefully and quietly through the crawl space, they find the skiff and slide into its small cockpit. Looking out of the windscreen of the skiff, they wait until the sun finally sets. Looking at Estelle, Isabella reaches for the handle, controlling the docking clamp. Smiling, Estelle nods and Isabella pulls the handle. Dropping away from the airship, they wait until they clear its engines before igniting their own. Slowly moving, they turn away from the course of the airship and head towards San Francisco.

Chapter Twenty-seven

Sitting down at the bar on the airship, Leon orders a whisky. Sliding onto the stool next to him, Shizuri has a quick look around before leaning close.

"I just received word from my contact in the underground. No-one can identify the creator of the piece I found in the Thames. It's like they're a damn ghost."

"Well, no surprises there. We figured that would be the case. How about the person who attacked the airship? Any news on them." Going silent as the bartender approaches with Leon's drink, she waits a moment for him to serve someone else before dropping her voice low and continuing.

"None. As best we can tell, they're still on campus but as to where, your guess, is as good as mine."

"Hmm. Can you get a message to Andrea?" Looking over Leon's shoulder, Shizuri catches sight of a blue bangled arm disappearing around a corner.

"I can. What do you need?"

"Tell her to be on the lookout for anyone acting stranger than normal, and not just in the school. In the town as well. And anyone with an injury matching the description. I know she probably already knows this, but tell her anyway. I have a bad feeling about this whole situation."

"Do you want me to send it now?"

"Please do. And after, go enjoy yourself. Relax a little. We've got a long flight ahead of us. I'm going for a walk. Clear my head. I'll catch up with you later." Not waiting for her reply, Leon gets up and cradling his whisky, heads toward the upper deck. Waiting until he's out of sight, Shizuri ducks around the corner and threads her hand through Iris's. She smiles as the black-haired woman squeezes her hand softly and leads her towards the cabins.

* * *

Standing alone on the top deck, Leon walks up and leans against the railing of the airship, nursing the whisky in his hand. Looking over the edge, he watches the ground slowly slide by as the airship sails on. Watching the skiff shoot out into the night, he follows its flight, taking a long sip of his drink. Losing it in the clouds, Leon's attention is drawn to the mountains. In the moon's light, the icy peaks seem to glow silver, their image giving the illusion of a beautiful and magical place. However, for Leon, they only bring about sadness. The peaks reminding him of the night in San Francisco where everything changed. Moving away from the railing, he sits down at a stool nearby, placing his drink on the bench in front of him. Looking at the mountains again, he begins to remember that night and the days leading up to it.

* * *

Reaching the ground floor finally, Leon and Farrah stop in the lobby of the building they landed on. From their vantage point, all they can see is the street. In the darkening light, the abandoned cars create shadows on the walls of the building. The screams of civilians and the sounds of fighting have long since faded, leaving behind an eerie silence. Gesturing for Farrah to stay hidden, Leon cautiously approaches the door leading out into the street. Cracking the door, he peers out, looking down the street in both directions. Closing the door softly, he ducks low and quickly returns to Farrah. Squatting down next to her, he talks quietly.

"Looks clear in both directions. Though I doubt it will stay that way for long. We need to hurry. If we go quietly, we can probably make it to the docks. With a bit of luck, there's still a ship moored there that you can use. Once you're safely away from here, I'll go back for Victoria."

"I'm not going anywhere without you. We go together or we don't go at all."

"Dammit, Farrah. This isn't the time for you to be a stubborn pain in the arse." Moving back from him, she puts a hand on her hips and gives him a stare that could kill.

"I'm been stubborn? Which one of us is the fool who's trying to run into the viper's den all alone? You're not leaving me behind this time."

"Fine. Let's get moving then. Last I checked in with her, she was at Andrea's. Pulling Farrah to her feet as he gets up, the pair move quickly to the door. Walking outside, Leon draws Fenrir in his dormant form and heads out into the road. Ducking down an alleyway on the opposite side of the street, Leon sets a fast pace.

"Leon. I'm sorry about your father. I know you wanted to believe there was still some good in him." Without looking over his shoulder as they dash through the alleyway, Leon replies with a heavy voice.

"Don't worry about it. It was a fool's dream. I think I always knew he was beyond help. I just didn't want to believe. Guess Andrea was right after all." The sharp intake of breath from Farrah is all the warning Leon needs. Summoning Fenrir in an instant, he turns and impales the nocturna's claw as it hits her. Pushing past Farrah, he pulls out his sword from the creature's claw and drives it into its chest.

"Howling wind." With a sickening sound, the wind tears the nocturna apart. Not wasting any time, he turns and runs over to Farrah. Getting up slowly, she clutches a cut on her left arm, that is spilling bright red blood onto the ground.

"Sorry Leon. I didn't hear it coming until the last second."

"Don't worry about that. Right now, we need to stop the bleeding. If my memory serves me correctly, there's a pharmacy near here. Come here and let me bind it so we can move on." Taking off his coat, Leon removes his shirt before tearing it into strips. Carefully, he binds the wound on her arm. Shrugging back into his jacket, he takes a firm grip on Farrah's hand before leading her further into the city.

Chapter Twenty-eight

The clink of the ice in his glass brings him back to the present. Finishing the remaining whisky in his glass with a sigh, Leon turns away from the mountains and heads inside. Avoiding the dining area, he places his empty glass on a passing waiter's tray and heads towards the ship's sleeping quarters. Walking down the empty corridors, he thinks about the pharmacy and everything he did after Farrah was injured. Bandaging the wound on her arm and finally making their way to Andrea's place, only to find it destroyed. The windows blown out and the building on fire. Lost in thought, Leon turns the corner and stops at the sight in front of him. Leaning against the wall, mouths locked together, are Shizuri and Iris. Quickly turning around the next corner before he disturbs the women, Leon carries on walking towards his quarters.

"Well, that explains a few things," he chuckles to himself as he arrives at his door. Entering his quarters, he quickly unbuckles his coat and anima, before walking over to the window. Looking out, he smiles sadly at the moonlit clouds before laying down on the small bed in his quarters. Laying there in the silence, sleep refuses to come. Before long, his thoughts turn back to San Francisco and everything else that happened there.

* * *

Staring at the burning building, Leon drops to his knees. Looking up at the flames billowing from the upper windows, tears come to his eyes.

"Victoria. I was too late." A bottle clattering across the pavement snaps his attention to the alleyway next to the building. Leaning heavily against the wall, Andrea staggers out, blood running down the side of her face. Getting to his feet, he runs over to the older woman and, propping her up, helps her walk clear of the wall. Reaching the kerb across the street, he carefully sits her down against a car. Pulling a bandage from his pocket, he hands it to her before turning back to look at the building. Before he can say a word, Farrah comes out of a different alleyway, with a soldier in tow. Before seeing Andrea and rushing over to her with a cry.

"Andrea, are you okay? What in god's name happened?"

"Alistair happened. He sent Baur and a platoon of men to the apartment. They took Victoria before torching the building on their way out. I only just managed to escape. I'm sorry Leon."

"Which way did they go?"

"Leon, you can't. It's too dangerous." Before Andrea can say another word, the soldier comes over.

"She's right Mr Aelfdane. The nocturna control everything east and north of this location. The World Council is still maintaining control of the port and Aerodrome, but we won't be able to maintain them much longer. My orders are to ensure you're on the next transport out, Sir." Leaving Andrea where she is, Farrah walks over and takes Leon's hand.

"Leon come on. There's nothing more we can do here. Your father has her. For now, she's safe. Well, as safe as she can be in your father's hands. But for the time being, there's nothing more we can do. Please?" Turning away once more from the burning building, Leon faces Farrah.

"Okay. Let's go." Gesturing to the soldier to lead on, Leon takes Farrah's hand and follows the man down the street. Climbing into a military vehicle as it pulls up next to them, Leon takes one glance back at the burning building. With a sinking feeling, he shuts the door and together they drive off into the night.

* * *

Arriving a little while later at the San Francisco airfield, the military truck they're in gets waved straight through the perimeter gates. Coming to a stop across from the hangers, they all get out of the car quickly. Coming over, the soldier salutes Andrea and Leon.

"Ma'am. Sir. The helicopter just over there is your transport. Please get on it as soon as you can. For the moment, the World Council still controls this area. But reports are coming in that Requiem's forces are advancing quicker than expected. We won't be able to maintain our position here for too much longer." Not waiting for them to reply, he turns on his heels and moves over to meet up with the soldiers helping civilians into airships. Starting towards the helicopter, Leon, Andrea and Farrah stop as an explosion fills the sky. Shouting from the soldiers reach their ears and Leon turns as a soldier comes running from the terminal.

"Requiem has breached the outer perimeter. Get the civilians on those airships now. And someone get the VIP's to safety." Coming over to the three of them, another soldier gestures for them to continue towards the helicopter.

"Hurry. We must leave. I'm your pilot. Running towards the helicopter, Leon stops as Farrah collapses to her knees and cries out.

"No more. I can't do this anymore." Turning back to her, he gestures at Andrea and the pilot.

"Go. We're right behind you." Coming over to Farrah, Leon squats down in front of her. Placing his hand on her forehead, a shock goes through him at the heat radiating off her.

"Come on. We have to go."

"Leon, I can't go any further. It's too late. The virus is running rampant through me. I can feel it." Taking her anima off her belt, she holds it out in front of her.

"Don't do it, you don't have the strength." Ignoring Leon's warning, she begins to chant.

"Done now is our contract, for the time has come for us to part. Aurora, I release you from this bond." Slumping forward against Leon's shoulder, she sobs. Pushing back from his shoulder, she looks Leon in the eye.

"Take Aurora and go Leon. It's too late and you know it. I'm going to turn it's just a matter of time now. I don't want to hurt you."

"Don't talk like that. I'll be damned if I'm going to let it end like this. We came here together and we're leaving together." Pushing him away, she opens her mouth to yell at him.

"Nocturna! Open fire! Don't let them past." As the shout reaches their ears, gunfire begins. Flashes of light and screams of agony come from the direction of the civilian transports. Getting to his feet, Leon turns towards the terminal. An explosion sounds from within the terminal and blows out a nearby window. Through the flames, a nocturna emerges and leaps from the window, landing heavily on the tarmac below. Stepping between the creature and Farrah, Leon draws and summons Fenrir.

"Farrah, get to the helicopter. Go now" With a roar, the creature runs towards them. Running at it, Leon sidesteps its first blow, his blade flashing out. Passing through the creature's chest with ease, blood sprays through the air as the blade completes its arc. Roaring in pain, the nocturna swings wildly around. Rolling under its swing, Leon drives his blade, point first, through the back of its chest as he rolls to his feet. Twisting the blade free, he leaps clear of its reach as it spins around to face him. Looking at him with dying eyes, it takes a single step forward before collapsing in a heap. Claws flexing, the creature breathes its final breath and falls still. Sighing with relief, Leon relaxes.

"Come on, we need to..." He stops talking as Aurora's dormant tube comes rolling past his foot. The growl behind him alerts him to the danger a moment too late. Pain lances down his back and he's thrown heavily against the ground. Ignoring the fire tearing across his back, he rolls over and tears spring to his eyes. Walking towards him, one giant claw already replacing her left arm, is Farrah. Her once blue eyes, now cold and black. Pushing himself to his feet, Leon leans heavily on the wolf blade. With a menacing growl, she advances towards him.

"Farrah. No. Please don't." With a roar, she charges towards him. Covering the distance to him before he can move, he watches, stunned, as her arm raises up. Claws reflecting the burning light from the fire, she swings her arm towards Leon.

"Leon!" Andrea's shout across the tarmac awakens something in him. Ducking under Farrah's swing, he steps forward and slices through the side of her leg. A roar dripping with anger and savagery, tears free of her throat. Spinning around with incredible speed, she drives the claws straight at Leon's throat. Dodging the claws by a hairsbreadth, he drives his blade through the middle of her chest. Light flashes from the base of his blade and with a cry of pain that becomes human, Farrah turns back to normal. Pulling his blade from her chest, he drops it on the ground and supports her weight as her legs collapse. Lowering to the ground with her held tightly in one arm, Leon puts his other hand against her chest in an attempt to stop the blood pouring from the wound. Looking around frantically for something to stop the bleeding, he goes to reach towards his blade but a hand weakly gripping his stops him. Looking down, he meets Farrah's blue eyes.

"Leon stop. That's enough, there's nothing you can do now. Take Aurora and go. I..." Her words cut off as a coughing fit wracks her body, causing blood to trickle from her mouth.

"Farrah, hold on!" As she finishes, another coughing fit, more blood bubbles from her mouth, and a note of fear enters her voice.

"Leon!" Reaching up, she wraps her arms around his neck and pulls herself against him.

"I love you." As her last words come out as a whisper, her body goes limp and she slumps heavily in his arms, the light fading from her eyes. Clutching her body to his chest, Leon's agonised cry echoes into the sky. As he cries into Farrah's hair, the sound of tearing metal breaks through his grief as a small host of nocturna rips through the fence closest to him. Picking up Fenrir and Aurora's dormant tubes, he runs towards the nocturna, the wolf blade appearing in his hand. Reaching the closest of the creatures, he lashes out with Fenrir. As the blade pierces the nocturna's chest, spikes of ice explode out of the creature's back. Stepping clear of the creature's frozen corpse, he charges towards the next nocturna, all reason lost to the rage consuming him. Watching from the helicopter, Andrea's heart races as fear grips her.

"Leon!" At Andrea's shout, he turns back towards the helicopter, wrenching his blade free from the chest of a nocturna. As the realisation of the distance now between himself and the helicopter sets in, fear replaces the rage previously consuming him. Lumbering into a limping run, he makes a line toward the helicopter. Explosions come from behind, and the air is filled with roars and running footsteps.

"My lady. He's not going to make it."

With a grimace, Andrea vaults from the helicopter, landing lightly on the ground. Holding out her hands, lines of light swirl around her fingers and quickly form sigils in front of her palms. Clapping her hands together, energy crackles between her fingers. Stepping forward, she pulls her hands apart and, crackling wildly, the energy quickly materialises into a ball. Taking another step towards Leon, she thrusts her hands skyward.

With barely a whisper, the ball of energy flies from her hands into the sky. Within seconds thunder roars overhead. Slowing to a walk, the nocturna pursuing Leon looks around in fear. With blinding light, bolts of lightning streak from the sky, crackling towards the nocturna. With agonised screams, the creatures burst into flame as the lightning connects with them. The nocturna's cries cut through the night air as they roll, burning on the ground. Raising her arm, lights already start, forming a sigil at the end of her fingertips. Andrea points her hand at the nocturna on the ground and from her palm, a red light shoots out, bouncing between the creatures. As it does, the flames expand out and climb into the sky, quickly becoming a wall separating the terminal from the helicopter. Ignoring the screams and the heat of the flames behind him, Leon staggers the last few metres to collapse against the side of the helicopter. Reaching out from inside, the soldiers quickly and carefully drag him inside. Starting first aid on his wounds, they signal to the pilot to take off.

"Lady Andrea, we need to leave. Hurry!" Turning from the wall of flame, she vaults into the helicopter as it begins to lift from the ground. With a flick of her wrist, the doors close behind her and she kneels next to Leon. Placing her hands on either side of the wound on his back, she channels her energy once more. As burning pain sears through his body, all Leon can see is the moon's silver reflection on the floor of the helicopter as it lifts into the night sky. Eyes closing, a single tear runs down his cheek as he falls unconscious.

* * *

Walking towards the wall of flame, Simon Baur wipes the blood off his hands. Dropping the soiled cloth on the ground, he smiles as the helicopter lights fade into the distance. Dropping into a small bow, he quickly straightens as footsteps approach.

"Until next time My Lady. What is it?" Saluting as he comes to a stop, the Requiem soldier straightens and gives his report.

"We've finished securing the city, Sir. It's now fully under our control." Looking at the woman's body lying on the ground nearest to him, he turns back to the soldier.

"Very good. Inform Alistair immediately. And bring her. She may yet be of some use. Quickly now, before her life force has completely faded." As the soldier runs off and begins issuing commands, Baur walks towards the hole in the nearby fence. Ignoring the death and destruction around him, he begins to whistle a tune as he leaves the airport.

Chapter Twenty-nine

Waking in his bunk with a start, Leon sits up.

"We are now beginning our descent into Athens. Please remain in your quarters or seats until we've finished docking. Thank you for your co-operation." As the P. A system crackles into silence once more, Leon leans forwards and a tear falls down his cheek. Starting at the feel of it, he wipes it away quickly, looking out the window at the pale dawn sky.

"Farrah, I'm sorry." Sitting there for a moment more, he gets up with a sigh and begins gathering his things. Outside, the city of Athens finally comes into view. Taking one last look out the window, he picks up his belongings and leaves his room. Stepping out, Leon sees Gilroy in the hallway heading towards the exit. Stopping his old friend, Leon gestures him into a nearby empty room.

"Gil, get the soldiers settled then meet me at my hotel room. I've got a few things to discuss with you before the council meeting."

"Has this got something to do with the attempted attack on the airship before we left?"

"Yes, and no. Just meet me there. I'll explain everything later. Ok?" Nodding his assent, Gilroy follows Leon out into the hallway. Reaching a T-junction in the hall, the two men go a different way without a word.

Stepping out onto the gangway at the Athens Aerodrome, Leon's breath comes out in a mist. Shrugging into his coat further to escape the brisk morning air, he slowly makes his way to the dock. As his foot touches down on the concrete, a deep voice calls out to him.

"Yo. Leon Aelfdane." Walking over to him is the American representative, Dion. Raising his hand in greeting, Leon walks over to the tall American man. Holding his hand out in greeting, Leon smiles warmly as Dion takes it.

"It's good to finally meet you in person, Dion. How was your flight to Athens?" Looking back at the airship grimly, he gestures towards it before replying. Giant tears in the metal scar the side of the airship and smoke still trickles out of one hole towards the engines.

"It wasn't a pleasant trip. Not long after we crossed the American coastline, we were attacked by flying nocturna. Luckily enough, we managed to drive them off. But we lost a few good men in the process." With a sigh, he gestures towards the exit and waiting a moment for his soldiers to take up position around him, he begins to walk. Falling into step beside the tall American, his own soldiers increase the men surrounding them and Leon draws a packet of smokes from his pocket as they head towards the exit. Lighting a smoke as they step outside of the aerodrome, Leon takes a drag.

"How did you go with gathering intel about the behemoth attacks? Cause to be honest I came up with nothing. I couldn't even track down any leads as to who has the capability to shield a behemoth like that. Anyone who's had any knowledge of such things seems to have vanished into thin air." Stopping in his tracks, the American turns towards Leon with a concerned look in his eyes.

"I encountered much of the same. All my leads seemed to have evaporated overnight. It's frustrating. But Leon, doesn't that strike you as strange? It's almost as if there's a…"

"Traitor in the council." Taking another drag of his smoke, Leon leans against the wall.

"If that's the case and there's truly a traitor in the council, then there's a good chance that this meeting is going to get interesting fast. If that happens, well, I guess we just deal with that bridge when we come to it." Drawing his anima out, Dion turns it over in his hands.

"You know, ever since the arrival of the anima, things haven't exactly been dull. And to be honest, given everything that's happened since you were elected to the council, I don't think I want to see your definition of interesting. What do you think about the World Council's plan to go to war with Requiem?"

"It's foolish. For starters, we have no intel regarding their forces. I think it would be the worst idea ever to make a move against them. My father's planning something. I can feel it. These attacks on the cities, as well as the increasing number of attacks around the world on transports and small settlements. They don't feel random. There's a kind of directed feel to them. Requiems up to something and I just hope we can find out what it is and stop it before it's too late." Crushing his cigarette out, Leon pushes himself off the wall.

"It was good meeting you, Dion. I'm sorry to cut things short but I have a few things to take care of before the meeting this afternoon."

"Likewise. I'll see you later at the meeting. Stay safe." Frowning at the Americans parting words, Leon sets off into the city of Athens.

* * *

Walking fast, Leon gets about a block from the aerodrome when Shizuri lands lightly next to him, startling a few of the soldiers.

"You took your sweet time getting rid of him." Talking quietly so the soldiers can't hear. She steps a little closer to Leon before he replies.

"I couldn't exactly just fob him off without arousing suspicion. And given we still don't know who the traitor is, I can't afford to unnecessarily alienate people. It'll be hard enough working it out as is without everyone working out what we're up to. I take it you got past the guards without incident then." Grimacing, she pulls a cloth wrapped object from behind her belt as they continue walking toward their quarters.

"It's pathetic how easy it was. If security is that lax everywhere, there's nothing to stop Requiem marching right into Athens and causing all kinds of trouble. So, do you suspect Dion is involved?"

"I don't think so. He's too earnest a person for that kind of thing. And he has a lousy poker face. No, I'm thinking Cassy is on the right path. Bernardo is the one we should look at." Reaching the hotel they're staying at, Leon stops at the foot of the stairs leading into the building.

"For now, put that away. We need to focus on the meeting. Go rest up. I have a bad feeling about this whole thing. Can you sense it? It's almost like there's a storm coming. One we're directly in the path of. Something we can't avoid."

"Of course, we can't avoid it. We're the Council of Nine. It's our responsibility to face everything head on. Whatever the world throws at us."

"Hmmm. Well anyway, I'm heading up. I'll see you at the council meeting later." Leaving Shizuri to ponder her thoughts, Leon ascends the stairs and enters the hotel. Dismissing his guard at the entrance, he walks towards the desk. Halfway across the lobby, he halts as a voice calls out to him.

"Leon!" Coming towards him is the blonde-haired leader of the council. Grabbing him by the arm, she drags him away from the check-in desk towards the lifts.

"I've already checked you in. I need a word with you."

"Cassy, couldn't this have waited until I at least got to my room? Please remember who you are when you're in public." Looking around quickly, she smiles mischievously at the looks the people in the foyer are giving her and Leon. Walking hand in hand. Hugging his arm to her chest, she leans into him heavily.

"And what if I do this, Mr Aelfdane? What then?" Looking up at him, she leans in towards his face. Before she can connect her lips to his, the door to lift opens with a ring. Smiling, she whispers into his ear,

"Maybe next time." Laughing, she breaks free and pushes him into the lift. Turning and winking at the people in the foyer, she steps in after him and closes the door. Pushing the button for his floor, the Australian woman rests against the railing on the opposite side of the lift.

"What have you discovered about what I asked?"

"Straight to the point, huh? Very little. Requiem seems to have gone dark, but I'm hoping to shed some light on that soon. But I assume you're referring to the message you left with Shizuri?"

"I am. It's the more important of the two."

"Well, that's another story. I've enquired into a few things regarding Bernardo. It seems his whereabouts on the night Sigmund was killed are sketchy, but not enough to warrant action. It's same with family and state meetings. He often disappears from them with little to no warning, but even though his excuses appear flimsy, it's still not enough to accuse him. If he is the traitor, he's being damn careful to cover his tracks. At this rate, it will be nearly impossible to uncover the truth, short of getting an actual confession from him." Sighing, Cassy rocks backward against the railing.

"I suspected as much. I know you've brought Guard Commander Roscoe with you. His reputation precedes him. Maybe see if he can do some investigating in town. If we're lucky, he'll be able to dig something up." Stopping the chatter as they reach the floor of Leon's room; the pair step out into the hall. Following Cassy, Leon's thoughts turn to Requiem and what his father has planned. Breaking from his thoughts, when Cassy stops, he looks up. Holding out a key card to him, she gestures at the door to her left.

"This is you. Room three-o-six. I'll leave you with what we discussed. And I'll see you later this afternoon, at the meeting." Smiling, the Australian woman skips off down the hall, turning to give Leon one last wink before turning the corner. Shaking his head, he swipes the card and enters the room, closing the door behind him. With a grimace, he walks into the bedroom and throws down his bags. Pulling off his coat and anima, he heads to the bathroom and begins getting ready for the meeting.

Chapter Thirty

Stepping off the elevator, Leon comes face to face with Gilroy. Smiling as his friend falls into step beside him, the two men head towards the city.

"So, I take it you're my guard? What happened to the others and what happened to meeting me at the room?"

"I am. The others are resting. I want them fully refreshed and ready for the big meeting tomorrow. It's just a minor council meeting today, so I'll accompany you there. And come collect you when it's done. It took a while to get everything sorted out. I've literally come straight from the barracks to here."

"No worries. Well, you'll have to keep going for a while longer before you get the chance to rest. I have a job for you, while I'm in this meeting."

"What's that?"

"I need you to sniff around. See if you can find out anything. Hit the bars. Do some digging. Something about this whole thing doesn't add up."

"I know the feeling. Since that Behemoth attack in London, I've had the feeling that something dark is moving behind the scenes. I'll see what I can find." Going quiet and retreating to their own thoughts, the two men make their way slowly through the city. Finally reaching the Council of Nine building, Leon stops and turns, offering his hand to the big man. Smiling broadly, Gilroy takes it.

"Good luck Gil. Stay safe mate."

"You too Leon. Good luck in there. I don't envy your position." Chuckling to himself, Gilroy turns and makes his way back into the city. With a deep sense of foreboding, Leon ascends the steps and enters the Council Chambers.

* * *

Walking into the Council room a few moments later, Leon looks it over. A large stone table sits in the middle of the white marble room. Devoid of anything else apart from the table and a small door, the room is plain with no furnishings. Making his way to his seat at the council table, Leon takes a quick look around at the assembled members. Most seem slightly agitated, but the Italian representative holds Leon's gaze. Leaning on the table he seems relaxed, almost bored, chin resting upon his hands. Something about the man makes him uneasy. As the council members finally take their seats, Cassy stands up and calls for quiet.

"Welcome everyone to Athens. I'm glad you all managed to make it here. The World Council is meeting tomorrow and discussing a plan of attack to stop Requiem. This is the only chance we will have to discuss everything before tomorrow's major meeting. What I need to know from everyone here, is where we stand on the Behemoth attack. Have any of you found out anything? If so, speak up so that we can finally make some damn progress on this incident." Finishing in a huff, Cassy gestures to the gathered council members before taking her seat. Rising slowly from her seat next to Leon, Shizuri pulls out the cloth-bound object.

"Regarding the attack on London a little under a month ago, I located this." Unwrapping the spearhead, she places it on the table for all to see. Shocked gasps come from a few of the council members as it thuds onto the timber.

"You all know it's like. Made from the remnants of destroyed anima. These devices are used solely to control nocturna. Despite my influence and abilities, I have been unable to track down the creator of this piece. But given what is happening in this city currently, now is the best time to track down the individual responsible." Standing on the other side of the table, Dion takes a deep breath before addressing his question to Shizuri.

"What makes you think the person responsible would be in Athens?"

"It's simple Dion. The World Council and The Council of Nine, both currently have meetings being held at this location. The sheer number of keepers that are currently present, give them the perfect place for peddling their wares. There is more than a single person who wants to be stronger than they currently are and who doesn't care how they get there."

"You make a valid point. How do you suppose we go about finding these individuals?"

"Well, I think the best plan is…" Whatever she was going to say is lost as the window above them shatters. Through the skylight comes a woman dressed in white. Face covered by a thick veil; she falls elegantly through the air. Halfway down to the table, she draws two anima. With a flick of her wrist's they become twin cutlasses. Turning to Leon and grabbing his sleeve, Shizuri has a panicked look.

"Leon. That's her. The one from my vision in London. The one who was controlling the behemoth." Leon rises from his seat as the girl lands in the centre of the table. Straightening up, she points her blades at Bernardo.

"You are a traitor, Bernardo. Your deals with Requiem have not gone unnoticed and now you shall be punished." Before anyone can move to stop her, she charges at the Italian man. Leaning back in his seat, he smiles an amused smile before tumbling backwards. Rolling to his feet as he hits the ground, a well-placed kick flings the chair into the girl's path. Not slowing down, she cuts the chair to pieces. Drawing an anima, Bernardo twirls it once through his fingers before activating it. Steel gauntlets run from wrist to elbow on both hands.

"Come, little girl. Big words for someone so puny." Rising to the provocation, she screams in fury and charges the Italian man. With ease, he dodges her, strikes as he slowly backs away. Finally, making a mistake and overextending with her attack, she gasps as Bernardo moves inside her guard and lands a strike to her midriff. Coughing, she lashes out with her blades. However, both blades come to a grinding halt as he grabs them in his gauntleted fists. Twisting his hands, he rips both blades from her grasp. Defenceless, she takes his first hit to the side of her head. Followed up by a power drive to her midriff that sends her bouncing down the floor. Hitting the wall hard, her vision swims in and out of focus as she slumps. Extending his right hand, Bernardo smiles a deadly smile.

"Time to die, you little bitch." Tracing a quick sigil, Bernardo brings a fireball the size of a small car to life. The heat from it is enough to wither the nearby plants. Standing in her seat, Cassy shouts.

"NO! Stand down, Bernardo!" But it's too late. Paying no heed to the leader of the council, he throws the fireball at the defenceless girl. Drawing Fenrir, Leon rushes across the table as Bernardo brings his arm back to throw the fireball. With a burst of speed, he makes it between the girl and the fireball. Landing lightly, the anima in his hand becomes the wolf blade. Extending his right hand, he lets the blade fall, speaking as it does.

"Howling Storm Barrier." Spinning the blade creates a shield of air and ice. As the fireball hits the barrier, steam erupts. Sensing the girl starting to move, Leon draws and summons Aurora. Without turning from Bernardo, he places the tip of the weapon against her neck.

"I'm sorry, young miss, but I'll have you stand down. Give me your word as a keeper, and I'll be satisfied. Oh, and I'd be quick with your answer, it isn't easy keeping this fireball at bay."

Rising to her feet, she walks to where Leon can see her and, hands in the air, gives a nod. Smiling his approval, Leon removes the rapier from her neck before getting serious once more. Shifting his right hand, he moves the shield slightly. Lashing out with the rapier, Leon cuts the fireball straight down the centre. Finally, having been released, it explodes violently, sending cracks running through the floor and knocking the young would-be assassin off her feet. Yells and cries come from the council members. Before the dust settles, Leon charges from the smoke and lands in front of Bernardo, levelling his blade at the man and preparing to strike. Finally, moving from her location, Cassy lands between the two men. Tracing a sigil before clapping both hands together, she creates a bubble of white energy that pushes them apart.

"That is enough, both of you. I will not tolerate fighting between members of my council." Staring coldly at Bernardo, Leon sheathes both his anima and backs down. Putting his hands up, Bernardo puts away his anima and smiles a sickly sweet smile at Cassy. Letting the bubble disperse, the Australian woman walks over to the Italian man. His smile turns to a sneer as her backhanded slap catches him on the cheek, knocking him to the ground.

"You ignored a direct order. I will not tolerate insubordination. Especially from you, given recent events. Now young miss. If you'd be so kind, please remove the covering off your face. I like to face people who accuse my council members of being traitors directly." Regaining her feet, the young woman reaches up and removes the veil covering the bottom of her face, causing a gasp from Cassy.

"Monica! Why? What do you think you're doing attacking your brother?" The young girl walks over to the Council Leader. Pointing at her brother, she talks loudly.

"Because he's a damn traitor. He's in league with Requiem. He's a disgrace to keepers, our family name, and the Council of Nine." Breathing heavily as she finishes, she lowers her arm. Slowly getting to his feet, Bernardo wipes away the trickle of blood from his split lip.

"Like you can talk about being a disgrace to the family, Monica. You're not even supposed to be here. And a traitor? That's exactly the kind of thing I would expect from a spiteful, jealous little girl."

"Why you!" As she walks towards her brother, Cassy places her hand on the young woman's shoulder, restraining her.

"Enough! Monica, you're coming with me for a moment. Leon, you come as well. As for you, Bernardo, take your place at the council table and wait until I give you further instructions."

"Like I'm going to…" any further arguments are silenced by an icy glare from the Australian woman. Steering Monica away and beckoning to Leon, she quickly leads them through the small door into a side chamber. As the two women exit the room, Leon gives one last look at the Council chamber. Noticing Shizuri giving him a questioning stare, he gives her a quick shrug in response and follows Cassy through the doorway.

Chapter Thirty-one

Stepping into a small room, Leon blinks in surprise as he finds Cassy hugging the smaller Italian woman. Waiting for the two women to part, he has a brief look around. The room is plain and simple. At one end is an old fireplace set in the blank stone walls, looking sad and desolate. Stepping back from Monica, Cassy turns around to Leon.

"Thank you for your intervention. If not for you, I'm certain Bernardo would have killed Monica." Turning from Leon, Cassy gestures at the young Italian girl.

"I've known the Grimani family for a long time. Monica is a close friend and nothing like what her brother just described. I already suspect Bernardo of treachery, but I've had no way to prove it. What do you know Monica?" Looking up and wiping away a tear, Monica looks Cassy in the face before replying in a strong voice.

"It started about six months ago. Before Lord Sigmund was murdered, back when everyone still thought Requiem were just out to sow anarchy in the world. Before the truth about San Francisco became known and they became the number one threat, that the world now faces. As you know, my father is one of the members of the Italian council. New Italy was struggling financially. The masses were starving, and the council started to panic. They were looking for any solution and didn't really care where it came from. That solution, was my brother. He came up with a large sum of money to bail out the country almost overnight. Of course, the council didn't look the gift horse in the mouth but, there was something about the way he delivered it to them that irked me. I had no reason to suspect him, but even so, I still began to monitor his activities. It didn't take long to discover, what he was up to. He met with a man that I've been able to identify as Simon Baur, who is a known associate of Alistair Aelfdane, the leader of Requiem." At the mention of Baur and his father's name, Leon clenches his fists and grinds his teeth in anger.

"Of course, it would be Baur who's involved. That filthy bastard. He's always been the one who does my Father's dirty work." Sitting down on a bench nestled so well into the wall that Leon didn't notice it before, Cassy sighs heavily. Raising her head, Leon sees the well-disguised tiredness in her eyes.

"Leon, I need a favour. Can you please investigate, Bernardo? I know you're new to the council, however, I feel I can trust no-one else with this task." Before he can reply, the door to the small room shakes violently. Turning, Leon immediately draws and summons Fenrir. Waiting for something more to happen, the following silence seems to stretch on forever. Slowly walking forward, Leon pushes on the door to find It stuck hard. Grimacing, he addresses Cassy over his shoulder.

"Doors jammed. What do you want me to do?"

"Destroy it. We need to find out what that was."

"Stand back then." As the two girls move to the back of the room, Leon focuses on the door in front of him. Ice forms a thin layer over the blade and with a swing, the door explodes outwards as the blade connects. Not waiting for the dust to settle, he rushes into the council room, finding it in a shamble. Chairs overturned and the table in the centre smashed into pieces. All around the room, council members are lying on the ground. Some appear to be unconscious, whilst others are just getting to their feet with dazed looks on their faces. Moving around, he sees a familiar arm sticking out from under a chair. Rushing over and throwing the chair clear, he gasps. Lying in a pool of blood, Shizuri is as pale as a sheet. Dropping Fenrir, he carefully picks her up. As he lifts her, a blood-covered piece of stone falls to the ground.

"CASSY!" At Leon's shout, she comes running. Shock lights her face as she sees the Council Chamber. Her shock is quickly replaced by worry as she sees Shizuri. Moving to an undamaged section of the table, she removes her jacket and lays it down.

"Bring her here. Quickly!" Being careful not to jostle her, Leon carefully places Shizuri on Cassy's jacket. Looking over the wounds quickly, Cassy grinds her teeth.

"She's lost a lot of blood, Leon. I can save her. I think. However, I am going to need a few things in order to do so. Hot water, clean towels and a suture kit. If you can get those or have someone get them, I'll start stabilising her." Vaulting over rubble, Leon runs for the door, as Cassy traces a sigil and begins to stabilize Shizuri's wounds. Bursting out into the main hall, he sees a serving girl standing behind a column looking at the door fearfully.

"You there. I need hot water, clean towels and a suture kit." With a yelp, the young girl leaps out from behind the column and runs off down the hall, screaming. Shouting in frustration, Leon continues further into the main hall. Turning down a random corridor, he almost crashes into an elderly serving woman as she steps out of a doorway.

"Excuse me, ma'am. I need hot water, clean towels and a suture kit to be brought to the Council Chamber immediately. It's an emergency."

"No problem lad. Is there an injured person?"

"Yes, one of the council members has been seriously injured. She's currently being given emergency treatment to stabilise her, but we need to close the wound as soon as possible."

"No problems Lad. Leave it to me. GIRLS!" At the old woman's yell, serving women come from everywhere. Within moments, she has them running in every direction to gather the needed supplies.

"Now lad. Show me to this girl. I was a field surgeon in the military when I was younger. Those skills may be of some use. Now let's go." Before he can even move, the old woman grabs him by the hand and drags him off towards the Council Chamber.

* * *

Arriving back at the Council chamber with the old serving woman, Leon sees serving girls running in with the requested items. Entering the door, he sees Cassy bending down over Shizuri still trying to stabilise her with arcana. The effort evident by the sweat running down her brow. Coming around to Cassy's side, Leon looks down at Shizuri's still frame. Concentrating intensely, Cassy talks to Leon through gritted teeth.

"I've managed to knit together the muscle and kick-start her marrow into producing more blood. I'm at my limit though. I can't close the wound, and I'm only just able to stop the bleeding. How long till the med-kit is here?" As if summoned, the old serving-woman appears at their side.

"You've done good, girl. Now if you would kindly move aside and let those with more experienced take over." Pushing her gently out of the way, the old woman takes Cassy's place and starts working on Shizuri. Fresh blood stems from the wound, but she quickly stops it with a towel. Stepping forward to object, Leon stops Cassy with a hand on her shoulder and a look. With a steady and practised hand, the old woman begins to clean and stitch up the wound. Watching the old woman work, Cassy finally relaxes, and all the tension leaves her. Stumbling as the exhaustion finally catches up, she falls heavily against Leon. Leaning against him, she closes her eyes sleepily. Slowly and steadily, Leon helps her walk over to an intact chair. Standing next to her, he moves away once her breathing slows and her eyes close, sleep taking her. Leon walks around the room trying to piece together the events, when he sees Dion sitting on a bench, having his head bandaged by a serving girl. As he walks over, the American waves away the girl and gets to his feet.

"I'm surprised to find you still here, Dion. Everyone else seems to have retreated to their quarters already." Smiling, the American holds his hands up.

"What can I say? I ain't one for sitting idly by when there's work to be done. Besides, someone had to fill you in on what transpired and Shizuri's in no condition to do so."

"I'm glad you're in one piece, mate. Now, what happened here?"

"It was Bernardo, Leon. He got up to leave the moment you guys left the room. He had this strange look on his face. A few of us told him to sit back down unless he wanted to face Cassy's wrath. But Shizuri was the one who tried to stop him. That's when everything went to hell. He drew his anima on us all, Leon. Blasted the table into pieces with a massive shockwave. Before the dust had even settled, he was already breaking for the door. Shizuri, even though she was injured and probably the closest to the blast-wave, she went at him with full force. He didn't even bat an eyelash when he hit her. Leaving me as the last man standing. I didn't even have time to draw my anima. Heard a noise from behind and I turned and next thing I knew it was lights out. I came to just after you smashed down the door." Before Leon can reply, the old serving-woman calls out to him.

"Lad, would come here a moment please?" Leaving Dion, he comes quickly over to the old woman.

"It is finished. As much as can be done for now. The rest is up to her, but she's strong. I think she will be fine with a little rest. Speaking of which, where did you want her moved to and is there anything else that you need before I organise this room to be put to rights?"

"Take her to my hotel room. It's the closest and if you could also have someone bring Monica to Cassy's room as well, that would be good. Thank you for everything, Ma'am."

"I'll see that it's arranged. And the names Hannah lad. Now if you'll excuse me, I need to get to work." Standing aside so the old woman can leave, Leon looks down at Shizuri. Paler than normal, she seems to be sleeping peacefully. Sighing with relief, he gestures to Dion and Monica. Moving away from the table, he meets them in front of the side room's broken door.

"Monica, you are to go with Cassy and remain in her chambers. That's for your safety as much as hers. She is tired and will need rest, so until I say otherwise, you're to remain there. Tell her I'll be back as soon as possible. Dion, I want you to stay with Shizuri if you can. She will need someone to watch over her until I return. If she wakes before I get back, tell her the same thing." Both begin to argue but go silent as a woman's voice comes sharply from behind Leon.

"Enough! Both of you." Standing on shaky legs, Cassy glares at the two in front of Leon.

"Leon's orders stand. Monica, you will return to my quarters with me, as I still have further questions regarding our earlier conversation. Dion, watch Shizuri. And Leon, I'm sure you don't need me to tell you what you need to do." Giving Cassy a quick nod, Leon vaults over a chunk of broken table and runs from the council chamber.

Chapter Thirty-two

Leaving a small bar, Gilroy rubs an ache out of the side of his neck. Sighing, he looks down at the dismal amount of information written on the small notepad. Moving over to a nearby chair, he takes a seat before pulling a pack of cigarettes from his coat pocket. Lighting one and taking a long drag, he leans back in his seat. Tearing the page from his notepad, he crumples it into a ball and tosses it in the bin next to him. Looking at the time on his watch, he gets up and walks back towards the hotel. Walking past the Council chambers, he stops as a serving girl comes bursting out of the double doors, running down the stairs as if her life depended on it. Coming down the last step too fast, she trips on her dress, ending up in a tangled heap at the base of the stairs. Putting out his cigarette, Gilroy runs over to the girl.

"Are you ok?" Getting to her feet, she straightens her dress and brushes her hair quickly from her face. Without a word or a glance at Gilroy, she dashes past the big man. Grabbing her left wrist out of reflex, he staggers backwards, dodging the slash of a dagger that came from the folds in her dress. Letting go of her wrist, he steps backward a few paces and creates some space between them. Turning to face him properly, she spins the dagger over her hand into a reverse grip. Pulling Leviathan from his belt, Gilroy brings the axe into being with a flick of his wrist, the edge of its blade gleaming menacingly in the sunlight.

"You really, don't want to do this, Miss. Trust me." Smiling wickedly, she twirls the dagger around once more before pacing around Gilroy.

"Commander Roscoe. You shouldn't have stopped me. Did you know there's a bounty on your head? And I'm going to claim it. For Requiem!" Screaming as she rushes the big man, a crazy look enters her eyes. Without moving from his position, Gilroy spins the axe, cutting her arm off with a spray of blood. Screaming, she clutches the bloody stump of her arm as the dagger falls to the ground, still clutched in her hand. Stepping forward, Gilroy strikes her with the butt of his axe, catching her as she falls backward, unconscious. Quickly tracing a sigil, he places it on the end of her arm. Bursting with light, the bleeding stops, and she regains consciousness, screaming loudly. Struggling, she tries to pull herself free but stops as he grips her good arm tightly. Sighing, he traces a second sigil and places it in the centre of her chest. From the point of impact, chains burst forth and within seconds bind the girl rigidly. Standing straight and stepping back, Gilroy turns at the sound of the doors being thrown open. Bursting through them, Leon takes the stairs three at a time.

"Leon!" Sliding to a halt as he hears his name, Leon turns and takes in the sight of Gil standing in front of the bound woman.

"Ummm Gil, what the hell?" Turning to look at the girl, Gilroy spits out his words.

"She's with Requiem. Her daggers over there. Tried rushing..." Pushing past Gilroy before he can finish, Leon knocks the girl onto her back as he dashes past. Grabbing the dagger out of her limp hand, he turns back to the girl, hatred etched on his face. Before Gilroy can say anything, Leon grabs the chains and drags the girl upright, pressing the dagger to her neck.

"Start talking. Where's Bernardo? Tell me what I want to know, and I'll save you the agony of a Requiem's execution." Staring him defiantly in the eye, she smiles sadistically as she replies.

"Leon Aelfdane. The prodigal son. You'll never catch him. I'll tell you nothing. You will burn along with the rest of the world when..." Gargling cuts her words off as Leon drags the dagger across her throat, silencing her forever. Dropping her on the ground, he throws the dagger down next to her.

What the hell did you do that for?" Turning to face Gil, Leon leans down and tears a piece of cloth from the woman's dress and starts wiping the blood off his hands.

"She wasn't going to tell me anything, and I don't have the time to deal with getting her to the authorities. And now neither do you. We have to track down Bernardo."

"Hold up. You just murdered her in cold blood. I'm not about to let that fly, Leon!" Stepping forward, Gilroy's grip on his axe tightens. Turning to face his friend, Leon fixes the big man with an icy stare.

"She had that coming. And there are bigger issues than one Requiem agent. Bernardo just destroyed the council room and injured half the members, including Shizuri. She barely made it. So if you expect me to have any sympathy or mercy for anyone working for them, think again. Now if you're done, Bernardo's in the wind and we need to catch him before he can finish whatever it is, that Requiem has him doing," Grinding his teeth, Gilroy lessens the grip on the axe, and burying the point into the ground, looks at Leon.

"Dammit. Well, what do you want to do?"

Before Leon can reply, an explosion rips through a building a few blocks over, spewing fire and rubble high into the sky. Pulling Fenrir from his belt, Leon runs towards the explosion when a second comes from the opposite direction. Followed quickly by a third and fourth. Stopping in his tracks, Leon looks up at the sky. Changing colour slightly, it seems to flicker in the light. Swearing, Leon turns back to Gilroy.

"New plan Gil. Grab Iris and bring her to Shizuri. Tell Cassy to get any council member still able to fight to the shield. It's failing. I want you to help them. It's the top priority." As he finishes speaking, another explosion blows the wall out from the building opposite the council chambers. As the smoke billows from what remains of the wall, Requiem soldiers come pouring out into the square. Gesturing to the soldiers as he hefts his axe, Gilroy grimaces at Leon.

"We should probably take care of these guys first."

"Yeah." Summoning Fenrir as the two walk toward the soldiers streaming from the hole, Leon gives the wolf sword a few test swings to loosen up his shoulder. Pulling blades from their sheaths, the Requiem soldiers rush the two men. Stepping forward to meet the soldiers, the sound of metal clashing echoes through the courtyard. Letting themselves get lost in the moment, the two men spin and slice their way through the charging soldiers. Blades flashing as blood sprays in the sunlight, everything goes quiet after a few moments. Standing in the middle of a circle of dead bodies, Leon and Gilroy survey their handiwork. Stretching the stiffness out of his neck, Leon wipes the blood off his face before turning to Gil.

"Well, now that's over, get moving and get to that shield. It's imperative we get that stabilised as soon as possible. Before the nocturna overrun Athens. I'm going to head to the main gate and rendezvous with any soldier that doesn't belong to Requiem. We need to stop this before it begins. Bernardo will have to wait." Turning from his friend, Leon heads towards the alleyway leading to the main gate.

"Leon!" Running over to his friend, Gilroy clasps him arm to arm.

"Be careful. These boys ain't playing." Gripping the big man's arm back, Leon smiles before releasing the grip and taking off down the alleyway. Watching his friends retreating back for a moment, Gilroy sighs and heads in the opposite direction towards their rooms. Before he can take more than a few steps, a voice calls out to him. Turning, he comes face to face with Iris. Blue bangles on her wrists, blood already stains her clothes and runs from a slight cut on her forehead.

"Was that Leon I just saw running off?"

"It was. He's gone to try and stop the attack at the main gate. Why are you here?"

"Requiem soldiers attacked the hotel. Nearly all the guards are wounded or dead. They hit us hard and without warning. After we fought them off, I left the remaining guards to attend to the wounded and raced here to inform the council of what was happening, but it seems like they already know."

"It seems that way. Come with me. I have a job for you." As if brought on by his words, another explosion rocks the city, causing the sky to flicker once more.

"We'd best hurry if we're to avoid this place being destroyed. You haven't seen Shizuri by chance, have you?"

"I haven't. But Leon said she was injured when the Council Chambers were destroyed. I don't know how badly she's hurt or where she is currently. Once we meet up with the Council, your job, is to guard her until all this is over." At the big man's words, a wave of panic rises in her throat. Suppressing it, she nods to Gilroy, and the two set off at a run towards the council chambers.

* * *

As the last of the injured council members leave the chamber, Cassy breathes an exhausted sigh. Slumping into one of the few remaining chairs, she watches as a handful of servants carefully lift Shizuri onto a stretcher under the old woman's instructions. Rubbing her forehead, she gestures to Monica to take a seat across from her. Opening her mouth to talk to the younger woman, she closes it and springs to her feet as an explosion shakes the room. Running towards the hallway, she staggers as more explosions shake the room. Looking up as a small amount of dust falls from the ceiling, she grits her teeth and yells over her shoulder.

"Monica, Dion. You're with me. Let's go. We need to find out what's happening" Not waiting for the two to follow her she bursts into the hallway, already drawing her first anima. Twirling it through her fingers, she flicks it to the side.

"Let's go, Arthur." In an instant, her whole body is covered in plate mail armour, with a white cape hanging from the shoulders. On her left hip, a thick double-edged broadsword hangs and a white shield rests on her left arm. Drawing the sword, she starts down the hallway at a run. It doesn't take long for the sounds of fighting to reach her ears. Turning a corner, she comes face to face with men wearing armour bearing Requiems symbol. As the closest soldier to her pulls his blade from the chest of a servant, she grits her teeth in anger and charges the man. He doesn't even have a chance to turn before her blade cuts him down. The sound of his body hitting the cold stone floor catches the attention of the remaining soldiers. Brandishing their weapons, they advance towards her. Taking a defensive stance, she waits for the soldiers to make a move. Coming up beside her, Dion draws his anima out.

"Let's go, Shiva." His deep voice echoes slightly through the hallway as the casing becomes a pair of katars. With a nod at Cassy, he walks forward. Smiling, she advances next to him. Worry shows on the faces of the Requiem soldiers and their advance halts. Using their fear, Dion and Cassy charge towards them. Easily sidestepping the soldier's blades, the two council members tear through the soldiers like a whirlwind. Leaving a trail of bloody destruction in their wake. Finally dispatching the last soldier, Cassy turns to find Dion standing next to her but Monica no-where to be found. Cursing to herself silently, she turns at the sound of heavy footsteps. Running around the corner, Gilroy and Iris come to a halt in front of the Council of Nine Leader. Dropping into a small bow, Gilroy doesn't hesitate before launching into an explanation.

"My lady. Leon sent me to find you. Requiem are attacking the shield that protects the city. It's already starting to fade. If we don't hurry and stop them, Athens will be another San Francisco."

"Dammit! Alright. You're both coming with us then. Our top priority is repairing the shield. We fight only those who stand in our way. The rest of the city will have to fend for itself," Stepping forward in front of Gil, Iris drops a curtsy before addressing Cassy.

"My lady. Leon requested I remain with Councilwoman Shizuri as a guard until all this is over. May I please have her current location?" At the young woman's words and the look of worry in her eyes, Cassy's face goes pale for a moment.

"As she was badly injured in the attack on the council chambers, right now, she's being transported to my private room." Stepping past Iris, she beckons to a nearby serving woman.

"Young miss. Take this young lady to my chambers. She's to watch over Council Member Shizuri until I return." Turning away from the serving woman, she embraces Iris tightly.

"Go there now and look after her until she wakes. Leon is right. We can't leave our injured members undefended. I can see in your eyes you care for her deeply. Go and look after her. Protect her with your life." As she finishes whispering in Iris's ear, she gives the shorter woman a light push. With a smile at the Council leader, Iris sets off down the corridor, closely following the serving woman. Turning back towards the two men standing in front of her, she releases her armour.

"Now then. Let's go stop these pricks from messing up the city." With a nod from both men, the three set off at a run into the city.

Chapter Thirty-three

As another explosion rocks the city, Leon looks up at the sky. Worry runs through him as it flickers purple for a moment. A shout ahead brings his attention back to reality as a Requiem soldier charges towards him. Recovering quickly, Leon dodges the man's clumsy slash and ends his life with a stab to the chest. Continuing forward, sounds of battle soon reach his ears. Breaking into a jog, he emerges out of the alleyway, into chaos. Requiem and world council soldiers clash in the middle of the street. Ignoring the soldiers clashing around him, Leon's attention is drawn to a redhead girl standing directly in front of him. Surrounded by a ring of Requiem soldiers, she holds a small knife in front of her. With the flick of her wrist, it becomes a flintlock style rifle. Spinning around, she fires a shot, killing the closest soldier. Leon shouts as a soldier rushes her from behind. Inches from splitting her head in half with his sword, the soldier is set upon by a white wolf, seeming to appear out of nowhere. Dodging the next soldier's slash, she cuts him with her knife. Backing up from the girl, the soldiers make a wider circle. From the back of their group, a giant of a man comes forward. With a broadsword in one hand and a spear in the other, he enters the circle with a menacing smile. Reaching out behind her, the girl places her hand on the wolf. With a word, the beast becomes a large knife in her hand. Raising both blades, she charges toward the man. Before they clash, a small group of soldiers moves to block Leon's view. Drawing their blades, they charge toward him. Summoning Aurora, he meets the men blade to blade. Twisting and turning, his blades slash and pierce, dropping the Requiem soldiers like flies. Finally cutting the last man down, he once again has a clear view of the fight in front of him. Sitting on the ground, the woman is clutching a wound in her leg. Standing in front of her, the wolf snarls at the man. With a kick, he sends the beast flying. As it hits the ground, it becomes a dormant anima case. Stepping forward, he pokes his spear into the girl's wound. With a scream of agony, she rips it out and shuffles back from the swordsman. With a deranged laugh, the man brings the spear up to his face and smells the blood on its tip. As it hits his nostrils, a crazy look enters his eyes and hefting his great sword, he advances on the helpless woman.

"Fenrir!" In answer to his cry, power surges through him.

"Leon, GO!" Not needing to be told twice, Leon launches himself towards the fight. Easily jumping over the ranks of soldiers, he lands next to the woman. Twisting, he swings the wolf blade and with a jarring impact stops the man's sword inches from the young woman's head. With a snarl, he pushes back the giant man and takes position in front of the woman.

"Don't you know, mate, it's rude to deprive a hunter of his kill?" Lifting the wolf blade in front of him, Leon gives the man a cold smile.

"I see no men here. Only corpses." With a snarl, the man swings the giant sword at Leon with incredible speed. Sidestepping the blade, he slashes towards the man's shoulder with the rapier, only to have his blade knocked away by the spear. Smiling, the man twists around and with no effort swings the blade back towards Leon. Leaping clear of the sword, Leon spins Fenrir as he lands.

"Howling wind shard!" Springing forth from the tip, a tempest of ice and wind cleaves toward the man. Unable to bring his blade back in time to defend against Leon's attack, he throws the spear into the ice. With a shrieking sound, the spear shatters and its fragments freeze in the air. Regaining his composure, the giant man smashes the ice in front of him with a swing of his sword and laughs a deep, booming laugh.

"If that's the best you have, then this fight is over." Sighing, Leon suppresses the power running into his two blades, returning them to their dormant states. Replacing them on his belt, he draws Valkyrie. Breathing out a slow breath, he holds the anima in front of him.

"From the halls of Valhalla where the heroes of old rest. The defender of all that is good, just, and right. Heavenly queen upon a steed of light. Warrior Queen, fight with us one last time. Before we shed this mortal coil and join the Warriors of old, bring forth your radiant light and smite all enemies that oppose us. Defend now and fight, VALKYRIE!" Lightning crackles from the sky and the anima lengthens into a double edge broadsword and shield. Taking a ready stance, Leon raises the sword above the shield.

"Leon, I'm ready to go phantasm as soon as you want me to."

"Hold for the moment. I have a plan. Once the time comes, you'll know." Bringing his focus back to the swordsman in front of him, Leon waits for the man to make the first move. Roaring, the man swings his sword in a wide arc. Blocking the blade with the shield, Leon presses the attack, following up with a lunging stab. Bringing the blade back with unbelievable speed, the swordsman blocks Leon's attack, shock ringing through him at the man's movements. Leaping backwards to create some distance, Leon barely has time to raise the shield in defence as the man's blade stabs towards him. With a jarring impact, it sends Leon sprawling into the dirt. Rolling away from the man, Leon springs to his feet and puts the blade to the shield.

"Now, Val!" At his shout, the sword and shield pull from his grasp and move towards the swordsman. Halfway to the man, Valkyrie materialises and takes hold of her arms. Shock crosses his face briefly before being replaced by a sneer.

"So, you have to get your anima to fight for you ey? What a weakling. Once I'm done with her, I'm going to enjoy killing you." Taking a step forward, he swings his sword overhead and brings it whistling down towards the anima. Easily sidestepping the blade, she steps forward and cuts him across the thigh. Roaring in anger, he brings the blade whistling back towards Valkyrie. Raising her shield, she meets the blade head-on with a crash. Twisting to avoid the stab from a soldier's blade, Leon grabs the man's wrist as he lunges past. With a twist, he breaks the soldier's wrist and takes possession of the man's sword. Slashing the man across the back of the neck, he raises the blade in front of him and turns to face the remaining soldiers.

"I don't have time for this!" he mutters inside his head.

"Then use me, Leon. If you lend me your strength, I can take care of these guys." Smiling at the vision that flashes through his mind from Aurora, he blocks a slash and kicks another soldier away. Throwing the sword at the soldiers, he reaches behind his belt and removes Aurora. Bringing her dormant form in front of him on outstretched arms, he chants.

"The light of the North, guider of those at sea and hope giver to all. The aura that washes away the darkness. Assist me now, AURORA!" Wings explode from Leon's back as he finishes his chant. Pulling the rapier from its sheath with his right hand, he traces a sigil with his left. With a few powerful strokes, the wings lift him off the ground and quickly propel him metres above the fight. Holding the blade upright, Leon chants.

"Using the light of the guide, let me reach thy enemies. Seraphs Assault!" Before the chant can finish, Leon stabs the blade through the incomplete sigil. As the blade pierces the sigil, feathers blossom into being at the hilt of the rapier and begin circling around the blade. As his chant finishes, he drives the blade into the air. Instantly the feathers become daggers of light. Exploding into the air with a burst of light, they quickly turn and drive back towards the ground with force, impaling the soldiers below. Light fading from the wings, Leon falls back down to the ground, landing heavily. Winking out of existence, the wings and rapier return to Aurora's dormant form. Dropping to his knees as a wave of exhaustion washes over him, Leon looks up with one eye as the giant swordsman lumbers over. Blood running down multiple cuts on his arms and face. Looking past the man, he sees Valkyrie's dormant form lying on the ground just behind him.

"Nice trick pal, but now, it's time for you to say goodnight." Raising his sword above his head, he pauses for a moment, waiting to swing. Before he can finish the movement, a single gunshot rings out behind Leon. Looking behind him, he sees the red-headed woman holding an old flintlock rifle, aimed at the swordsman. Turning as the blade clatters to the ground, Leon just has time to roll away, as the man collapses into the dust. Getting to his feet slowly, Leon walks over to the woman, still sitting on the ground. Stopping near her, he offers out his hand. Once she takes it, he pulls her to her feet.

"That was some shot. Thanks for the assist." Laughing lightly as he helps her to the nearby bench, she replies.

"I should be the one thanking you. If you hadn't intervened, I'd be history. The names Renee. But everyone just calls me Ren. And unless I'm mistaken, you're Leon Aelfdane. The newly appointed Council of Nine member for London. What brought you in this direction?" Sitting her on the park bench, Leon retrieves his anima and rummages through the soldier's corpses nearby, looking for medical supplies, talking as he moves.

"I'm pursuing a dangerous man who turned traitor and fled. Injuring a friend of mine and destroying half the council chambers in his escape. At this very moment, he's trying to flee the city. If he gets away, it will be next to impossible to track him down. So, I must stop him. But first I had to reinforce the main gate. Finally!" Pulling a small first aid kit from a soldier's pack, he turns back to Ren. Stopping briefly as World Council soldiers appear and take up positions at the main gate.

"I'll patch you up, but then I'm going to have to leave you to fend for yourself. No offence but I need to catch him." Coming over as he finishes speaking, he kneels next to her and begins bandaging the wound on her leg.

"Are you a believer in coincidences, Mr Aelfdane? Because I'm not. I believe everything happens for a reason. It just so happens that my anima has an ability, that allows her to track people. Keepers are especially easy to track. All I need is a name and Nova can track them, to the end of the earth if need be." Tying off the bandage and standing, Leon sighs for a moment before replying.

"The man I'm tracking is incredibly dangerous. If we manage to catch up to him, I can't guarantee your safety. I suppose there's no point in not telling you the name, as it will be all over the city soon enough. I'm chasing after Bernardo Grimani." A look of shock crosses her face and her mouth falls open.

"As in Council member from Italy, Bernardo Grimani? Damn! Surely, he can't really be the traitor you're chasing. It seems so unreal that one of the council members would turn like that. Don't get me wrong, I'll still help you track him down. It's just so, unbelievable."

"Yeah, well, I'm not having that hard of a time believing it. There was always something about him that didn't sit right with me. His sister came forward with claims that he was working with Requiem. Before we had the chance to question him about it, he fled. And in my opinion, innocent people, don't run. Now that you know who we're tracking, how soon can we start after him."

"Right now." Getting to her feet, she walks over and collects her dormant anima off the ground. Holding it in her right hand, she flicks it up and clicks her fingers. With a burst of wind, the anima turns into the white wolf again. Padding over to her, it sniffs her hand. Speaking to the wolf in Gaelic, her voice takes on the air of command. With a howl, the wolf runs off down a nearby street.

"He's that way. We'd best hurry if we're to keep up. Nova doesn't enjoy waiting." With a nod, Leon comes over and supports Ren lightly and together, they follow the wolf down the street, heading towards the outskirts of Athens.

Chapter Thirty-four

Echoing in the distance, explosions rock the city and the sky flickers purple for a moment. Breathing heavily, Monica leans against a wall for a moment to catch her breath. Looking back towards the smoke rising above the city, a feeling of remorse comes over her for leaving Cassy and the others to deal with everything on their own. Shaking her head to rid herself of such thoughts, she pushes clear of the wall and begins walking down the street. Turning the corner, she ducks into a shadowed alcove as she catches sight of a man walking down the street towards her. Drawing both her anima, she grips them tightly, pushing further back into the doorway. As the footsteps get closer and louder, she recognises the sound of Bernardo's voice.

"Yeah, I got it. You just make sure you hold up your end of the bargain Baur or this relationship of ours may be very short-lived indeed." As the voice grows louder, Monica peeks around the edge of the doorway. For a moment, she sees no one, then Bernardo comes into view. A small flip phone pressed against his ear.

"My position here is compromised. I thought you had sent someone to deal with Leon. What the hell happened with that? Of course she's in place. My operatives are not so easily dissuaded from their objectives. Athens should fall within the hour. Ha, so you claim, but I've yet to see the proof. Yeah, I'm on my way there now. This intel had better be good Baur. I'm sick and tired of running in circles looking for her. I'll let you know when I have it." Closing the phone, he puts it into his pocket. Stepping out of the doorway, Monica summons both her anima and charges at her brother. Swinging the first blade at her brother's exposed back, the cutlass whistles slightly as it flashes through the air. Quicker than she can follow, he summons his anima, turning and blocking her blade with the back of his forearm.

"Hello, Sister." Before she can react, his other fist connects with her midriff, knocking the wind out of her and sending her crashing into the hard ground. Getting to her feet shakily, she leans against the nearby wall to support herself.

"If you think I'm going to let you leave after everything you've done, brother, you had best think again." Trying to ignore the shakiness in her body, Monica pushes herself away from the wall. Twirling her second anima, she steadies herself and raises the blades. Smiling sadistically, Bernardo loosens his shoulders and stretches slightly before focusing on his sister. Without warning, energy crackles over his gauntlet and stepping forwards, Bernardo punches towards Monica shouting.

"Sonic Crescendo." Bursting from his fist, a bolt of energy heads towards Monica. Diving to the side, she rolls to her feet as the bolt passes through the spot where she was standing. As it flies past, all the hairs on her body stand on end. Not hesitating, the young woman launches herself forward towards her brother, swinging one of her blades. Raising his arm, he steps forward to meet her attack, deflecting the blade away. Releasing her grip on the cutlass, she dives under his following attack, sliding past his defences, swinging the other blade in an arc as she turns. Completing its arc, the blade cuts deeply into the back of Bernardo's shoulder. Leaping backwards at his enraged cry, she creates some space between herself and her brother. Turning towards his sister, a look of rage covers Bernardo's face.

"I would've been content to leave you out of this, Monica. I would have even overlooked those times you've stood against me. But now, you're between me and my exit and there's no one here to save you this time, Sister. But don't worry, you won't be alone in the afterlife for long. Mother and Father will soon join you there." Squaring his shoulders, Bernardo advances towards Monica, energy crackling over his gauntlets. Swallowing to suppress her rising level of fear, Monica holds her blade in front of her. Closing her eyes, she reaches inside of herself.

"Let's do this, Ed." From the back of her mind, a man's deep voice answers her.

"Are you sure Monica? This will hurt a lot."

"I don't see any other option."

"So be it." Opening her eyes, a look of focus comes over her face. From the hilt of her blade, water bursts forth and spirals up around the blade. Twisting her wrists, Monica drives the blade into the ground. As the blade pierces the stone, water explodes outwards from the tip. Creating a small pool of water around the Italian girl. Slowing his advance, Bernardo takes a defensive stance. A look of amusement crossing his face for a moment. Stepping back from her sword, Monica holds her hand out and a lit torch materialises at the end of it. Grasping the torch, she places it against the hilt of the cutlass. As the flames touch the steel, there's a hiss, and the air fills with sounds of creaking timber and flapping sails.

"Carronade Nine, FIRE!" At Monica's shout, an explosion appears above the blade, firing a cannonball towards Bernardo. Stepping back, Bernardo claps his hands together.

"Sonic Finale." From between his hands, a shockwave explodes outwards, stopping the cannonball inches from his chest. Stepping past the ball, he clicks his fingers and the iron ball crumbles to dust. Dropping the torch, Monica staggers as a wave of pain and exhaustion washes over her. As her vision blurs she steps forward, reaching for the cutlass. As her fingers brush the hilt, cold steel clamps around her neck. Looking up into her brother's hate-filled eyes, Monica grasps his wrist as he lifts her clear off the ground.

"Nice try. But once again you fall short. This is goodbye." A feeling of weightlessness settles over Monica as her brother tosses her towards a nearby building. Slamming into the brick wall, she feels her ribs crack, and her consciousness goes black for a moment as she hits the ground. Pain lances through her entire body as she lies on the stone pavement, gasping for breath. Twisting her head slightly sends pain lancing through the back of her skull and down her back. Watching as her brother walks away, a surge of strength fills her. Tracing a sigil on the ground in front of her, she pushes against it. Smiling as a wall of flame blossoms in front of him, she coughs violently and blood sprays onto the ground. Turning from the flames, she sees her brother's lips move, and he punches the ground. From behind her dust falls, floating in front of her eyes. Pushing herself over, she turns her back to her brother and looks up. Time slows as the ground heaves and the wall starts to fall apart, bricks and mortar bursting into the air. As the first piece of rubble strikes her, the world goes black in a haze of dust.

* * *

Stepping back as the wall collapses on his sister, Bernardo smiles as the wall of flames splutters out. Turning on his heel, he walks away and is soon out of sight. Emerging from an ally further down the street a moment later, a white wolf stops and stiffs the air. Turning, the wolf looks back at a man supporting a woman on his shoulder, following closely behind. Stepping out of the ally into the street, the pair looks around cautiously. Coming over to the woman, the wolf rests its muzzle against her leg.

"Leon. Nova says Bernardo's close. He was here moments ago. That direction." Gesturing up the street, Renee lets go of his arm and pulls clear of his support.

"I'm slowing you down. Hurry after him." Following the red-haired woman's gesture, Leon frowns as he notices the signs of battle. Drawing Fenrir, he advances up the street slowly, alert for anything out of place. Stepping through a small pool of water, he notices an anima lying dormant on the ground next to it. Leaning down to pick it up, he gasps as a wave of sorrow and pain washes over him. Dropping the steel to the ground, he staggers backwards. From deep inside his mind, Aurora's voice bursts forth.

"Leon, the broken wall just over there. HURRY!" At the urgency in Aurora's voice, Leon hastily looks around, spotting the collapsed building wall. With a growing sense of dread, he dashes to the pile of bricks and digs through the rubble. Within moments, he exposes a hand underneath.

"Leon, Phantasm Now!" Listening to Fenrir's command, he stands back and chants. Emerging from the ground, Fenrir quickly transforms into his human form, the wolf blade gleaming at his side. Drawing the blade, he holds it out and ice coats the blade in a sparkling layer. Stepping up to the rubble, he drives the blade into the ground. From beneath the rubble, a rumbling sound emerges, and the bricks fly into the air, supported on thin lines of ice. Looking down, Leon gasps at the state of the small Italian girl lying there.

"Leon, grab her now! I can't hold this forever." Dashing forward, he puts his arms underneath Monica as carefully as he can. Hoisting her light frame, he quickly moves clear of the wall. Not even turning as all the bricks crash back into the ground, Leon moves down the street to where Renee is sitting on a cottage step. Gasping as Leon places Monica softly against the ground, she shifts forward, coming over to Leon.

"Is she still alive?" Leaning forward, Leon places his ear against the girl's mouth at the same time as his fingers brush her wrist.

"There's barely a pulse, and she's not breathing." Placing her arm against the ground, Leon leans back and closes his eyes.

"Aurora, can you stabilise her?"

"I can, but Leon, it will only buy you enough time to get her to proper medical attention. It means letting Bernardo get away though."

"So be it. We can't leave her here to die."

"Okay then. You know what you need to do." Opening his eyes, Leon reaches behind and removes Aurora's cylinder. Holding it out in front of him, he chants quickly. Bursting forth from his back, wings of white flap lazily. Looking at the white gloves now adorning his hands, he grimaces. Leaning forward, he carefully places his hands on Monica. From the point of contact, warm white light spreads across her body. Within seconds she's enveloped in a cocoon of light. Sweat beads on Leon's forehead and starts trickling down his face as the strain of healing Monica takes its toll. Concentrating hard, he doesn't hear the clatter of anima next to him as Fenrir goes dormant, dropping Monica's anima as well. Seconds stretch out into forever and the sound of Leon's heartbeat fills his ears. Watching for any sign, he starts as she gasps in a breath of air. Removing his hands, he leans back.

"She's stable, for now. But you need to hurry Leon, she won't last long without medical treatment." As Aurora's voice fades from his mind, her anima appears in his hand as she goes dormant. Grimacing as a sharp pain stabs through his head, he looks down at the Italian girl. A peaceful look on her face, she could be sleeping, not laying there with her life hanging precariously in the balance. Picking up the anima off the ground, Leon gets to his feet, ignoring the wave of dizziness that washes over him. Clipping Fenrir to his belt and pocketing Monica's anima, he frowns as heat washes over his top lip. Reaching up, he wipes away the blood trickling from his nose.

"Is she ok? Are you?" Glancing at Monica, Renee looks up at Leon with concern.

"She's stable. I have to get her to a medical facility." Swallowing to remove the croak from his voice, Leon continues.

"I'm fine. Just overdid it a little. Though Bernardo will have to wait for now. This takes precedence." Getting to her feet, Renee shakes her head.

"No, he doesn't. You take her to a medical facility. I'll continue tracking that bastard. Just don't be too far behind me."

"Are you sure? You're not exactly in a fit state yourself..." Leon's words are cut off abruptly as the wolf lets out a warning growl.

"We're sure. Now go, get her out of here." Smiling, Leon bends down and picks up Monica carefully, but with ease. Turning, he walks away, stopping after a few steps. Glancing back over his shoulder, he catches Renee's eye.

"Stay safe." Without waiting for her nod, Leon turns and heads back into the city. Smiling as he disappears around the corner, Renee bends down and pats the wolf on the head.

"Come Nova. Let's find us a traitor." With one last look at the corner Leon walked around, she turns and follows the white wolf away from the city.

Chapter Thirty-five

Wrenching her blade free from the body on the ground, Cassy looks at the carnage around her. The broken and twisted bodies of Requiem soldiers litter the ground all around the area in front of the shield generator. Coming over towards her, wiping the blood from his face, Gilroy looks around with a grim expression.

"That seems to be the last of them. For regular soldiers, they sure put up one hell of a fight." With a creak, the nearby door swings in the wind, as it balances on one remaining hinge. Glancing towards it, Dion starts cleaning his blades on the uniform of a dead soldier.

"What did you expect, Commander? These men were the last line of defence. They're all that was standing between us and repairing the shield." Looking around once more, a feeling of unease settles over Cassy. Catching Dion's eye, she gestures around.

"Still, this seemed a little too easy. Even with how long it took us to clean up the forces here, it's not enough to destroy the shield. They had to have known, that it was going to be a keeper that came to investigate the shield. So why leave ordinary soldiers to guard it. It makes no sense." Opening his mouth to reply, Dion is cut off as a woman's laugh fills the air.

"Should have known it wouldn't have been enough to fool you, Cassy. Always the smart one. Guess you're not the Leader of the Council for nothing." Turning towards the voice, a chill runs down Cassy's back, as a woman dressed all in black and wielding a thin rapier steps out into the open. Walking towards the council leader, her heels click on the pavement with every step. Catching Gilroy looking her over out of the corner of her eye, she stops and looks at him.

"Get a good look, big man. It'll be the last piece of ass you'll see in this lifetime." Snorting, he lifts his axe and points it towards her.

"I must admit, I do like the leather. Shame, I'm going to have to bury my axe in it." Taking a step forward, Gilroy is stopped by Cassy's outstretched arm.

"That's enough Commander. It's been a while Teisha. What the hell are you doing here?" Laughing, the woman flicks her hair back and waves her rapier around before replying.

"What can I say Cassy, Requiem made me an offer I couldn't refuse. And, it comes with the benefit of your head on a platter. What more could I want?" Grinding her teeth, the Council Leader levels her blade towards the woman.

"Commander, you and Dion take care of the generator. I'll deal with her." Eyeing the woman in black, Dion draws his katars.

"Are you sure, My Lady?"

"I'm sure. She's more than you two can handle. Now go." Nodding, the two men take a step toward the shield generator.

"Not happening boys. Not on my watch." Before anyone can react, she moves in front of the two men, black and red energy crackling over her body. Stepping forward, she drives her sword into Gilroy's shoulder. Grunting, he grabs the blade with one hand, swinging his axe with the other. Releasing her grip on the sword, she bends at the hips, ducking beneath the axes blade. Shoving Gilroy aside, she moves towards Dion, the energy gathering around her fist. Stepping back, he raises his arms in defence as she punches him. With a gasp of shock, he's thrown back through the air, landing with a dull crunch on the ground. With a clatter, the Katars fall from his hands and return to their dormant form. Pulling the blade from his shoulder and throwing it to the side, Gilroy turns to see Dion crunch into the ground. With a roar, the big man swings his axe towards the woman. Turning, she easily sidesteps his downward swing, laughing as the axe buries itself in the ground. Exploiting the moment before he can recover from the swing, she drives a punch into Gilroy's stomach before bounding onto his shoulder and propelling herself into the air. Falling backwards gracefully, she twists once, landing lightly on her feet. The rapier flying from where it was thrown to land in her grip as she stands. Getting to his feet, Gilroy traces a sigil quickly and a small blue light appears at the end of his finger. Pushing it against the wound on his shoulder, he grimaces in pain as it sizzles for a moment. Removing the ball of light, he looks down at his handiwork before letting it dissipate. Flexing his shoulder, he steps forward and pulls his axe free of the ground. Standing casually, Teisha brings the point of the rapier up in front of her face. Gilroy's blood still glistening on the tip. Smiling a sadistic smile, she waves the tip of the sword towards him.

"Come play some more, big man. I do believe my partner likes the taste of your blood." At her words, the blade glints red for a moment and the blood disappears. With a snarl, Gilroy raises his axe and advances towards the laughing woman. Stepping in front of him, Cassy raises her arm, stopping him in his tracks. Turning towards him, she speaks and an air of authority radiates from her.

"Commander Roscoe! Stand down! She's far more than you can handle. Stand aside. I'll handle it from here." Walking forward at a deliberately slow pace, golden radiance blooms all around her. With a flash of golden light, a white and blue scabbard appears at her hip. Grinning maniacally, Teisha dances a little jig at the look on Cassy's face.

"Oh, you're finally getting serious, Cass. This will be fun." With a laugh, she flicks her black hair over her shoulder and brings her rapier to bare in front of her. From its hilt, blood-red energy explodes outwards in a tempest, enveloping Teisha almost instantly. From inside the wall of crackling energy comes her voice.

"Come forth Countess. We shall bathe in blood once more, and their screams will fill the air." As her words end, the tempest ceases. Blade glowing red, Teisha steps forward and, with no warning, leaps with blinding speed towards Cassy. Spinning her broadsword, the blonde woman brings it around and meets the attack head-on, energy bursting from their clash in a shock-wave. Bracing himself, Gilroy grits his teeth as it washes over him, forcing him back a few feet from where he's standing. Squinting through the dust in the air, he watches as the two women move apart and come back together, blades flashing in the sunlight, shockwaves bloom from the impacts. Moving away, the big man makes his way over to Dion. With a grunt, he picks the American man up and moves him further away down the street, leaning him against a vehicle. Squatting down with a frown, Gilroy traces a sigil on his palm. With a small grin, he slaps Dion, energy bursting forth from the sigil upon impact. With a gasp, Dion's eyes open. Looking around for a moment in confusion, he starts when he sees Gilroy.

"Wha... Commander Roscoe? The hell is going on?"

"See for yourself." Gesturing over the bonnet of the car, Gilroy waits until Dion gets to his feet and looks in the direction of Gilroy's gesture.

"I think it's best if we stay here for now. I think we'd only get in the way." From their vantage point, the two men watch as shock-waves ripple through the air from the two women fighting in the middle of the street.

Chapter Thirty-six

Bursting through the door of the hospital, Leon shouts for help as he enters. A nurse nearby grabs a bed and wheels it over, its wheels squealing in protest. Stepping forward, Leon carefully lowers Monica onto it.

"What happened?"

"Her name's Monica. She was involved in a fight with a keeper from Requiem. I did what I could in the field." Putting her hand to Monica's neck, the nurse feels her pulse for a moment before grabbing another nurse nearby. Pushing the bed away from Leon, the first nurse talks to the second.

"She's a keeper and her pulse is weak. We need to get her into surgery right away. Possible internal injuries." Standing in the middle of the waiting room, Leon watches as the two nurses wheel Monica through the doors, down the end and into the restricted area. Taking a deep breath, he turns to walk out but is stopped by a hand on his shoulder.

"Not so fast there, sonny. We need some more information from you." Turning, he looks down into the eyes of an elderly lady.

"Do we have to do this right now? The city's under attack and the person responsible is getting away." Frowning, the old lady draws herself up to her full height.

"Do I look like I care, boy? Look around. There are people here because of the attack. And we need to know everyone who comes through that door so we can contact there next of kin if worse comes to worst. Do you really think your job is any more important than anyone else's? No. Now get over there and fill out that girl's information. At the old lady's words, Leon looks around the room. People are propped against walls or sitting in seats all around. Covered in bandages, or holding wounds closed with what they can. Without a word Leon walks over to the information desk, but before he takes two steps, a man's voice calls out.

"Leon?" Turning, Leon comes face to face with a familiar face.

"Uncle Rick?" Stepping forward, the older man embraces Leon. Stepping back, he holds Leon at arms-length.

"It's good to see you, boy. What's it been? Ten years?"

"Give or take. Rick, I'd love to stay and chat, but I've got to give the people here the details about the girl I brought in and then I've got to go. The person responsible for all this is getting away, and he needs to be stopped."

"The girl was Monica Grimani, correct?" At the use of Monica's name, shock runs through Leon.

"You know her?"

"Aye. Our paths have crossed a few times. If she's here, then her attack on the council succeeded and that means that Bernardo has made a move and fled Athens." Pulling free from his uncle's grip, Leon takes a step back and reaches his hand to his side, placing his hand on Fenrir.

"How do you know about that? It's only just happened."

"Who do you think gave her the plans to get in? Now remove your hand off your weapon, we need to talk." Stepping past Leon, Rick goes up to the reception desk and has a quick word to the lady seated there. Turning from her, he gestures to Leon and walks through a nearby door. Removing his hand from Fenrir, Leon follows him cautiously. For a moment, the two men walk in silence down the corridors before arriving in a small room. Opening the door, Rick leads the way inside, taking a seat on the couch against the far wall. Following his uncle, Leon closes the door and takes a seat in a wooden chair opposite.

"Now you've probably got a lot of questions but for the moment you'll just have to keep em to yourself. We've got a lot of things to discuss and not much time to do it. Now tell me, what do you know of your father's plans?"

"Not much. I know Requiem is on the move. And I know Bernardo is working for them. Above and beyond that, I don't have much to go off." Sighing, Rick pulls a flask from inside his jacket pocket and takes a swig, offering it to Leon as he starts talking.

"Well then, that's we're we'll start. Bernardo is just Requiems errand boy. For months now they've been getting him to gather things here and there. He's good at covering his tracks, I'll give him that. Unluckily for him, I'm good at following things like that. He's trying to get an anima for Requiem. I don't know what they want it for exactly, but I do have an idea of where it might be. Do you remember the town of Pyrgos?"

"The name rings a bell. It was the settlement that was destroyed a few years ago, right? Not far from here?"

"Correct. It's about a hundred and twenty miles east of here. Though the town was destroyed and overrun by nocturna, some people still live in the ruins there. Like in other cities that have fallen over the years, there's always a few that don't move to the next major settlement. Instead, they live as nomads. There's one such settlement there, and I believe that is most likely where Bernardo will go. I heard a rumour of a keeper who lives on the outskirts of the city, as her anima generates too much energy and is dangerous to people around her. I can't be certain but I'd bet my last dollar her anima is what Requiem are after and they must not be allowed to get it." Opening his mouth to speak, Leon pauses as a commotion comes from outside. Getting to their feet, the two men jump as the door bursts open and a young nurse steps in, a grin across her face.

"The shield has been stabilised, we're safe." Jumping forward, she hugs Leon and gives him a kiss on the cheek before darting out of the room once more. Closing the door behind her, Leon sinks back into his seat, a feeling of relief washing over him.

"Looks like the others made it in time, then. That's a relief. Now Rick, back to what we were discussing. Can you get a message to Andrea?"

"I can, and I will, but I've seen that look in your eyes before, Leon. Forget about going after Bernardo on your own. It's the kind of foolishness that will get you killed. Even if you are a Council of Nine member, there's a limit to what one man can do. Go and see Cassy. Let her know what's going on before chasing after Bernardo. I dare say she will send some people with you, just to be sure." Sighing, Leon looks up at Rick.

"You make a fair point. I have someone tailing Bernardo as we speak, so I'd best get going and get after her. Hopefully, we can make it in time to stop him." Getting up from his seat, Leon extends his hand out to Rick. Clasping his nephew's arm in a warrior's grip, he looks into Leon's green eyes.

"I won't be far behind you. There are a few things left to tidy up here, but I'll see you soon. Stay safe, boy. You're about the only family that I have left."

"Likewise, Uncle Rick." Releasing the older man's arm, Leon turns and leaves. As the door shuts behind him, Rick turns away and opens a hidden panel in the wall. Pushing the buttons on the machine inside, a small holographic image of Andrea appears moments later.

"Rick. I'd like to say this is a pleasant surprise, but I'd be lying. What do you want?"

"Well now... Where should I start?"

Chapter Thirty-seven

Blinking the dust from his eyes, Gilroy walks through the streets looking for any sign of the council leader. Dust still fills the air, from the aftermath of the fight between the two women. Tightening the grip on his axe, he steps around the corpses of the Requiem soldiers from the earlier fight. Starting as he catches movement from the corner of his eye, Gilroy spins, axe glinting through the dust. Halting his momentum, he stops the blade of his axe a whisker away from the side of Cassy's neck.

"Well now, Commander Roscoe. I know I'm kinda scary looking right now, but that's a little bit of overkill, don't you think?" Lowering his weapon, he takes a step back and allows Leviathan to go dormant. With a sigh, Cassy releases her armour and takes a stumbling step forwards. Moving forward, Gilroy catches the arm of the Council Leader as she stumbles.

"Thank you, Commander. Damn Teisha. She got me good and then escaped. Help me over to the shield. We need to fix it before Athens falls."

"You can barely stand. How in the hell, are you going to repair the shield?"

"I'm not going to, you are."

"Me? I don't even know the first thing about fixing that thing. I'm not really versed in the advanced uses of arcana."

"Well, fortunately enough Commander, I am. I'll cast the arcana, you're going to supply the energy." Supporting her with his shoulder, Gilroy helps Cassy over to the building, housing the crystal for the shield. Stepping inside, he catches his breath at the sight of the multifaceted gem sitting on a pedestal in the middle of the room. Gesturing to a small dais a few feet away from the pedestal, Cassy leans heavily on Gilroy as he helps her over to it. Stepping clear of his support, she stands up straight in the middle of the dais. With a grimace, she extends her hand out to Gilroy.

"Now, this is the fun part. Give me your hand, Commander Roscoe." Reaching out, he takes hold of the blonde woman's hand.

"This is going to be loud, but no matter what, don't let go of my hand." Nodding, he widens his stance and tightens his grip on Cassy's hand. Extending her arm out towards the crystal pedestal, Cassy closes her eyes for a moment. Opening them, she takes a deep breath and light blossoms at the tips of her fingers. Moving her arm, she traces a complex sigil of light in front of her. Pausing as it changes colour, she moves slightly and raises her hand above her head. From the centre of her palm, light begins to blossom upwards, as sigils trace themselves in complex patterns all around the council leader. Sweat breaks out on Gilroy's forehead as he feels his energy been drawn from him through the connection with Cassy. With dazzling light, the sigils flare and pulse as they continue to grow in number and size. Releasing her grip on Gilroy, Cassy steps forward and extends both arms out to the side. The moment she does, blinding light fills the room and a spine-tingling shriek comes from the lips of the Australian woman. Shielding his eyes, Gilroy tries to peer through the light. Taking a step forward, he's thrown from his feet across the room, as an invisible force strikes him. Gasping as the breath leaves his body from the impact, he rolls onto his side, looking towards the pedestal. Through the light he can see Cassy slowly being lifted off the ground, arms still outstretched. With a rumble and a final flash of light that shoots into the sky, everything stops. As the light fades, Cassy slumps and falls to the ground. Leaping to his feet, Gilroy rushes over to the council leader. As he leans down and lifts her slightly, her eyes flutter open.

"Did we win?"

"I think so."

"That's good." As the words leave her mouth, her eyes close and she slumps into the big man's arms. Panicking, he leans forward and puts his finger to the side of her neck. Relief washing over him as he feels a faint pulse. Looking up at the sky, Gilroy smiles slightly as the sky flickers one last time before settling into its regular colour. Carefully, he lifts the unconscious woman off the floor and, with one last look at the crystal pedestal he leaves the room, kicking the door closed on his way out.

* * *

Slowly opening her eyes, Shizuri looks around at the room she's in, finding nothing familiar about it. Attempting to push herself up, she gasps loudly as pain lances through her. Carefully, so as not to aggravate her injuries, she lifts the blanket up and looks down. Bandages criss-cross her chest and arm. Letting the blanket fall, she puts her arm against her eyes. Even pressing it against her face, she can't stop the tears running from her eyes into the pillow. Moving her arm as the door opens, she turns her head away as Iris enters, carrying a tray. Placing the tray down, Iris comes over and sits on the bed next to Shizuri. Leaning forward she interlocks her hand with the Japanese womans and squeezing Iris's hand softly, Shizuri breaks, the tears flowing into her pillow. Without a word, Iris moves carefully and gets off the bed, turning to place her arms around Shizuri. Squeezing Iris's hand more tightly, Shizuri continues to weep. After some time, the tears stop and Shizuri turns back towards the door, her voice coming out as a croak.

"I'm sorry."

"You have nothing you need to apologise about. I'm honestly just glad you're ok."

"What happened after I was injured?" For a moment, a strange look comes over Iris's face.

"I think it's best if someone else explains." Leaning in and giving Shizuri a soft kiss on the forehead, Iris gets up and moves over to the door, opening it a fraction.

"She's awake and asking about what's happened." Stepping back as the door opens, Iris sits on a nearby chair as Leon walks in.

"Leon!" Moving to rise from her bed, she cries out and pain lances through her once more.

"Woah! Take it easy. You're lucky to be alive. Don't try to move."

"The Council Chamber, Leon. Bernardo is..."

"We know. Now calm down and I'll explain everything that happened." Coming over at Shizuri's gesture, Iris helps her into a sitting position, before taking her seat again. Seeing everyone settled, Leon begins.

"At the same time as Bernardo attacked the council, Monica was telling us everything. And afterwards, everything went to hell. Requiem launched a full-scale assault on Athens. The World Council is in shambles. They've called an emergency meeting and are pretty much deciding to go into open war against Requiem as we speak. To facilitate Bernardo's escape, Requiem attacked the shield directly. Athens almost fell. But thanks to Cassy and Gilroy, the shield was stabilised, but unfortunately, Bernardo escaped. On top of that, he severely injured his sister. I found her buried under a wall, shortly after their fight. She's in the ICU now. And at this point, it's touch or go whether she will make it. Now the only positive out of all this. I came across some intel as to where Bernardo may head to next. At the moment, I have someone tracking him. And Cassy has spoken to Luka. He's going to use the power of his anima to get us to where Bernardo is likely to go. I think that about sums everything up. I'll let you know how we go."

"Leon, I'm coming with you. You're not benching me."

"Shizuri, you've been laid up in here for over half a day already. You're in no condition to travel, let alone fight and there's no doubt in my mind that there will be plenty of that to come." Refusing Iris's help, Shizuri pushes herself up out of the bed and looks Leon in the eye.

"I'm coming Aelfdane. End of discussion."

"You truly are a fool, Shizuri, but hey, it's your funeral. I can't stop you. I'll let the others know. Get some rest. We leave first thing in the morning, day after tomorrow. I'm not waiting for you if you're not there..."

Turning away from the Japanese woman, Leon leaves the room, slamming the door in his wake.

"That was a foolish thing to do Shizuri."

"Probably, but I'm not sitting on the sidelines just because a man thinks I can't take it. He would still go, even if his limbs were falling off. You should stay..." Stepping forward, Iris places a finger over Shizuri's lips, shaking her head.

"Where you go, I go remember."

"What did I ever do to deserve you?" Smiling, Iris steps closer, her lips meeting Shizuri's. Breaking away, Iris wraps her arms around Shizuri's neck softly and looks into her eyes.

"I don't know but I'm glad."

Chapter Thirty-eight

Sitting by a small campfire, the young woman shivers as an owl calls out into the night. Getting to her feet, she stretches and pulls the anima case out of the pocket of her oversized coat. As she rotates it in the firelight, a woman's voice enters her mind.

"Are you okay, Eustolia? I know you didn't want to leave your family."

"I'm fine Nic. And I told you, just call me Lia. I know it was for the best. The fact that I'm a keeper meant I would eventually attract more nocturna than I could handle. Which would be the death of myself or someone I care about. Besides, I think it's better if we go somewhere, we can get some training."

"I'm sorry Lia. I wish this fate didn't have to fall on your shoulders. Or that we had even appeared in your world." Before the girl can reply, a twig snaps close by. Starting, Lia peers into the darkness. For a moment her heart leaps into her chest as a figure appears, before materialising into a man as he nears the fire. As he comes closer, she calls out to him in her native language.

"Come no closer." Stopping, she's shocked when the man answers back in Italian.

"I'm sorry I didn't mean to startle you, Miss. I saw your fire and thought you wouldn't mind if I shared it with you."

"Okay. Come closer but I'm warning you no funny business." With a visible nod, the man steps into the firelight and Lia gasps softly.

"Lord Grimani? What are you doing out here?" Stepping closer to the fire, Bernardo leans down and warms his hands over it before looking at the girl and replying.

"I'm surprised you know who I am. Most of the people out this way who live in camps have no idea who's on the Council of Nine, let alone being able to identify one of its members. I'm impressed. What's your name girl?"

"Eustolia. But everyone just calls me Lia. I know who you are, Sir, because I studied up about the local Schola. It's actually where I'm currently on my way to. My anima is powerful, and I need the training to help me master it."

"Well, you definitely decided to head to the right place. You're a brave girl for travelling alone, lots of nocturna around this area."

"I travel during the day, My Lord and rest at night. It's easier to avoid nocturna during the day. You didn't tell me why you were out here, My Lord. Is it a secret mission?" Rubbing his jaw for a moment, Bernardo looks the girl over before replying.

"Well, sort of, you see, I've been sent to retrieve something of high value." Standing from the fire, a dangerous gleam enters his eye. Taking a step back, Lia clutches her anima tightly to her chest.

"What have you been sent to retrieve?"

"About that..."

"Lia, look out!" The shout enters her mind and instinctively reacting, she dives to the side, energy crackling over her head and destroying the wall behind her.

"Tsk. Stay still would you, I really want to finish this." Stepping around the fire, Bernardo flexes his gauntleted fist before firing off another bolt of energy at the girl. Rolling aside as it impacts the ground where she just was, Lia leaps to her feet and starts running back towards the town she came from earlier that day. Running without looking back, the ground disappears from under Lia's feet as an explosion comes from behind, throwing her into the air. In the darkness, the ground comes out of nowhere. Rolling as she falls, she hits the ground on her shoulder with a sickening crunch. Crying out as pain lances through her left side. Rolling to her feet, she continues running as Bernardo rains down bolts of energy upon her. Each one narrowly missing in the dark. Reaching the outskirts of the city, Lia turns and draws her anima.

"From the depths of the past to the light of the future. Let all phenomena be scattered now to the wind and let the guides way be clear. I command the fires that light their way. Ignite!" As her chant finishes, a red light flashes and a small red disk appears on the back of Lia's hands. Ducking behind a wall as another bolt of energy flies past, Lia raises her good arm above her head. From the small disk in her hand arcs of lightning appear, crackling out in every direction and stepping clear of the wall she turns to face Bernardo. Taking a single step back, she drops to her knees, driving the lightning covered fist into the ground. From the point of impact a small iron rod sprouts from the ground, purple lightning crackling across it. With the click of her fingers the lighting arcs from the rod towards Bernardo. Stopping in his tracks, he quickly traces a sigil and summons a shield in front of him. With an ear-splitting shriek the lightning clashes against the shield, blinding him. Using the rod, Lia drags herself off the ground and turns away from it, retreating into the small town. After a moment, the energy stops. Releasing his shield, Bernardo looks around and swears under his breath. Taking a step towards the city, he stops as the phone in his pocket rings.

"Yes?"

"Mr Grimani. It's Baur. I need you to meet me. Near sunset. Small bar on the other side of town called Maid Mead's, I think. My Greek is a little rusty. Anyway, looking forward to seeing you. Ta-ta." Before he can reply, the receiver clicks as Baur hangs up on the other end. Grinding his teeth, Bernardo sets off into the city as the first rays of sunlight break over the horizon.

Chapter Thirty-nine

Stepping into the small antechamber, Leon frowns at Shizuri, leaning against the wall just inside the door.

"So, I see you made it."

"Did you honestly think I wouldn't? Like I said before, you're not leaving me behind. You owe me that. And I owe Bernardo."

"That's what worries me. If you lose your head, it could cost us or you everything." Looking over at Iris to emphasise his point, Leon waits a moment before turning back to Shizuri.

"Remember what's important and don't screw it up." Leaving Shizuri where she was standing, Leon walks over to Luka, taking the Russian man's offered hand.

"Good morning Leon. How did you sleep?"

"About as well as expected, given what's riding on this mission. I've got one question before we go. How does this power of yours work, in a nutshell?"

"It's kind of like teleportation. But not the kind you see in old sci-fi films. There's a small-time displacement that goes along with it. It's the reason my power causes travel sickness to those I send to places. The further away it is, the longer the time displacement. Normally, this distance would only be a few minutes. But as we are sending more than one person, it will be more like a few hours. Does that cover your question?"

"It does. I think everyone's good to go. What do you need us to do?" Standing in the centre of the room, Luka calls everyone over.

"Everyone, gather around me, please. Now, this is going to be noisy and cold. For those of you who get motion sickness, well, I would not want to be you. Good luck." As everyone gathers, the Russian man pulls out his anima and summons a giant broadsword. Holding it with two hands, he points the blade directly down.

"Everyone ready? Okay then. In..."

"Three..."

"Two..."

"One..." As he reaches one, he drives his blade into the ground and the whole room fills with light. Roaring wind fills everyone's ears and the entire world seems to flex and wane. After a moment the whistling stops, and they find themselves in a square in an abandoned town.

"Okay everyone, please back away from me so I may return to Athens." Stepping clear of Luka, they watch as he once again drives his blade into the ground, disappearing in another flash of light. Looking around at the small abandoned town, Leon takes a deep breath. Drawing Fenrir, he turns and walks over to Gilroy.

"Gil, I need you to take the girls and find someplace to set up camp. I'm going to take a quick look around. Mark the way from here like we used to as kids." Waiting only a moment for his friend's nod, Leon heads off into the city.

* * *

Stepping clear of the broken wall, Renee looks down the hill towards the city. At that moment, a bright flash comes from somewhere not too far away inside the city. Ignoring it, she bends down and studies the markings leading away from the campsite towards the city. Looking over at the white wolf next to her, she grimaces.

"What do you think, Nova? Looks like there was a decent fight here. Probably Bernardo. Well, we best follow the trail, for now. See where it goes." Standing, she stretches her back and makes her way down the hill to the city. Stopping by a hole in the ground, she bends down and examines the burn marks on the ground around it. Getting to her feet, she stops as a footfall sounds from nearby. Dashing to the wall, she summons her knife and peeks around the corner, relaxing at the sight of Leon walking towards her. Stepping out from behind the wall, she raises her hand in greeting.

"Took you long enough." Barely flinching at her sudden appearance, he greets her back and continues walking over to her.

"Sorry about that. Athens was in pretty bad shape after Requiems attack. Any sign of Bernardo?"

"Not for a couple of days. He always seems to stay a few steps ahead of me. There were signs of a massive fight leading from a camp up there on the hill and into the city. Can't be more than a few hours old."

"So Bernardo has most likely found the girl he was looking for. I swear, if it wasn't for bad luck, we wouldn't have any luck at all. Alright then, well first things first. We need to regroup with the friends I brought along. Then we can work out which way Bernardo went. Can Nova track him independently of you?"

"She can."

"If you could, please get her to do so. I think it best if you're brought up to speed on everything that went down in Athens after you left." Looking toward the wolf, Renee nods after a moment and gestures for Leon to move on. Looking at the wolf once more as it pads off silently into the city, Renee falls into step next to Leon. Studying him silently as they walk, she focuses on him as he speaks.

"So, a lot has happened since you left."

"It's been all of three days. What could have possibly happened? Speaking of which, did you bring some food with you? I've been living off the lean pickings of old supermarkets and service stations, trying to keep pace with your friend. He moves fast by the way."

"Plenty has happened. First, Athens is safe. The shield was successfully repaired. So, for now, Athens will remain nocturna free. Onto Requiems attack, I'm certain it achieved their goal. The World Council has decided to launch a direct strike on Requiems base in San Francisco. If they go through with it, I fear we will be handing them the world on a silver platter. It's imperative we stop Bernardo at the very least. Whatever Requiem have planned for the anima that Bernardo is trying to acquire isn't good. I'm sure of it." Sighing deeply, Leon puts a hand into his pocket, drawing out a deck of smokes. Stopping and taking a seat on a nearby wall, he lights the smoke and takes a massive drag.

"On top of all that, the rumours flew faster than the wind. Almost every city knows by now that Athens was attacked by Requiem. The populace is panicking, and riots are starting everywhere. What's left of the world is tearing itself apart, when the need to be united, is stronger than ever. The council have all returned to their respective homes to calm what they can."

"Sounds like that was Requiems plan all along. Divide and Conquer."

"Well, it's a good plan. Certainly, sounds like something my father would cook up."

"I had heard that one of the Council members had family that was high in Requiem. I didn't realise it was you. I'm sorry to hear that."

"It's fine. I made peace with it a long time ago. And he's not just some higher up. He's the leader. Anyway, we should keep moving. Time's not on our side and if we can I'd like to get a beat on where Bernardo's heading before the day's out." Crushing out his cigarette, Leon gets to his feet and starts walking. Taking one last look behind her at the blazing sun, she hurries to catch up to Leon.

Opening the door to the council chamber, Rick lets out a whistle at what's left of the destroyed room.

"Mr Aelfdane. Glad you could join us." Looking towards the voice, Rick smiles at the blonde woman, walking over to her and the man standing next to her.

"Good to see you, Cassy. Who's your friend?"

"Ah, Sorry. Rick this is Luka Yakovich. He's the Council of Nine member for Russia."

"A pleasure to meet you, Sir. I've heard a great deal about you. They tell stories of the Pillars in my country. You're famous." Taking the young man's hand, Rick smiles warmly.

"The pleasure is mine and please, call me Rick. The Pillars were a long time ago. We just did what needed to be done. So, Cassy, I assume this isn't a social call?" Sighing, the young Australian woman slides onto an upright section of the broken table.

"You heard about the council's decision, I assume?"

"I did. And a foolish decision it was. I've already spoken to Andrea. She's reaching out to old friends now to see what can be done. Best case, we stop them before they hand Requiem the world. Worse case, we take the world back after the Council screws up."

"That's good to know. But that's not why I called you here. I was merely curious whether you'd heard. What do you know of the mission I sent Leon on?"

"I know all of it, including what it is he's been sent to retrieve. And so does he now. I passed on all my information to him before he left. He's as well prepared as he can be, to face that mission."

"Hmmm... that's what worries me. You've heard of the soldier that Requiem's been using lately yeah?

"The black armoured female knight. I've heard of her."

"I just received word that she and Baur were sighted not far from where we sent Leon earlier this morning. Rick, I want you to go there and provide whatever support you can. I know it's a lot to ask, but if that knight shows up, there's a good chance it will be too powerful for Leon and the others to handle. I'm sorry to put this on you."

"It's fine. He's family. I would have heard about the knight and Baur soon enough and would have probably sought you out to ask to go. That boy is the only blood I have left. I'll not let any of it be spilt. Not while I have strength left to prevent it." Smiling at Rick's words, Cassy vaults off the table and gestures to the window.

"When do you want to leave?"

"Tomorrow morning, before dawn. I need to gather a few things first."

"No worries. That work with you, Luka?"

"It's fine with me, Cassy. I'll see you tomorrow morning, Rick." With a nod, the old man walks out of the council chamber, his eyes burning brightly in the low light of the hallway.

* * *

Opening the door of the abandoned building, Leon steps back as a wave of heat assaults him. Stepping inside, he stares at the bright blue fire burning inside the remnants of the old fireplace. Stepping inside, Leon speaks loudly, causing everyone to jump.

"What the hell is going on in here?" Turning from the fire, Shizuri stands and with the click of her fingers, extinguishes the flame.

"Scrying. I'm sure you've heard of it."

"I have. But what has that got to do with turning the place into a damn sauna?"

"I use fire to scry Leon. I was trying to locate Bernardo but had no luck."

"You didn't need to worry about it. I have it sorted." Stepping aside, Leon gestures for Renee to enter. As the red-haired woman steps inside, Leon introduces her.

"Everyone, this is Renee. She's the ones who's been tracking Bernardo. Renee, that's Council member Shizuri and Iris is a keeper from London. And...." Looking around in confusion for a moment, Leon pauses.

"Where's Gil..."

"Right here." Stepping through the door at the other end of the room, Gilroy smiles as he enters.

"Bit hot in here for my tastes, mate. Nice to meet you. Renee was it?"

"It was. A pleasure to meet you all. I look forward to..." Cutting off mid-sentence, a look of concentration crosses over her face.

"Leon, I've found him."

"Bernardo?"

"Yes. he's close to here. He just entered a small bar. Nova says she detects others inside."

"How far exactly?"

"Maybe three or four blocks. I can guide you there if you want."

"You've done enough. I'll take it from here. Gil, I need you to stay here and monitor things."

"The hell I am, Leon. There's no way you're facing that bastard alone. I'm coming with you."

"Not this time, old friend. I need someone I can rely on, to hold this position. And that someone is you. If things go south it will be up to you to get them out of here." Stepping forward, Shizuri places herself in front of Leon and draws herself up to her full height.

"I'm coming then. If you won't take Gilroy, then take me at least." Holding up her hand to quell his argument, she waits a moment until he closes his mouth before continuing.

"I know what you're going to say. I'll stay clear of any fight that breaks out and support you from the side. Even being unable to fully fight, I can still support you with arcana." Hiding his grimace, Leon nods in agreement.

"Fine then. Gather your things. Renee, do you have some other way to lead me to Bernardo?" Closing her eyes for a moment, she moves her hand and a small silver orb appears.

"This will lead you to nova once it reaches her both will disappear. Leon if you get in trouble, we won't know until it's too late."

"Thank you. Gil, if I'm not back by morning, head back to Athens. Cassy will need to plan accordingly." Stepping forward, Leon embraces Gilroy in a warrior's grip.

"Good Luck. Stay safe." Turning from his friend, Leon gestures to Shizuri and the two of them step out through the door. As it closes with an ominous thud, Gilroy sits down on a nearby stool and lights a smoke.

"Might as well settle in for the time being, ladies. It could very well be a long night." Breathing out his first drag, Gilroy shivers as a chill runs down his spine. Looking through the window, he watches a raven fly away from its nearby perch. Pushing away the dark thoughts filling his head, the big man gets up and begins unpacking food from the bags against the wall.

"So who's hungry?"

* * *

Stepping into the dark bar, Bernardo blinks to get his eyes to adjust quicker from the light outside. Before he can take another step, a voice calls out from his left.

"Ah, my good friend, Bernardo. I was starting to wonder if you'd ever show up." Turning, the Italian man hides a look of disgust at the man sitting at the table leaning back on a chair.

"Baur. Why did you call me to meet you here? You're wasting valuable time when I could be finishing the job I've been assigned."

"Yes, about that job. You seem to be having some trouble. Surely one girl can't be that hard to acquire. And really, we don't even need the girl, we just need her anima."

"It's not and you're not telling me anything I don't..."

"Then why did you allow her to escape your grasp this morning? Hmmm? Surely the great Bernardo Grimani, wouldn't struggle to kill one little girl. That would be ludicrous." Anger quickly fills Bernardo, and he steps towards Baur, reaching into his pocket. Before he can draw his anima, the thin man moves and covers the distance to Bernardo, gripping his wrist. Trying to step back, fear fills him as his back pushes up against cold, hard steel. Looking over his shoulder, he looks into the cold eyes inside a suit of black armour.

"Now pay attention, Bernardo, as I'm only going to say this once. Requiem does not tolerate failure. Given how you screwed up in Athens and let your sister live, another failure will not be tolerated. If you let the girl escape again, my associate here and I are going to have to get involved, and that won't end well for you. So, just to be clear, Kill the girl and retrieve her anima." Releasing the Italian man's hand, Baur steps around him and heads towards the back door, the armoured knight following closely behind. Reaching the door, Baur pauses, his hand on the handle, and turns to look back at Bernardo.

"And do remember, Mr Grimani, I'll be watching. Ta-ta for now." With a little giggle, Baur opens the door and steps out into the afternoon light, leaving Bernardo standing shell-shocked in the middle of the bar. Swallowing heavily, the Italian man tries to calm his nerves. Moving behind the bar, he grabs an unopened bottle of whisky from a broken shelf and uncorks it, pulling a long drink from the bottle. As the whisky warms him to his stomach, his nerves begin to settle. Looking towards the back door, Bernardo shakes his head and, placing the bottle down on a random table, leaves through the front.

Chapter Fourty

Stepping out of the abandoned bar, Bernardo pulls a cell phone out of his pocket and begins dialling. The feel of cold steel pressed against the side of his neck stops him before he can push the call button. Closing the phone, he puts it back in his pocket before raising his arms in surrender.

"Well now. Haven't you been a pain to track down?"

"Hello, Leon. Cassy sent you to bring me in, I take it? How's Monica doing? I hear she survived our little encounter." Grinding his teeth, Leon walks around to the front of Bernardo, keeping his blade pressed against the Italian man's throat as he does so. Stepping out from the shadow of the building to Leon's left, Shizuri summons her katana as she approaches the two men.

"I wouldn't worry about your sister right now. I would start worrying about yourself. Cassy wants you brought back, preferably alive. Do you have any idea how many people died because of yours and Requiems actions in Athens?"

"Am I supposed to care? What is this? Are you seriously trying to appeal to my good side? Hah, that's laughable. You're both pathetic. Running around, playing at being a hero. You really think you'll make a difference?" Pushing the tip of his blade forward just enough so it draws blood, Leon gestures with his free hand.

"Maybe, maybe not. I could just put an end to you. I'm sure that would be a good enough start. Now start talking. What's Requiem up to?"

"Leon screw talking, that doesn't get anywhere with the likes of him, besides..." Lifting her shirt just high enough to expose the bandages covering her chest, Shizuri lifts her sword and points it at Bernardo.

"I want a piece of this arsehole. Let's call it compensation for what happened in the council chamber." Dropping her shirt, she takes a step forward before being stopped by Leon's raised hand.

"Enough! Put it away Shizuri. Now's not the time." Backing down from the two men, Shizuri lowers her blade.

"There you go doing as you're told, just like a good little lapdog. No wonder the Kawamura family is in such a pathetic state. If I was your father, I would've done myself in by now. Oh, wait..." For a moment, a shocked look crossed Shizuri's face before being replaced with blind fury. Screaming, her katana bursts into flame. Ignoring Leon, she charges at Bernardo.

"Shizuri, NO!" Stepping away from the Italian man, Leon spins, coating Fenrir in a thin layer of ice. With a burst of steam, he meets Shizuri's blade with his own. Twisting, Leon deflects the flaming katana and, shoving her roughly, knocks the Japanese woman off her feet, causing her to land heavily a few feet away.

"Enough!" The sound of grating steel and a surge of power are the only warning Leon needs. Spinning back to face Bernardo, ice and wind swirl around Fenrir as he turns.

"Howling wind shard!"

"Quaking Overture!" Both men's voices shout out at the same time. Bursting forth from Leon's blade, a wave of ice and wind meets Bernardo's sonic shock-wave in mid-air. Explosively cancelling each other out, the resulting shock-wave from the blast shatters nearby windows and creates a wave of dust that billows outwards from the two men. Recovering quickly, Leon reaches to his belt and unclips Aurora. Summoning her without the wings, he pulls the rapier from its sheath just in time to meet Bernardo's second attack.

"Not bad Aelfdane. But let's see how you deal with this!" Stepping back, Bernardo drives his left fist into the ground. As the ground rumbles, a strange feeling comes from under Leon's feet. Listening to his instincts and leaping backwards, Leon only just avoids being impaled by a spike of rock that bursts from the ground where he was standing seconds earlier. Landing lightly, Leon slashes forward with the rapier, cutting the pinnacle off the spike. Running forward, he leaps and rides the falling piece of rock towards Bernardo. As it lands, a wave of dust springs up from the impact. Using the dust to cover his movements, Leon charges Bernardo. Clearing the dust, he finds Bernardo waiting for him, energy crackling over his right fist. Leaping into the air, he spins Fenrir.

"Sonic Crescendo!" At Bernardo's shout, a bolt of energy bursts from his right fist straight toward Leon.

"Howling Storm barrier!" at his shout a shield of ice forms at the front of the blade. Holding the blade in front of him, he releases his grip on the hilt as Bernardo's attack connects with the shield. Using the force of the impact, Leon thrusts himself towards the ground. Twisting as he lands, Leon switches the rapier to his right hand.

"Sonic Dissonance!" Before Leon can move, the second bolt of energy enters the ground in front of him. With a small hiss, the energy fizzles out. Smiling as Leon takes a step forward, Bernardo clicks his left hand. As Leon's foot touches the ground, light blooms from underneath and with a small explosion throws him off his feet. Landing heavily on his back, he loses his grip on the rapier. Rolling backwards to his feet, he searches for the rapier. Spotting it lying a few feet from the wall where Fenrir is impaled.

"It's too late Aelfdane. You're mine." Charging energy in both fists, Bernardo steps back.

"Not a chance, Bernardo. Suns Wrath!" Emerging from the smoke, Shizuri stabs her Katana towards the Italian man. Bursting from the tip of the blade, a beam of light streaks towards him. Crossing his fists across his chest, he takes her beam head-on. Taking a stance, Shizuri increases the energy pouring out of the tip of her blade, pushing the Italian man back to the wall behind him. Not waiting for another chance, Leon runs over and picks the rapier up. Placing one foot on the wall, he leaps upwards, tearing Fenrir out before landing lightly on the ground. Making Fenrir dormant once more, he clips it back to his belt. Gripping the rapier in both his hands, he focuses on the blade. With force, the wings explode from his back, feathers filling the air. Running back towards Shizuri, Leon scribbles a sigil and drags his left hand across the blade. As his hand clears the tip, feathers appear at the hilt and begin spiralling around the length of the blade. Dropping to one knee, Shizuri's strength gives out and the beam ceases. Smoke coming from his jacket and arms, Bernardo pushes off the wall and, staggering forwards, charges energy over both his arms once more. Reaching Shizuri, Leon steps past her and, sliding to a stop, brings his blade to bear.

"Using the light of the guide, let me reach thy enemies. Seraphs Assault!" At his shout, the feathers burst away from the blade, hanging in the air around Leon. Thrusting the blade forward, the feathers become blades of light and streak towards Bernardo.

"Sonic Quake Finale!" Clapping his hands together, Bernardo cries out, and a shock wave of sound booms outwards from where he stands. As the shock wave hits the feathers, they turn into particles of light. Throwing up rubble and dust, it hurls Leon into the air as well. Landing heavily amidst a pile of rubble, he gasps as the wind is knocked out of him. Ducking the shock wave, Shizuri hunches over and watches as it reaches the buildings. With a rumble, the worst condition building's collapse at the edge of the square, filling the air with dust and debris.

"Looks like you fall short once more, Aelfdane. Be seeing you." Bernardo's voice echoes through the dust as Leon slowly gets to his feet. Staggering through the rubble-filled square, Leon makes his way to Shizuri. Looking her over quickly, he notices a dark spot growing on her top. Leaning down, he puts his arms underneath and carefully lifts her up. Head resting lightly on his shoulder, she speaks to him as if half unconscious.

"Leon, he's getting away. We have to go after him."

"We can't right now. We're going to regroup with the others. Besides, we need to get out of here before nocturna show up." Stepping free from the dust, Leon breathes in a breath of fresh air. Coughing lightly, he re-adjusts his grip on Shizuri before walking down the street and away from the dust-filled square.

Sitting quietly by the fire, Gilroy looks out the window at the fading light. Sighing, he gets up and stretches out the ache in his back. At his movement, Iris starts from her position against the wall. Looking around, she catches Gilroy's eye, and a look of worry covers her face.

"They should've been back by now, Gil. Something's happened. You know it and so do I. You heard the booms and felt the ground shake. I'm going." Before he can move to stop her, the door opens and Leon steps in, carrying an unconscious Shizuri. With a small sob, Iris races towards the pair to be stopped by a look from Leon.

"She's fine Iris. She collapsed from overdoing it. Popped a couple of stitches as well. She just needs some rest." Stepping into the small area, Leon carefully lays Shizuri down on the ground next to the fire. Stepping clear, he smiles as Iris makes the Japanese woman comfortable and looking at her wounds. Catching Gilroy's eye, Leon gestures to the exit with his head. Gesturing to Renee, he waits for her and Gil to come over before heading outside. As soon as the two are outside of their hiding place, Leon starts.

"He got away again. We were so close. If Shizuri hadn't lost her cool, we would've had him." Lighting two cigarettes, Gilroy hands one to Leon before replying.

"So, what now, what's the plan?" Taking a drag of his cigarette, Leon frowns for a moment and turns to look at Gilroy.

"We chase him down. He must be stopped. I doubt he'll be going too far tonight. He's injured and even if he does, I can find him. I put a tracer on him. So, Renee, I need you to do me a favour."

"What do you need?"

"I need you to take a message back to Cassy. Tell her we tracked Bernardo to here. And we'll most likely catch him tomorrow. And tell her there's more to this than a simple attack. Tell her I said look into San Francisco. Find out what Requiems up to. If we don't, I fear we may well live to regret it. Can you do that for me?"

"I can. When do you want me to head back?"

"First light tomorrow will be fine. We'll all get going then. No point chasing after Bernardo now. The nocturna are more active at night and I'd rather not face any, given how exhausted everyone is." Nodding, Gilroy looks at the setting sun.

"Well, if that's the plan, we'd best get settled in for the night." Crushing out his cigarette, Gilroy turns and heads back inside the small abandoned building, followed closely by Renee. Turning to look at the city surrounding him, a look of anger crosses Leon's face and he clenches his fist. Turning away, he heads inside and joins the others.

Chapter Fourty-one

Rising just as the sun peaks over the horizon, Leon creeps past the others and slips outside into the chill morning air. Taking a deep breath, he removes his shirt and unclips Fenrir from his belt. With the flick of his wrist, the wolf blade appears. Taking a stance, he begins to move slowly, blade spinning through complex patterns. Letting his mind go blank, his body flows from pattern to pattern, the chill fading. Slowing to a halt, covered in sweat and breathing heavily, Leon starts as clapping comes from behind. Spinning, he frowns as Renee laughs.

"Very impressive, Mr Aelfdane. With skills like that, I can see now why you were selected to become the successor to Lord Sigmund as the London Council member."

"How long have you been standing there?"

"Long enough. Listen, the others are starting to wake, and I wanted a moment to speak with you." Shrugging into his shirt, Leon gestures to a nearby bench and takes a seat. Shaking her head, Renee replies.

"I'm not staying long. I mean to get underway and cover as much ground as quickly as I can. You need to be careful. I had a dream last night. Now before you interrupt, hear me out. Everyone dreams, I know that. But I occasionally have these, weird, vision-like dreams. I believe it's another of Nova's abilities. A foresight of sorts. I saw a storm coming over the horizon. Of the likes I've never seen before and you were standing before it, blade raised to the sky. I believe it means that you may be the only hope. Please, stay safe." As she finishes, she extends her hand out to Leon. Rising from his seat, he grasps her hand.

"You too." Smiling, she releases his hand and walks away. Turning away as she walks out of sight, Leon takes two steps towards the door before it opens, Gilroy stepping out into the sunshine.

"So, she's gone then?"

"Yeah. On her way back to Athens. Are the others awake?"

"They're beginning to rise."

"Good. We need to be on the move as well." Turning from his friend before he can say anything, Leon heads inside the small building. Opening his mouth to call out, he shuts it as his sight catches Shizuri standing in the middle of the room, bandages laying on the floor at her feet. Face burning, he turns his back on the Japanese woman.

"How are your injuries this morning?"

"They are considerably better. Thank you for carrying me back here last night." From behind him, the sound of a stool hitting the wall makes him flinch.

"You can turn now." Turning back, Leon finds the Japanese woman clothed and sitting on a stool against the wall.

"How long until you're ready to leave?"

"Iris is just freshening up. I'd say within the next ten minutes, we should be good to make a move."

"Good. In that case, I'll meet you outside." Without another word, Leon turns and walks out the door. From outside, the sound of his voice can be heard. Ignoring it as giggles come from her right, Shizuri turns to find Iris standing there, dressed and ready to leave.

"That was awkwardly amusing. I don't think I've ever seen a look of such shock on the new Lord Commander's face." Giggling, Shizuri gets off the stool and grabs her pack before sauntering over to Iris. Giving the woman a deep kiss, she stares into her eyes.

"And thank you for last night." With a smile, Iris kisses Shizuri's hand and gestures towards the door, whispering as she turns.

"You're welcome." Stepping outside into the weak sunlight, the two women look around. With a word from Leon, they all turn and head deeper into the city.

* * *

Waking with a start, Lia blinks at the sunlight streaming through the window. Groaning, she rolls over and moves to the edge of the bed. Slowly, she pushes herself into a sitting position as the aches and pains from the previous morning's battle come back to her in full force. Moving her shoulder, she winces as it begins to loosen painfully.

"Hmmm I would prefer more movement, but it will have to do."

"Given it was broken just yesterday, you're lucky you can move it at all."

"I know and I'm glad Nic. It's the one ability of yours that hasn't caused us trouble.

"I know. Now best be up. We should not linger here." Climbing out of the bed, she staggers into the adjoining bathroom. Leaning heavily against the basin, she puts the plug in, tracing a sigil with her free hand. In seconds it fills with crystal clear water. Taking a deep breath, she plunges her face in, the icy coolness a welcome shock to her system. Pulling her head out with a gasp, she stares at the reflection in the cracked mirror. Her black hair is plastered to her forehead. Between all that, her blue eyes seem to glow in the light streaming through the window. Twisting her head, she looks at the scrape marks alongside her neck. Shivering, she pushes away all thoughts of the previous morning. Brushing her hair back from her face, she pulls the plug and heads back into the room of the abandoned hotel, catching sight of herself in the full-length mirror. With a sigh, she looks down at the remnants of her clothing and walks over to the cupboard, stripping off her torn and dirty clothes. Opening the doors, she rummages through, quickly finding some clothing in her size. Pulling her hair back, she ties it in place with a blue ribbon, before shrugging into a white coat and leaving the room. Making her way to the stairs, she grabs a sharp knife off a trolley in the middle of the hallway, tucking it behind her belt. Slowly wending her way through the hotel, she stops and looks into open rooms as she passes.

"We really mustn't linger Lia."

"I know Nic. But can you imagine what this place must have looked like before the cataclysm? I'm sure music and laughter would have filled these halls. Stopping, she reaches down and picks up a child's doll off the ground. Brushing dirt off its skirt, she sighs and places it on a nearby planter box sitting up.

"I hope whoever that belonged to made it out." Turning from the plant box, she only takes one step when a savage roar startles her. Spinning, she barely raises her arm in time as the nocturna's clawed fist connects with her chest. Ribs aching from the impact, the wind whistles past her as she soars through the air, finally coming to a sudden stop against the wall. As darkness begins to take her, the nocturna leaps through the air towards her. As if stuck in slow motion, she watches as it nears. Fear wells up inside and from deep down, power explodes outwards with a blinding light. With the sound of timbers crashing, her consciousness fades.

* * *

Blocks away, Bernardo leans against the wall of a small apartment building. The edge of the nearby balcony shading him from the sun. Wiping the sweat from his forehead, he glances from his phone and the message he was reading as a plume of smoke starts to fill the sky. With a smile, he tucks the phone into his pocket and starts wending his way through the streets towards the echoing sounds of rubble collapsing.

* * *

With a groan, Lia slowly comes to, pain filling her.

"Are you okay Lia?"

"Somehow." Ignoring the pain coursing through her body, she pushes herself to a sitting position. A sense of shock fills her as she finally catches sight of the giant hole in the side of the hotel. With a gasp, her memories come back, and she jumps to her feet, looking around for the nocturna.

"Relax Lia. It's dead. But now we really need to leave. You've been out for a few minutes and that explosion would have bought us the wrong kind of attention." Agreeing silently, Lia pushes herself free of the wall and slowly makes her way towards the lobby of the hotel. As she reaches the ground floor, a timber crashes down on the floor above, sending her ducking behind the reception desk. When no sounds or steps follow, she calms herself and carefully peeks over the edge of the desk and glancing around the area. Taking a deep breath, Lia dashes to the door, bursting through it out into the street. Without slowing, she turns and keeps running, passing abandoned cars and desolate shops in a blur.

"Lia, you need to slow down. We can't keep this pace going."

"I know, Nic, but I slept too long. I want to get out of this city as soon as I can."

"I know but it won't help anyone if you collapse from exhaustion." With grim acknowledgement, Lia slows to a walk, emerging out onto a street leading into the factory district. Stopping as a voice calls out in Italian, a feeling of dread overwhelms her.

"Well well. Found you." The feeling of energy building above her comes before she can react. With a deafening explosion, she's thrown from her feet, landing heavily on the pavement. Ears ringing, she slowly climbs to her feet as Bernardo lands on the ground a few feet away.

"You've been a real bitch to track down, you know that. This time, just die." Looking directly at Bernardo, fear paralyses her as he raises his fists above his head, energy crackling over them. With a sickening smile, he brings both fists down and a wave of energy releases towards her. Closing her eyes, images of her parents and siblings flash before her eyes. Images from before the world went to hell. Images of a better time.

"Bernardo!" Opening her eyes at the shout, she steps back as a man lands in front of her, his single-edged blade spinning in front of his hand.

"Howling storm barrier!" At his command, the blade forms a blue shield and bringing it to bear, he meets Bernardos attack head-on. Hitting the shield with a screech, the attack sends shock waves rippling outwards, blowing dust and debris away in every direction.

"Are you alright, Miss?" Turning at the sound of another voice, Lia finds herself face to face with two women and a large man. Looking over his shoulder, the man catches the eyes of the others.

"Shizuri, take care of the girl. Gil, let's finish this." With a flick of his wrist, a giant battle-axe appears in the big man's hands.

"Lets." Striding past, Gilroy stands next to the other man.

"Well, it's so nice to see you, Leon. But you see, your once again in the way of what I came here to do. Except, this time you won't escape."

"Oh, and how do you figure that, Bernardo? There's four of us and one of you."

"That's easy. I'll just give you a distraction to deal with." From his pocket, Bernardo pulls out a small black vial. With a muttered word, the vial begins to pulse with red. A look of fear crosses Leon's face as Bernardo throws the vial behind him. For a moment, the vial seems to spin in slow motion through the air, before shattering on the ground, its sound echoing around them. After a moment of silence, the air fills with an ear-splitting shriek. Covering his ear with one arm, Leon leaps towards Bernardo, his blade flashing in the afternoon light. With a smile the Italian man blocks the blade one-handedly, driving his other fist into Leon's midriff, dropping him to the ground. Not waiting for another opening, Lia springs to her feet and runs between the two girls, ignoring their shouts. As she sprints away from the group of people, she looks back, her eyes widening with fear as the first of the nocturna crawl out of nearby buildings and converge on the people who came to her rescue.

"They'll be fine Lia, now run. This is our only chance." Taking heed of Nic's words, she puts her head down and sprints harder. Her blood pounds in her ears and the impact of her feet hitting the ground begin to blur her surrounds. Finally slowing as a stitch lances through her side, she finds herself in an abandoned industrial area. Stopping, she looks around and takes in her surroundings. In the late afternoon light, the buildings loom ominously. Making a snap decision, she slips up a metal staircase and into the office part of the closest building. With barely a whisper, the door closes behind her. In the gloom of the building, fear fills her, and she reaches behind her back and removes the knife from its place behind the belt, surprised to find it still there. Walking slowly, she makes her way deeper into the building, ducking away from the deepening shadows. Finally reaching the end of the offices, she carefully opens the door leading out onto the scaffolding above the factory floor. Stepping out, she looks over the edge at the old machinery workshop below her. As the height makes her vision swim, she steps back from the edge. Brushing against the wall, the shadow looming over her is the only warning she receives. Spinning towards the shadow, she gasps as a gauntleted fist connects with the side of her head.

"Do you have any idea the shit I had to go through after you left? Time for this to end" Through the haze of pain, she can only just make out the Italian man's words. Before she can react, a sense of weightlessness fills her as she's roughly hauled off the metal scaffolding and lifted into the air. Throwing her over the edge, a sense of terror fills her and a blood-curdling scream tears free from her throat, echoing menacingly through the factory. For a moment, she blacks out as the impact with the ground overwhelms her with pain. Coming back to reality, black spots edge her vision as she tries to crawl further into the factory, all feeling gone from her legs. From behind, the sound of Bernardo landing heavily causes her to try to pull herself along faster. With a chuckle, he walks over and lifts her off the ground roughly, ignoring her shriek of pain. Putting his arm around her throat, he pulls her tightly against his chest. From somewhere deep inside the office, the sound of a door splintering off its hinges can be heard. Reaching forward with a bloodstained hand, she barely feels the pinch of the knife as it enters her.

"Sorry, Mother and Father. I'll see you soon." Her lips barely form the words as blackness rushes in and coldness overwhelms her. Closing her eyes, she falls into the darkness and everything disappears.

* * *

Hearing a scream, Leon hurriedly runs up the stairs of the old warehouse. Reaching the top, he kicks the door, stopping with a painful thud.

"Gil I can't get through."

"Step aside." Leaping away from the door, Leon watches as Gilroy takes a deep breath and, summoning the axe, he steps forward. Swinging the axe with a whistle, he hits the door with tremendous force, shattering the frame and sending it crashing to the floor.

"Have I ever told you how glad I am that we're friends?" Without waiting for the big man's reply, Leon dashes into the building. Making his way through a small block of offices, he quickly reaches the edge of a small metal walkway running between two offices and overlooking the warehouse floor. Stopping, he looks down into the warehouse, seeing Bernardo behind the small woman from earlier, his hand around her throat.

"You're too late Aelfdane. It's done." As he finishes, he pulls his free hand back, the blade coming free of the girl's body without a sound. Letting go, he laughs as her body falls to the ground. Tossing the blood-covered knife to the ground, he reaches down and removes the anima from her belt. Tossing it into the air, he looks at Leon and Gilroy with a crazy glint in his eye as he catches the anima.

"Now all that's left, is to deliver this. And then Requiem will rise and there is nothing any of you can do to stop them. Once they have this little beauty, it's all over." Brandishing a bloody hand, he waves at Leon, ignoring the blood splattering on to the floor. Arriving at that moment, Shizuri and Iris gasp at the sight in front of them. Stepping all the way to the edge of the walkway, Shizuri points at Bernardo.

* * *

"You're one sick bastard, Bernardo. The council will not let you get away with this. And neither will I. This is as far as you go."

"Hahaha. That is where you are wrong Shizuri. This is as far as YOU go." With a flash of light, his gauntlets appear. Before they can react, Bernardo's fists crackle with energy.

"Sonic Crescendo." With the shuddering of the steel and a tearing sound, the supports collapse. A moment of shock crosses the faces of Leon's group, before the scaffolding disappears, burying the four of them under it. Turning from the carnage before the dust has even settled, Bernardo runs from the building as fast as his legs can carry him. Coming out into the alleyway behind the factory, he turns left and after a moment finds himself in a square. Ruined buildings cover three edges of the square. With the fourth opening up into an overgrown park. A run-down children's playground edges the park and a smashed fountain lies in the centre. Standing near the fountain is a female knight in black armour, giant broadsword embedded in the ground in front of her. Suppressing the chill of fear that runs up his back, Bernardo walks over to her.

"I have it." Producing the anima, he holds out his hand to give it to her. Moving from her position, she pierces his chest so fast. Were it not for the spray of blood hitting his face, he would never have known he'd been stabbed. Letting out a cry of agony, he grabs the blade sticking from his chest. Stepping forward, she cuts off his shout as her gauntleted hand closes around his throat. Lifting him off his feet with ease, the female knight tightens her grip on his throat. As his consciousness fades, the anima falls from his right hand and lands with a soft metallic clatter on the pavement.

Chapter Fourty-two

Blinking the blood from his eyes, Leon slowly crawls out from under the wreckage. Coughing from the dust, he wipes the blood from his forehead. Ignoring the pain, he slowly gets to his feet and turns to survey the damage.

"There's no going back that way," Muttering to himself as he looks at the wreckage of the scaffolding and the door now fifteen feet above them. A heavy grunt, followed by clattering pieces of metal, comes from the wreckage as Gilroy stands up, pulling the two women with him.

"You guys alright?" Sitting down heavily, Gilroy replies.

"Just barely. That bastard. I'll kill him next time I see him." Says Leon through gritted teeth.

"I'm not." Replies Shizuri sitting down heavily against the wall.

"My leg's broken. Leon, go after him. He cannot get that anima to Requiem. We can't let him."

"What about you?"

"I'll follow as soon as I can. Now get going. You need to catch up to Bernardo and stop him,"

"Okay then. Iris stay here with Shizuri. Gil mate, you're with me. Let's go get that bastard." The two men run off towards the back of the factory and within moments, they're out of sight. Coming over to Shizuri, Iris slides down the wall next to her. Reaching over and taking her hand, Iris leans her head on Shizuri's shoulder.

"Give me your arm My Lady and I will help you up. We need to bind your leg."

"Don't worry about my leg. Go after the boys, Iris. I have a bad feeling about this whole situation."

"With all due respect, My Lady, I refuse to go anywhere without you. Now let's get your leg sorted out." Supporting Shizuri with her shoulder, Iris stands and moves them to a nearby bench. Setting Shizuri down on the bench, Iris goes to work, gathering supplies to bind the Japanese woman's injured leg. With a heavy feeling of foreboding, Shizuri looks out the skylight at the fading sunlight.

Stepping out into the alley, Leon and Gil look both ways. Shrugging, they turn in opposite directions and begin to run when a scream of pain rings out from Leon's direction. Turning to shoot Gilroy a look, Leon sprints in the scream's direction. Exiting the alleyway, they come out into a square that was most likely a park once upon a time. Standing in front of the smashed, dusty fountain is the black knight from Leon's vision. Bernardo is hanging from the knight's hand a few feet off the ground. Stepping forward and brandishing Fenrir, Leon calls out with a voice steadier than he feels.

"Release that man at once." Turning toward Leon, the knight pulls her blade from Bernardo's chest and throws his body aside. Reaching down, the knight picks up the anima that Bernardo had been holding and, without taking her eyes off the two men in front of her, throws it over her shoulder. From the shadows near the park, a man's hand extends out and catches it. Stepping from the shadows out into the light, Simon Baur smiles a greasy smile at Leon and Gilroy before waving his hand in greeting.

"Long time no see, boyo. I hear you held your own with your sister. Not too bad considering the state you were in. Given that, I am sure your father would overlook your past misdeeds and let you join Requiem. You'd have to swear fealty of course." Gritting his teeth, Leon points Fenrir towards Baur before responding.

"I've no interest in joining that megalomaniac or his band of whack jobs and psychos. What I will do though, is take that anima back and stop whatever disaster he has planned." Without waiting for a response from Baur, Leon leaps into action. Bursting forward with blinding speed, he drives his blade towards Baur. Before Leon's strike can hit home, the knight moves in front of the man. With a reverberating sound of metal colliding and a shoulder numbing impact, the Knight catches Leon's strike on the flat of her blade. With tremendous force, she swings the blade away from her, sending Leon sprawling in the dirt at Gilroy's feet. Hurrying to his friend, the big man helps him up and together they watch in horror as the knight advances.

"Well, Leon, as much as I'd like to stay and see this end, I'm a busy man. I've got things to do, ya know? Like places to see, people to kill. Tis a tiresome thing taking over the world. But any who, ta ta, say hi to your mother for me." With an evil smile, Baur turns and walks away from Leon and the knight. Drawing Leviathan, Gilroy squares off in an offensive stance alongside Leon.

"Any ideas?" Drawing Aurora, he summons her in rapier form.

"Yeah. Don't get dead." With a grimace, the two men look away from each other at the approaching knight. With a nod from Leon, Gilroy attacks first. Closing the distance to the knight, he swings his axe, only to have it parried away with force. Quickly regaining his footing, he launches a flurry of strikes, the axe becoming a whirlwind in his hands.

At every turn, her blade blocks his axe. Coming out of Gilroy's shadow, Leon launches an attack with his two swords. Knocking Gilroy's axe up, she lands a kick to his stomach, knocking him off his feet. Before twisting around and catching Leon's first strike with Aurora on the edge of her sword. His second strike with Fenrir slips past her guard and strikes the armour on her left arm.

"Howling wind shard!" Leon's cry echoes out through the arriving night and the blade explodes with shards of ice and blades of air. Twisting the blade with all his strength, he tries to turn it towards her chest. All his effort, however, ends up for nothing. As the knight twists out of the path of the blade's storm, she lashes out at Leon with a fist, catching him on the chest. Feeling some of his ribs crack from the force of the impact, he lands heavily on the ground, facedown, his breath gone. Gasping for air and clutching his chest, Leon rolls onto his side to see the knight, with blood dripping down her left arm, advance steadily towards him. Pain lancing through his body, he struggles to rise. Without warning, Gilroy rushes her. Axe flashing, bloodlust is thick in the air as he attacks with a fury that Leon has never seen. Without ever breaking her stride, she parries every axe stroke of the Chaos Guard Captain. Finally, rising slowly to a sitting position, Leon tries to cry a warning to Gilroy as he goes for a deliberately left opening. With no mercy, her blade pierces his right shoulder, followed by a blow to the face that breaks his nose. Staggering backwards, Gilroy tries lifting his axe for another strike, but blood sprays from his wound and with a grunt the axe falls from his now limp grasp and he falls to his knees. Raising Aurora Leon chants.

"Light of the North, keeper of the stars. Let now your radiance shine down and guide those that are lost. Reaching wide and far, to all who are lost in the dark places. Guide them to the places they call home and back to those who make it so. Let the light of the North save now those that are in peril." With a burst of white light, Aurora takes her phantasm form. As she appears, the pain in his chest lessens and Fenrir goes dormant. Standing tall, her wings flap angrily behind her. Turning toward the knight, she draws the rapier from her hip and advances.

"You have harmed my Master for the last time. Now you will taste cold steel." With a burst of wind from her wings, she closes the distance to the knight almost instantly. Rapier a blur she strikes at the knight. Just managing to get her sword up in time, the knight falls back from the anima's onslaught. Getting to his feet, Leon rushes over to Gilroy's side. Putting pressure on the wound, Leon helps Gil to his feet. With a grunt of pain, the big man talks through gritted teeth.

"Damn bitch, got me good."

"Yeah. Can you summon Leviathan in phantasm form?"

"I can, but I won't be able to hold it for long."

"That's fine. I need to summon Valkyrie if we're to have any chance of winning. Aurora only seems to have the upper hand. Her attacks have no real impact, though. She can buy us a few minutes at best." Placing Gilroy down against the fountain to start chanting, Leon kneels on the ground a few feet away. Closing his eyes, he concentrates on releasing his energy. Within moments, it begins to flow. Opening his eyes, he chants Valkyries summoning chant. As he begins, Gilroy finishes summoning Leviathan. Catching the battle-axe, Gilroy uses it to push himself upright. With a command and a gesture from the big man, the giant serpent attacks the knight in tandem with Aurora. The flashing beams of light from Leviathan light up the surrounding darkness. Dodging the beams, the winged woman dashes in and lands light strikes on the knight. Bellowing in anger, the female knight lashes out at Aurora. Leaping backwards and narrowly avoiding the black blade, Aurora retreats high into the sky. Reaching a good distance between herself and the knight, she holds her rapier in front of her and quickly chants.

"Light of the North. Bend now to my will and smite all who hinder those returning home. Seraph's end!" As she finishes the chant, she swings the rapier downward. From her wings, a cascade of feather-shaped lights launch toward the knight. Standing her ground, the black knight drives her blade into the ground and holds her hands to either side of the hilt. A bubble of black energy instantly envelops her and the feathers of light bounce off it, vanishing harmlessly into the air. Grabbing the hilt of her sword, she barely raises it in time to block the impact from the giant serpent. Unable to negate the force of the impact, however, the black knight slides backwards across the ground, coming to a stop against the metal fence next to the children's playground. Regaining her footing, the black knight doesn't have a chance to move, as Leviathan continues its attack. Firing off a beam of energy, Leviathan twists and lashes out with its tail. Deflecting the beam, the knight takes the impact from the tail. Hitting the knight in the chest, the impact lifts her off the ground and throws her into the playground, causing it to collapse on top of her. Looking around at Leon, Leviathan seems to nod before dispersing into particles of green light. The particles of light gather around the axe in Gilroy's hand and with a flash, it returns to its dormant state. Stepping backwards, the big man collapses onto the edge of the fountain. Finishing his chant, Leon extends his last anima in his left hand. Lightning crackles overhead. With a thunderclap and a burst of light, the warrior appears. Drawing her sword, she takes her place next to Leon.

"Leon, this isn't going to be an easy fight. You're aware of this, I take it?"

"I am. Regardless of how hard the fight is, we must stop her here. For the safety of everyone." Nodding her head, Valkyrie readies her sword. At the signal from Leon, Valkyrie moves over to the edge of the fence surrounding the playground. Sword at the ready, she slowly advances towards the wreckage of the playground. Moving over to Gilroy, Leon squats down next to him.

"Thanks, mate. I'll end this as quickly as I can. Just rest for a moment."

Opening one eye, Gilroy barely nods at Leon before his eyes close once more and he slumps against the fountain. With the sound of tearing metal, the black knight's blade pierces through the centre of the playground's wreckage. Throwing aside the broken bits of play equipment as if they weighed nothing, she rises steadily to her feet. Walking towards Valkyrie, black miasma pours from her blade. Putting some distance between them, Valkyrie retreats to just in front of where Leon is stabilising Gilroy's wound. Alighting on the ground next to the armoured knight, Aurora steps over to Leon and with one movement drags him clear of Gilroy. Before he can protest, she reaches down, and a golden light envelops his shoulder. Within moments the wound stops bleeding and with a click of her fingers, bandages materialize and rapidly bind the big man's shoulder.

"Sorry, Leon, but we need you here. It's going to take all three of us to even have a chance of stopping her." Getting to his feet, he unclips Fenrir from his waist and summons the wolf blade.

"I know. How do you want to do this?" Raising her shield Valkyrie responds.

"I'll create the distraction, and you and Aurora attack her as hard as you're able to. But don't get injured, that reduces our chances of victory significantly." Walking over, Leon claps her on the shoulder. Smiling, Leon raises Fenrir and points at the black knight as she steps over the wreckage of the fence and walks toward them.

"Great speech, chick. Now, shall we?" At Leon's words, everyone springs into action. Valkyrie closes the distance to the knight in an instant. Blades clashing together, lightning seems to ark off the two women as they fight. Looking at Aurora, Leon gives her a helpless look.

"How the hell are we supposed to attack with all that going on?"

"From a distance," shouts the winged woman as she takes to the sky. Grumbling, he turns back to the fight and, gripping his sword, moves closer to where the two women clash, waiting for his chance to strike.

Chapter Forty-three

Sitting by an old car and sipping on his flask, Rick looks over at the storm forming a few blocks away. Lightning crackles through the air and the electricity can be felt. Watching as the hairs stand up on the back of his arm, he sighs and picks up an anima lying on the bonnet. Without a word, a pair of revolvers appear on his waist. Drawing one, he points it towards a nearby alleyway. Firing a single shot, he doesn't even look around as a nocturna collapses in a heap next to the edge of the building. Holstering the weapon, it switches to its dormant form once more. Clipping it to his belt, he removes a second black anima from the bonnet and clips it in as well. With a sigh, he looks over at the lightning crackling through the sky and walks towards it.

Rolling clear of the fight once more, Leon ignores the smoke billowing off his chest. Looking at the raging fight between Valkyrie and the black knight, Leon wipes the sweat off his brow. Valkyrie leaps backwards as the knight cleaves her shield in half. Chasing after the warrior woman, the knight barely stops in time as a pillar of fire sprouts from the ground in front of her. The pillar quickly becomes a wall, cutting the battlefield in half. Raising his hand to guard against the heat, Leon steps away from the wall of flame separating them from the knight. Turning, he sees Shizuri with her katana glowing red, stuck point first, into the ground.

"It's about time you showed up." Leaning heavily on Iris, Shizuri has her hand above her katana. Flames licking up the edge of the blade, she clicks her hand and the fire roars, increasing in heat. Turning his back on the wall of flame, Leon walks over to the two women.

"Leon! The fire!" At Valkyries shout, Leon turns back to the wall of fire. From the centre of the wall, the flame flickers and wanes. As it starts to die, a black vortex appears behind it and sucks the remaining fire into its centre. Swearing under his breath, Leon runs over and takes his place next to Valkyrie. Digging his feet in, Leon pushes back against the suction of the vortex. Finally, driving Fenrir into the ground as a final effort to remain on his feet. As quickly as it appeared, the vortex vanishes with a burst of air. Standing where it was is the black knight, her left hand outstretched. Before anyone can move, she drives the blade into the ground and places both her hands on top of the hilt. From under the earth, black chains burst forth and snake towards Leon and Valkyrie. Leaping backwards, Leon slashes the approaching chains with Fenrir, freezing them solid. Landing awkwardly, he scrambles to his feet and backs away as more chains burst from three ground. Summoning her shield, Valkyrie raises it as the first of the chains reach her. Blade a blur, she cuts through the approaching chains with ferocity and determination. Bursting from the ground beneath her, black chains snake around her legs and arms, halting her advance. Before she or Leon can do anything to break them, she's lifted into the air and slammed heavily into the ground, the black chains wrapping around her and staking themselves into the ground. Struggling furiously against her bonds, the armoured maiden makes no impact on the chains. Pulling her blade from the ground, the black knight turns towards Leon. Ignoring Valkyrie on the ground, she advances towards Leon. Suppressing the rising wave of panic, Leon readies himself to fight. Raising her sword above her head, the knight stops as lightning crackles above them. Before Leon can make a move, lightning comes lancing from the sky onto the tip of her blade. Taking a step back, she drives the sword into the ground. From the point of impact, black lightning erupts out of the ground and makes a line towards Leon. Leaping to the side, the hairs on his body stand up from the passing electricity. Rolling to his feet, Leon turns around and uses his sword to block the rocks and stones being thrown up. A split second later he realises his mistake. Watching in horror, as the lightning carries on towards Shizuri and Iris, he cries out. Stepping close together, they clasp hands and Iris quickly traces a sigil. Just before the lightning reaches them, a shield of blue blossoms into existence around them. With a piercing sound, the lightning crashes against the shield and arcs in every direction. Using her free hand, Shizuri draws fire from the katana embedded in the ground. With a movement of her wrist, the fire bursts into a blue fireball. Without hesitating, she throws it toward the black knight. As the fireball leaves her hand, the lightning crackling against the shield intensifies, forcing Iris and Shizuri to their knees. Without batting an eyelash, the knight pulls her sword from the ground and deflects the fireball towards Leon. Leaping out of its path, Leon rolls to his feet and can only watch as the knight levels her blade towards the two women. Thunder crackles overhead and before anyone can move, a bolt of lightning strikes from the sky. Tearing the shield to shreds, it hits the ground between the two women and explodes. Tossed through the air, Shizuri hits the fountain, as Iris bounces along the ground, stopping a dozen feet away from the fight. As he looks at the destruction around him and his friends lying injured, all Leon can hear is his heart pounding in his ears. Red covers his eyes, and all fear forgotten, he charges at the knight. Barely getting her sword up in time, she parries his first attack. Continuing, Leon viciously attacks the knight. Unable to find an opening to counter his onslaught, the knight steps back, parrying his attacks. Leaping back as frost forms a layer over his sword, Leon traces a sigil with his left hand.

"Howling Storm!" at his shout he drives his blade into the ground in front of him. Spikes of ice sprout from the ground and head toward the knight. Stepping back, she swings her blade towards the advancing ice, shattering it just before it gets to her. Before she can move, Leon steps out from behind the ice, spears of light protruding from the sigil. Holding his hand high, Leon opens his palm. Trailing tails of blue light, the spears shoot from his hand. Like missiles, they curve and head directly towards the knight. Not waiting for them to hit, Leon grabs Fenrir from the ground and charges the knight once more. Dodging the spears, the knight summons a sigil of her own. From her palm, red orbs blossom into the air and intercept the approaching spears. Causing them to explode into golden sparks. Closing the distance to the knight, Fenrir glows blue as Leon approaches. Swinging her blade around towards him, he brings his blade down, locking her blade against his. As they push back and forth, a thin layer of frost forms over the knight's blade.

"Howling wind tempest." From the edge of Fenrir, blades of ice slice forward, piercing the knight's chest plate. Pushing Leon away, she steps back and tries to block the attacks. Pressing his advantage, Leon swings Fenrir towards her blade with all his strength. With the sound of cold steel breaking, the wolf blade shears through the knight's blade. Kicking her in the chest, Leon backs up a few paces and, driving the point of his sword into the ground, rests on the hilt for a moment.

"Leon, I need to rest for a while. My power is spent. Don't draw this out too much longer, you don't have the strength either."

"I know. Thanks for holding out this long. I'll finish this now." Clipping the dormant Fenrir to his belt, Leon traces a sigil. Looking down at the shattered remains of her sword, the knight clenches her other fist. Lightning crackles down from the sky and for an instant, she disappears, reappearing in front of a stunned-looking Leon. Swinging her lightning coated fist, she drives it deep into Leon's stomach. Knocking the wind out of him and numbing the centre of his body. Unable to move, he cannot block her lightning charged backhand. Lifted off the ground from the blow, Leon feels weightless before gravity comes rushing back with a vengeance. Crashing into the ground, his head bounces off the ground and for a brief second, everything goes black.

"Leon!" Aurora's shout brings his conscious back and opening his eyes he sees the knight draw back her broken blade and prepare to strike. Stepping forward, she drives the blade down. Moving at the last second, Leon rolls aside as the blade pierces through the ground, cracking it metres in every direction from the force of the impact. Staggering to his feet, he holds his stomach to lessen the pain radiating from the place where he was punched. Landing next to him, Aurora places her hand on his shoulder. At her touch, the pain lessens, and he stands straight.

"Leon, we need to retreat. We cannot win. This one goes to Requiem." Stepping back a few steps, they get ready to move. But before either of them can, the knight picks up and hurls the broken tip of her blade at them. Leon twists to the side and Aurora leaps into the air, as the blade comes whistling through the space he just vacated. Before he can move another inch, the knight grabs Leon by the front of his shirt. He looks into her cold eyes as she raises a hand above her head. A look of sadness crosses her eyes briefly as the blade re-appears and she gets ready to strike. Time slows as the blade flashes toward him. Moments before it hits, Aurora slams into them, knocking him clear, the broken blade piercing her chest. From her left hand the white rapier falls. Grabbing the knight's shoulder, Leon catches the dropped rapier and, twisting her around, drives it home. With the sound of tearing metal, the sword pierces the knight's chest plate. Lifting the knight into the air, the rapier glows white. The knight's pressure vanishes as the rapier starts to disappear into particles of light and the black chains holding Valkyrie disappear. Stepping back, Leon watches as Valkyrie, now released from the chains, rushes over to Aurora who's laying a few feet from him. Turning back to the knight, he watches as the armour flakes away and disperses into a smoke-like substance. First, the gauntlets and pauldrons go. Revealing battered hands and legs of someone held captive for a long time. Next is the chest plate. The woman's clothes are torn and grubby. Barely more than rags that provide the barest of coverings. Finally, the helmet begins to disperse. A shock runs through Leon as dirty golden hair flutters out behind her. Moments later the helmet finishes dispersing and his heart plummets into his stomach. Stepping forward, he catches her as she descends. Landing softly in his arms, she briefly opens her eyes and looks into his. Raising a hand to touch the side of his face, she smiles.

"Leon. I knew it would be you. I always knew." At her last word, the breath leaves her body and arm falling, she slumps heavily into his arms. Hugging her tightly, he whispers into her hair.

"Farrah, god no. Not again. Please, I can't do this."

"Leon. Bring her here." Aurora's voice, though faint, reaches him clearly, cutting through his panic. Standing, he carries her over to the dying anima.

"She's still as beautiful as I remember. Leon, I am truly sorry that I must leave you soon. But before I do, I will impart my final gifts." Reaching her hand out, she touches the side of Farrah's face. Light blooms at her touch and colour comes back into the blonde woman's face. Moments later she inhales a sharp breath of air before settling into a regular breathing pattern.

"I have done what I can for her, Leon. She is alive; however, she remains under some sort of curse. My last gift is to you Val." Reaching out once again, she places her hand on Valkyrie's breastplate. Particles of light gather and cover the warrior woman. As the light disperses, wings appear on her back and her armour turns white.

"I have given you some of my power. You truly are a warrior queen now. My time has come. Goodbye." A tear falls from the warrior's eye as Aurora fades into nothing. With a dull flash, she returns to her dormant form. As they look on, the casing breaks in half, before bursting into particles of light that quickly fade away. As the lights finally wink out, the darkness sets in. Coming over to Leon, Iris looks over at Farrah briefly before sitting down in front of him.

"Leon, we need to move from here. Gil needs extensive medical attention, the kind I'm unable to do in the field and so does Shizuri." She gives Leon a quick look over before continuing.

"You yourself look like you could do with a rest and some basic medical treatment as well. LEON!" At Iris's yell, he snaps out of his stupor. Before he can respond, a low, menacing growl comes from the direction of the park. Turning towards the sound, he curses to himself as a small host of nocturna come out of the shadows and begin to approach. Straightening, Leon readjusts his grip on Farrah and has a brief look around at the others. With everyone so badly injured, he sighs.

"Fen, I need you. At this rate, we will never make the shelter of the building, let alone a safe place before we're run down." His voice echoes emptily in his mind, and standing defiantly in place, Leon can do nothing but watch the nocturna approach.

Chapter Fourty-four

Standing on a roof overlooking the park, Rick looks down at Leon. Standing defiantly, even as the nocturna converges on his exhausted party. Moving forward to the edge of the roof, Rick pulls an anima casing from his belt. Activating it, a pair of revolvers appear on his hips, resting in their holsters. As he readies himself to jump, a female voice comes through strongly in his mind.

"Are you going to save them?"

"Don't see how I have much of a choice. I can't just leave them." Without another word or hesitation, he leaps from the building, landing lightly on the ground behind the two injured people leaning against the fountain. Sensing him, Leon turns in his direction. Eyes widening in surprise, he goes to take a step toward the older man but stops at an angry growl from the direction of the trees. Lumbering towards them is a large bear-like nocturna. Cursing internally, Rick jumps over Gilroy and Shizuri drawing his first revolver. Taking aim, he gently squeezes the trigger. Aiming true, the first shot hits the first nocturna in the eye, killing it. Placing his aim carefully, Rick fires the next five shots quickly, nocturna falling where the bullets hit. Looking at the revolver, he grimaces at the two remaining shots. Focusing on the biggest of the creatures, he takes aim and fires, the bullet ricocheting off the creature's head. Firing the second shot, he aims directly at its eye. Twisting at the last moment, the nocturna once again deflects the bullet with its armoured head. Holstering his first revolver, he draws his second. Before he can fire it, Leon stands in front of him.

"Rick, take Farrah. I'll deal with that big one. Can you provide cover fire and take care of the few little ones remaining?"

"I can, lad. But be careful. That big fella is built like a tank." Stepping forward, Rick gently takes Farrah from Leon. Turning towards the nocturna, Leon draws Fenrir. Coming over to the two men, Iris places a hand on Leon's shoulder.

"Leon, it won't be much, but I may be able to assist you a little from here."

"I'd appreciate that, Iris, but don't push yourself." Nodding, she steps back and draws her anima. With a dull flash of blue light, the bracelets appear on her wrist. Nodding to Leon, she takes a combative stance. Turning to face the nocturna, Leon closes his eyes for a moment and focuses internally.

"Hey, Fen. I know you're tired, so am I. But I need your strength, just for a little while.”

“Leon, I don’t know if we can do this, but I will give you what strength I have left. I can hold my form for a time, but anything beyond that is impossible. You do not have the strength left for anything fancy and I do not have the energy.”

“I know Fen. But I can’t just let these bastards overrun us.” Opening his eyes, Leon summons the wolf blade once more. Taking a firm grip on the hilt, he adjusts his footing and gets ready to charge. Kicking off, he closes the distance to the nocturna quickly. Stepping to the left of a small nocturna, he twists and brings his blade down. With a spray of blood, the blade cleaves through the creature’s head with ease. Kicking it aside, he steps into the space where it was and slashes at the large, armoured nocturna. Just before the blade connects, ice forms a layer over the top and instead of bouncing harmlessly off it sinks deep into the armour. Roaring in pain, the nocturna takes a swing at Leon. Dodging the creature’s claws by a hairsbreadth, he pulls his blade out with a twist, opening the armour more. Leaping backwards out of range of the nocturna’s attacks, he turns and faces Iris.

“Do it now!” turning from her, he closes the distance to the nocturna once more. Blade becoming a blur, Leon launches a relentless barge of attacks to keep the creature from moving. Dodging its wide swings, Leon’s strikes bounce harmlessly off the armour. Tiring, Leon’s movements get slower until finally he dodges the creature’s claws but not the blow. Taking it to the chest, he gets knocked off his feet. Raising his sword to fend off the next blow, he’s shocked and then relieved as a blossom of ice sprouts out of the hole in the creature’s armour. Tilting his head backwards, he sees Iris with her hand outstretched, blue bangles glittering. Getting slowly to his feet, Leon looks at the edge of the park and the dead nocturna laying all around. Turning away from the sight, he clips Fenrir’s dormant form onto his belt and walks over to Rick and the others.

“Thanks for the help, Rick.”

“No worries. By the looks of things, lad, you and your friends could do with a place to rest and regroup. I’ve got a vehicle parked not far from here. We should be able to reach it without too much trouble. Once we reach it, I can take you to my place. It’s not much but you’ll be able to rest easy and decide what to do after you’ve cleared your head.” Looking over at his friends, it only takes Leon a moment to decide.

“Okay. Lead on, Rick.” Slowly gathering the wounded, they make their way out of the park back towards the city. The gloom of the dark and the weight of their failure at stopping Requiem settles heavily upon them. Without another word, they leave the dead behind.

* * *

Standing next to the table, Leon looks at Gil seated across from him. Arm still in a sling from the night before, pain is etched in the big man's face. Glancing outside at the morning light, Leon takes a seat across the table from Gilroy. Taking a sip from his coffee, Leon places the cup down before talking.

"We need to get word to the council. There's no telling what Requiem will do with that anima."

"I agree, but Leon, what are you going to do about Farrah?" Looking towards the door at the end of the small hallway, he sighs.

"I don't know. I don't think there's much I can do." The door opens and Rick walks out, followed closely by the two girls.

"You'd be right about that, lad. She is in a coma. And likely to stay that way until we can remove whatever foul curse your father placed on her, in order to bend her to his will. I know some of what goes into that curse and though it may not be much consolation Leon, she is stable. And likely to stay that way for a long while yet. I'll keep her here and continue trying to break the damn curse, but don't pray to hope, lad. You may be disappointed with the outcome. Now, what's your plan moving forward from here?"

"Thanks, Rick. Hmmm, I was just thinking about that. Shizuri, who's the closest council member from here?"

"Hmmm, that would be Lady Ennelyn in Zurich. We can make it there in a few days."

"Good. I know we're all not fully recovered from the fight last night, but we have no choice but to keep moving. Now that Requiem has that anima, I feel that whatever they have planned is going to keep us busy. No point delaying any further. It's time." Standing up from the table, he turns to Rick and offers his hand.

"Thanks for everything, Rick. Please keep in touch regarding Farrah."

Taking the younger man's hand, the older replies.

"Don't worry about it. Now get going, lad. You've got a world to save."

With one last smile, Leon and company turn away, walking out of Rick's small house and without looking back, set off toward Zurich.

Epilogue

Walking down the stairs, Simon Baur whistles a merry tune to himself. Stepping into the main room of the Requiems Base, he pulls the anima obtained from Bernardo out of his pocket. Looking over a map covered in counters, Alistair doesn't even look up.

"I take it you were successful." Placing the anima on the table, Baur sits on a nearby chair before replying.

"Yes, and no. We got what we wanted so yes but we also lost the girl sooo... I guess we broke even there." Looking up from his map, Alistair lights a smoke and leans against the table. Taking a long drag of the cigarette, he scratches his chin before turning to Baur.

"The girl is of little consequence. A useful pawn. Do you still have contact with your supporters from Foundation?"

"A few. I can reach out and get in contact with a few more, though. Why? What are you thinking?"

"Reach out and gather those you can. Then I want you to set up outside London and wait for further instructions." Nodding, Baur gets up from his chair and leaves the room, pulling out a cell phone as he does. Taking the last drag of his cigarette, he crushes it out on London's spot on the map.

"Victoria!" At his bellow, the young girl comes bursting through the far door.

"You called father?"

"I did. It's time for you to redeem yourself. I want you to go to Tokyo. I have a job for you." Victoria's heart sinks into her stomach as her father outlines his plan. Sending her on her way, she leaves the room with a heavy heart, horrified by her father's plan, but compelled to do his bidding by the curse. Looking down once more at his map, Alistair smiles a sickening smile.

"My turn."

W.P Angus

211